The Lords of Absence

The Lords of Absence

Dan Williams

ISBN: 978-0-9909452-3-9
Library of Congress Control Number: 2015950312

Cover Photo Courtesy of EdgeOfReason/Shutterstock.com
Manufactured in the United States of America

Ink Brush Press
Temple and Dallas

For All Those Left Behind

Books from Ink Brush Press

Jerry Bradley, *The Importance of Elsewhere*
Brown, Nathan and Ashley Brown, *Agave*
David Bowles, *Shattering and Bricolage*
Laurie Champion, ed., *Texas Told'em*
March Coffield, *The Very Special Christmas*
Terry Dalrymple, *Fishing for Trouble*
Terry Dalrymple, ed., *Texas Soundtrack*
Millard Dunn, *Places We Could Never Find Alone*
Chris Ellery, *The Big Mosque of Mercy*
Dede Fox, *Postcards Home*
Alan Gann, *Adventures of the Clumsy Juggler*
Andrew Geyer, *Dixie Fish*
Andrew Geyer, *Siren Songs from the Heart of Austin*
H. Palmer Hall, *Into the Thicket*
Charles Inge, *Brazos View*
Dave Kuhne, *The Road to Roma*
Robin McCorquodale, *Falling into Harmony*
Myra McLarey, *The Last Will and Testament of Rosetta Sugars Tramble*
Jim McGarrah, *Breakfast at Denny's*
Jim McGarrah, *The End of an Era*
J. Pittman McGehee, *Growing Down*
John Milkereit, *A Rotating Equipment Engineer is Never Finished*
Karla Morton and Alan Birkelbach, *No End of Vision*
Eric Muirhead, *Cab Tales*
Brett Riley, *The Subtle Dance of Impulse and Light*
Robert Rynearson, *Time to Listen*
Jim Sanderson, *Faded Love*
Jim Sanderson, *Dolph's Team*
Steven Schroeder, *a dim sum of the day before*
Steven Schroeder and Sou Vai Keng, *a guest giving way like ice melting*
Jan Seale, *Nape*
Jan Seale, *The Wonder Is*
William Seale, *Texas Riverman*
Melvin Sterne, *Zara*
W.K. Stratton, *Dreaming Sam Peckinpah*
Charles Taylor, *At the Heart*
Charles Taylor, *One True Cat*
Charles Taylor, *Saving Sebastian*
Caroline Watanabe, *My Many Sisters*
Jesse Waters, *Human Resources*
Dan Williams, *The Lords of Leftovers*
R. Scott Yarbrough, *A Sort of Adam Infant Dropped: True Myths*

Chapter 1

"What do they call you?"

I shrugged. "Whos they?"

The old man looked hard at me for a moment, then lifted his gaze across the land below us. Patches of cattle grazed off to the right on a series of rolling hills. Off to the left a broken spine of redrock cut a line across the hills like some kind of prehistoric fence left by a race of giants. The scrub grass stood thick and green from the spring rains.

"You find lost things, you and your partner? Thats what I was told. Youre some kind of wizard at finding lost things. That right? I heard stories about you and your partner."

This was his ranch. He owned it, lorded over it, and ever since the Fires he had worried over it. I imagined he was not used to losing things, and I wondered how much he was willing to pay to get back what he had lost. He seemed like a man who liked to calculate, only somehow he had miscalculated.

I sipped his leftover coffee from a heavy mug and turned back to him. "Sometimes when people lose something, Ill go hunting around for it, and sometimes if I am lucky Ill stumble over what they lost. But most times, whats gone stays gone."

The old man nodded. I had come about the reward. He had probably talked to a hundred scavs and grubbers like me. Most everyone along the front ranges had heard about the lost boys and the reward, and most were looking. Joe was already hunting around in the hills, poking the liars and stragglers with questions, buying answers with whiskey shots. But I had come out to the ranch to talk to the old man. One of his clan, a nephew, had brought me. He had heard about me and Joe and had cornered us in a little lanternlit room, where we shared a bottle of bad whiskey. We pumped him as best we could about the ranch and the reward, and he spilled about all he knew and then invited us out to meet the old man, thinking maybe a couple more fools out searching wouldnt hurt, especially notorious old fools like us. He was a young man, one of many the old man kept working his ranch, and he thought maybe we could do what all the others hadnt been able to do. The old man was desperate.

"I want them back, and I want them sumbitches who took them. My two baby boys, my littlest grandkids. Two little boys, just five and seven, sons of my daughter Jena. They up and vanished. Some thieving sumbitches come through and took them. You find them little boys and bring them back. You kill them sumbitches who took my grandkids, or bring them back here so I can kill them."

I wanted to tell the old man that one way or another everyone was a sumbitch. Everyone who had come through the Fires was scarred from the hard times, and some so misshapen and monstrous that it was hard to tell what made them human. I didnt doubt for a moment that the old man would enjoy killing anyone involved in taking his grandkids.

The old man didnt know anything except that his boys had vanished. One morning one of the older girls had taken them and a couple dogs out to the redrocks to play, and they had suddenly disappeared. No one saw them go or saw them taken. The girl had let the boys climb up a notch and play in a maze of boulders and cracks, and they had disappeared. She and the dogs had run through the rocks searching for the two boys, and then she and the dogs had raised the ranch to search. But the boys had vanished.

For weeks the old man and his extended families had searched the hills and the flats, but they had never found any trace of the kids except for the youngest boys sweater dropped up in the redrocks. Nor had any sort of ransom note or word come back to them. The old man had offered a reward of fifty horses, a fat bag of silver, and a sweet portion of land for the return of the children. The horses, silver, and the land were more than enough to incite all the dustscrubbers and whiskeysoakers all along the front range to take up the search. The horses, silver, and land were more than enough to take up ranching or whiskeydrinking for a good long while. It was enough of a reward to equal a lifetimes worth of backbreaking picking and scraping.

I wondered why a ransom note had never come back to the old man. Child snatching was common enough. Wackers and skinners were always happy enough to carry off young recruits. And there were still strings of slavers creeping around who would steal and sell. I also wondered how many scammers and tricksters had already turned up to claim the reward, claiming some sort of sick thing like a gnawed finger or chunk of ear was proof the boys had been found. The old man was supposed to be sharp, but he seemed like a fool.

"I have also been told that you are a horse thief and that you are hunted up north."

I think it impolite to respond too quickly to accusations, so I sipped his bitter coffee and waited, wondering when the days would begin to blister and dry up. It would be hard going this far south during the hot months.

What he had heard was nothing, but it was enough of nothing so that me and Joe had come down south along the front range, trading and scavenging as we went. We had a string of horses and mules fixed in a stable back to the west at a small ramshackle crossroads, and we had hid our packs in a splintery cabin up in the hills. We thought we would give the old mans reward a few days look. Hundreds of others were out turning rocks over everywhere within a hundred miles. We thought giving a look wouldnt hurt.

Why the boys were taken was a mystery. There was no ransom or leads. No indication why someone would snatch two little boys and vanish. Even the damned slavers wouldve known how much the old man was worth and wouldve offered him a chance to buy the boys back. I didnt see much profit in snatching and keeping. Most everything gets traded or bartered, even people.

"I am a trader of lost things and leftovers, but once long ago I was a starving throwaway, street trash stealing to survive. But I am no worse than most that survived the Fires. What you might have heard is a misunderstanding. Back in Aurora a worthless swindler calling himself a banker misplaced a storehouse of leftovers, crates of canned food unopened and untouched since the hot times, boxes full of old books and clothing, some tools and household stuff, and a large hoard of old military weapons too. Me and my partner got blamed when it all disappeared one night. The amount of blame heaped on us was unjust."

I didnt think the old man cared about particulars, or if the Prince and all his Rangers were tearing down after me and Joe. Which they werent of course, since more than half of those lost leftovers had found their way into one of the Princes compounds.

All the old man cared about was if me and Joe could find his little boys, which didnt seem likely. It had been nearly a month since the boys vanished, and not a word from them or about them had been heard. But there were wild rumors, and everyone along the front range had an opinion or story. I didnt have a good feeling about finding the lost boys. Bad things can happen to little children.

"The earth didnt swallow them kids up. That just dont happen. Theyre out there somewhere, waiting for someone to come get them. I know theyre still alive." The old man gestured out towards the plains, sweeping his hand in an arc that contained more than half the world.

I guessed he was right both times. I never heard of the earth cracking open and swallowing up kids, though there were plenty of old mines up in the hills that could hide a body or two. Dead or alive, those boys were someplace. Only that someplace might be anyplace within a radius of a fourweek journey. Me and Joe needed a direction.

Chapter 2

The girl kicked at a rock twice her size, then kicked it a few more times. She wore old scruffy boots, leftovers from before the Fires, and I thought there was a chance she could hurt herself. She was about twelve or so and had dark hair tied back, blue eyes, and a pretty face pulled into a scowl. When the old man called her to take me down to the rocks, there hadnt been much warmth in his voice, and she had been silent and sullen when we walked out. I imagined that she had been much the same when she had walked out with dozens of other gawkers, idlers, and loafers.

She had been with the boys when they had disappeared, and she had come back alone with the dogs, and now she was being punished by returning every time some fool wanted to look at the spot. She was not happy about dragging me out.

I whistled a little bit of song I half remembered and thought more about the rocks than the boys. The rocks formed a long broken spine that ran more than a mile parallel to the foothills, then disappeared over a small ridge. At times the formation seemed to vanish into the earth only to reappear fifty yards or so farther down, and at times rocks piled up into jagged pyramids and at other times flattened out. But what struck me was that the rocks were old. The whole broken spine was rounded and smoothed out, the effect of wind and rain over thousands of centuries. Long ago, much longer than I could rightly imagine, the whole spine had been one continuous crust of rock shoved up out of the earth in some sort of worldbusting cataclysm. But now it was worn down and broken, filled with gaps and cracks and narrow passages, the perfect place for two little boys to play with their dogs while an older girl sat daydreaming in the warm spring sun.

This was a hot day, though not one of the hottest lately. The sky was spotted with large white clouds, and I thought the day might darken up and storm by the late afternoon. But the late morning was still pleasant, and I enjoyed its prettiness. I wandered through a narrow slot of shadows and dust and came out near the opening where I had started. The girl was not far off, still kicking her rock. I walked over to her and gave it a kick too.

"Maybe I aint getting the same enjoyment out of kicking this rock as you." I said.

The girl kicked once more, hard, and then turned away. I kicked her rock again and waited some.

"Maybe I aint doin it right? How you kick it?"

"Aint you going to ask me any questions?" she asked.

11

I looked at her and then looked back over the spine toward the ranch. I thought the old man was still perched on his porch. He probably had some old binoculars and was watching us, hoping against all hopes that I would suddenly reach down and pull two boys up out of the earth. The old man thought I ought to see where the boys had been, although after weeks of weather and people there wasnt anything to see that hadnt been seen and crawled over a thousand times. Maybe he just wanted the girl to drag me along while she did one more tour of penitence. Or maybe he maybe just wanted me to meet the girl.

"What kind of questions should I ask?"

She kicked a bit of grass and weed and frowned. I thought if you had to be kicking something that a clump of dirt was a better choice than a big rock.

"I dont know. I aint some old magic man that finds lost boys."

"I aint either."

She kicked and frowned some more.

"Everyone else asks me about Jemmy and Ben, where they were when I last saw them, where I was, what they were doing. Stuff like that."

Reasonable questions I thought, reasonable and dumb. The first ones to come roaring down from the ranch had probably destroyed all traces of the boys as they raced around searching and hollering. Anyone after that was merely a damn fool gawker. I thought that the real looking had to be done elsewhere, somewhere far off. But eventually the searching would come back to the ranch. Most times you have to go off somewheres just to get back where you started, and its usually the getting back that brings the answers.

"I got one question for you." I turned back to the girl and gave her what I thought was a kindly uncle sort of look.

"What?" She looked a bit pained.

I spread out my arms and flapped at the rocks.

"How old are these rocks?"

She stared at me like I was speaking a different language. I thought I would poke her a little more.

"Im wondering how old these rocks are. Now rocks are usually so old we cant imagine how old, but some rocks are older than others. And these here rocks strike me as older than most. Maybe theyre creation rocks. A human life is nasty and short, averaging no more than a small handful of decades. And that aint even a blink or twitch in rock time. We measure in years, but rock time is measured in millions of years. Think about how many times these rocks been rained on."

She stopped kicking and frowning and looked at me like I was some kind of strange bug. I poked some more.

"What do you think? Five hundred million years? A billion maybe? I like thinking about rock time. Sometimes, most times, we get so caught up thinking about ourselves that we start thinking we are the center of all creation. But rocks tell us a different story. A human life aint even a tiny flicker of light to a rock. These rock have been rounded out and broken up for centuries upon centuries upon centuries, long before the Fires, long before things got built up before the Fires, even long before people started stumbling around on two legs. These rocks have been here since the beginning of time."

"Are you crazy? What are you asking me about a bunch of dumb rocks for? I dont know nothing about a bunch of rocks. Rocks aint people. Aint you gonna ask about the boys?"

She was stubborn, hearing but not listening.

"I know rocks aint people. Thats what I been saying. I wanted to hear your thoughts on how old these rocks are. What can I ask about the boys that you aint already answered a hundred times or more?"

She looked at me mean, but then she softened.

"I aint got any thoughts on rocks."

She walked over a few steps towards where I was and leaned against a large boulder.

"I dont like coming out here. I dont like answering all the questions. I answered them a hundred million times already. The district manager is the worst. He keeps asking me the same questions over and over again, as if I am going to say something different. He yelled at me, said I was lying. How many times can I say I didnt hear anything or see anything? I had to come out here with him a dozen different times, and always answering the same dumb questions. I hate him."

She looked at me hesitantly. I turned away and considered the rocks.

"I thought youd ask the same dumb questions. But you ask crazy questions about rocks."

I looked back at the ranch house. I thought the old man was still watching, still hoping I would snatch up his boys, even though the smart part of his brain told him I wouldnt and couldnt. You cant keep from hoping.

The girl was probably hoping I would go away, or maybe she was hoping she could go away. I was hoping the girl would stop kicking rocks, and hoping that Joe mightve found a trail and that my belly would be half full when I went to sleep and that my sore back wouldnt hurt when I woke up. Theres always hoping. Every sumbitch lives hoping.

"Guess today Im more interested in dumb rocks than dumb questions."

Chapter 3

I knew he was going to take a run at me before we even started to walk past the corral. He had been watching us steadily as we came up slowly from the rocks, he and half a dozen others buzzing around him, pushing him. He watched us with an expression that was both sullen and arrogant, and never once turned his gaze away. He was young, thickchested, and muscled, probably the bully of the barnyard, the hero of his friends, but not smart enough to know when to turn his gaze away or when to let a stranger pass.

Theres always someone who thinks hes stronger and faster, always a rooster that likes to strut and crow for his friends. Before the Fires people strutted around with bank accounts and piles of stuff, the bigger the better. Now that the world has been scorched youre just as likely to get measured by who you can knock down.

Most time when Joes around there aint much occasion for strutting or measuring. Hes too big, too quick, and too strong, and not even the dumbest rockheads or pebblebrains will mess with him. But here I was on the rich mans ranch and Joe was back in the hills somewhere, and I knew I was going to get measured by a fool roosterboy. But I didnt know why, or how I would react. I aint always the most pleasant or smartest of people when I get pecked on.

The clouds had burned off and the sun was hot in the afternoon sky, and I was looking forward to a drink of cold well water, or maybe another mug of the old mans coffee. The girl was a couple paces ahead of me, hurrying to get back to wherever she had been, and then get rid of me. I stopped by the pump. Overhead a rusty windmill creaked slowly, a whiny raspy sound.

"Aint no one said you can drink our water," the roosterboy called. He squawked before I had even touched a drop.

I gave the pump a couple more hard pulls, and water gushed into the trough. I stuck my head underneath the pump and let the water run down my neck and back. When I straightened up I could hear him strutting towards me. His cheerleaders were on his heels, wild for the fight. He stopped a couple of paces from me and fluffed out his feathers.

"You sumbitch, I warned you."

I stepped towards him. "You warned me what and for what?"

He stopped puffing and flexing to consider me a moment. I guess I was supposed to scurry away apologizing for my disrespect. He smiled and circled a few steps.

"I warned you not to touch this water. We dont want none of you raggy thieving scavs around. This here waters for our horses. You dont look like no horse. But maybe Im gonna have to saddle you up anyway. Who gave you permission to come on our land?"

There were reasonable answers to his questions, but he didnt want anything reasonable, neither the asking nor the listening. I would have been wasting my breath. I squeezed the water off my head and wiped my hands across my shirt. It was an old blue shirt, a leftover that had faded and softened after several years of sun and wear. I favored the shirt and felt regret over having it ripped off my back.

"My kind of what. I aint rightly sure what kind of what I belong to? What kind are you, a grandkid, a nephew, or maybe something misbegotten? Maybe the problem out here is not lost boys but the fact that there aint enough branches on the family tree. Can you read or do your numbers yet? You dont talk any better than a wild skinner with a spear running naked across the hills."

He came at me then, a brawler who wanted to grab me and ride me into the mud where he could get on top and beat me. I stepped quickly around the pump, grabbed a handful of mud, and slung it at him, splattering his chest. Behind us his chorus hooted. The girl screamed at us to stop.

"Im gonna kill you for that," he said and wiped his chest, circling around the trough.

I kept the pump between us and swiped another handful of mud up as I circled.

"Dont you throw any more mud, you sumbitch."

I threw it, splattering him some more.

"Are you going to kill me after you kill me? I bet youre too dumb even to know how to spell sumbitch, which aint even the correct usage of an incorrect word. Go on, spell it, roosterboy. Show me you can spell." I picked up a third handful chucked it at the fool.

"Im gonna kick the stuffing outa you, you sumbitch."

Maybe he didnt say stuffing, but his exact words dont matter none. His meaning was clear, and I was giving more attention to what he was doing than to what he was saying. I stopped circling, packing another mudball, and let him come a couple steps closer to me before I faked one at his head. He ducked, and I was on top of him before he could right himself, pushing him backwards, smashing my mudball in his face as he fell back. He kicked out twice, the first time catching me solid in the leg, but the second time I wrapped an arm around his foot and dragged him around the pump. His chorus kept screeching.

"What is it with this family? Yall got some kind of kicking gene? You got some jackass kicking blood mixed in?

I was yelling and yanking on his leg, dragging him through the mud, when suddenly his ratty boot came off in my hands. I started swatting at his head with his boot, and he was crabbing away from me, kicking with a bootless foot.

"Here, take your boot back, you brainless kicking fool."

I swung hard and caught him on the side of the head just as he was turning to scramble up. He wobbled and rose up, stepping off a couple of paces. Then he steadied himself while he cleared his head. I could have been on him, but I let him go.

"You want your boot back? Ill sell you this one, real cheap. Its kind of scruffy and nasty. What you got to trade?"

"Im gonna kill you."

He pulled out a knife from somewheres, a hunting knife long enough to slice me open. I aint fond of getting cut. One time long ago a man I had fought got up off the floor and sliced my back open with a broken bottle. I nearly bled out. If I had known the fool had a knife I would have used a fence post on his head instead of his nasty boot.

"Well, come on then you blabbering bootless mudbrained fool. Ill kick the stuffing out of you with your own boot."

A boot and a knife aint much of a match, but I was mad. More than mad. I was whitehot reckless mad. Yet I felt good, like being whitehot stupid mad was a good thing, like I was strong and in control and no matter how many knives he had I was going to pound him into the mud. I was reckless and stupid, and yet I felt fully alive for being so close to what could end my life. The whole world had narrowed to a mudpatch around a rusty pump, and all I wanted out of this world was to hurt this boy that was trying to hurt me. All I wanted was for him to come at me so I could begin my work.

"This will stop."

I heard the words. I vaguely knew that others had come up to the circle and that they were clucking and jabbering. I wasnt giving anyone any attention except the bootless roosterfool with the knife. The thiswillstop words werent much different from all the shrieks of cuthim and riphim and killhim that filled the mudpatch. I didnt pay much mind to any of the whooping and snorting.

But then suddenly there was an explosion and a splattering of mud about my feet. And I stopped.

I didnt want to look too far away from the fool with the knife, but I glanced over and there were three variously blond boys with leftover military cutters. They were half smiling in a sort of Igotyou way and pointing their rifles in my direction. Two were so blond and blueeyed that they might have been angel twins, except one was a little older and stouter than the other. The third wasnt nearly so angelic looking. But none of them had to worry about scraping whiskers in the morning. They were dressed out in gray, shirts and pants, and had polished black boots.

I was about to request that the blond assassins shoot the fool with the knife when a little baldheaded man with a bushy beard and air of selfimportance pushed his way between the blond boys.

Chapter 4

"This will stop." The little man said and pointed to a middle point between the fool and me. The fool backed off a step and lowered the knife to his side. I eased up some, feeling the hot rage slip away.

"What will stop? Your thising is vague." I asked.

The little man eyed me and then ignored me. He turned to the fool and told him to go on back up to the house and clean himself up.

"Hes got my boot, and he knocked me in the head with it when I wasnt looking." The fool said and raised his knife enough to point at the boot in my hand.

"Give him back his boot," the little man commanded. For some reason his blond assassins thought this was funny, and they smirked and jiggled their cutters.

I have always tried to be fair in a trade, but I am always mindful of not giving without getting. Getting an edge, getting back more than you give, is the nature of business. But I try to be fair when it dont hurt none. So I held the boot up with two fingers.

"It aint much of a boot. Kind a nasty even. But what will you give me for it?"

The little man in the blondboy sandwich didnt miss a beat. "I will give you the chance to walk away from this with your life."

I quit worrying about the roosterfool and threw him his boot. I wanted to give the little man my full attention.

"Aint much of a trade. Who are you to be allowing me to walk or talk or spit?"

The little man puffed up his chest and raised his shoulders. He was also dressed out in gray, only he had some shiny black thread running up his arms and knotted up fancy on his shoulders. He had a little mouth and white teeth in the forest of his thick beard.

"I am Joseph Unger, the district manager for the northern territory of the National Recovery Alliance."

I thought there was something beaverlike to his face, though I hadnt ever seen a bald beaver. I had heard stories that down south there was some movement to organize into territories, that some people were claiming authority over some other people. But now that the Fires are cooling off you hear a lot of such nonsense.

There were too many people claiming authority over too many other people. Half the wackers that roamed up and down the eastern slopes claimed they were authorized by some sort of authority, and some of them even carried greasy wedges of paper that declared their authority, even though few or none could read. Im sure the cacklebrained clowns that lit up the Fires strutted around with their own little paper wedges. The Prince didnt much care about who claimed what authority. He hung them all. I didnt care much either.

"What happened to your head? Did all your hair grow on your face? Did you get frighted bad when you were little? Well, youre still little, but I mean when you were younger. Were you a bedwetter?"

He stuck a cap on his head. It had a little black bill and some more of the fancy black thread.

"I will have you chained and taken to the Canyons. If you resist, I will have you shot."

I looked around for a moment. The kicking girl had moved closer to what was now a circle around us. She looked upset, and I smiled at her. I wasnt feeling upset. I was starting to feel whitehot ragey all over again. I wish I had a little silver coin for every time some selfinflated bugbrain threatened me.

"Whats a district manager anyhow? I am familiar with the words, but I aint getting much meaning out of the way you string them together to puff yourself up. What does a district manager do to manage his district? I got a pretty good idea of what these ranchboys do, even that bootless brainless fool with a knife. They ride out and tend stock, gather strays, mend fences, and get fallingover drunk once or twice a week. I know the work. But whats your work? I aint never met a district manager before in any sort of size, large or small.

"You should not disrespect my authority. I am sanctioned with the civil authority of the National Recovery Alliance to maintain peace and order in this district. I will have you shot."

"Youre going to maintain peace by shooting me? That aint peaceable. "

"I will have . . ."

"I dont care what you will have or have not."

The little man stuck his lips out in a snarl but then relaxed and smiled.

"I have informed you who I am. Now will you be so courteous to inform me who you are?"

I tend to avoid names. Back at the ranch house I had a horse tied up, and I had a couple of guns tied up with the horse. Lately I had been favoring a little semiautomatic carbine I had picked up somewheres. It was light and did a fair job of hitting what I pointed at. But I didnt suppose the little beaver and his blond boys would allow me to get my rifle and shoot them. Yet I considered asking them.

"Yall mind if I get something out of my saddlebags?"

The little beaverman waited on my answer.

"You want a name? Pick any one you want. Over the years I picked up a few. Some more polite than others. Who I am aint steady."

"What is your birth name, the name your mother gave you?

There are times when somebody wants an explanation, and I aint never had much of an explanation. I smiled again at the girl, and she halfsmiled and halffrowned back at me. I thought it would be fun to get her going on rock time all over again. I thought she might do a fair job of kicking a little strutty beaverman a time or two. I turned back to the district manager.

"I aint nothing but a child of the Fires. I dont know who my parents were or what they named me. I dont know if I had brothers and sisters or aunts and uncles. I dont know what my birthday is. I am a trader of leftovers and lost things, and I trade up in the mountains with Joe Cruz. A nephew brought me out here to see about the lost boys."

The little beaverman nodded.

"Ive heard about you and your freak friend. Youre the Princes thief, whose nothing but a thief himself. I got word about you. You are a murderous thieving scavenger. I will have you arrested. And soon the National Recovery Alliance will arrest and hang your Prince. All of you thieves and raiders will be eradicated."

I smiled at the girl, and she headshaked a no back me, but I wasnt sure what she was noing about. I thought about asking the little district manager what he meant by eradicated just to hear what he would say. But it was clear what he meant.

But then I thought that what I really wanted to tell him was that everyone was pretty much the same, that one persons thief was another mans prince, and that after all the huffing and puffing gets done everyone gets eradicated, a feast for flies. But I wanted to say and he wanted to hear werent reconcilable.

"Its going to take a lot more than a little dandythreaded beaverfaced fool and three blond choir boys to eradicate me."

But the kicking girl dragged me off before any eradicating could start. While I was considering how to take down the three blond boys who were pointing automatic weapons at me, she came between us and started dragging me off with both hands.

"Grandaddy wants to see you right away." She turned to the little beaverman and offered him the same. "Grandaddy wants to see him right away."

And then without waiting for a reply she started hauling me towards the house. One of the blond boys, the lesser twin, started to head us off, but she just wedged up a skinny arm and pushed past him, tugging me along after her. We were halfway to the house when I spoke.

"You couldve gotten hurt coming between us. Those blond boys couldve cut loose. I believe I irritated the little bald man."

"You couldve gotten dead."

She looked grim, and a little angry. She kept pulling at my arm. Looking back I saw that the beaverman was gesturing to one of the bigger blond boys. I thought we would soon meet again, and I gave them all a wave. The kicking girl didnt break her stride until we reached the steps to the old mans porch.

Chapter 5

"They were taken."

I said it, and the old man acknowledged it with a slight nod.

Below us near the corral half a dozen horses grazed lazily in the afternoon sun. From where I sat they looked like good horses, and I wondered what it would be like to have so many good horses. And a ranch house with a big front porch set on a rise overlooking all the horses and cattle and kin. I wondered what it would be like to look out towards the horizon knowing I owned everything I saw.

Most times everything I own stuffs into a couple saddlebags. I aint never had much of anything that I didnt trade off after a while, including horses and people. Except Joe and all his clan, and maybe now a woman up in the high peaks I met a year back and a couple others we picked up when we came down from the Magic Mountain. You cant stumble too far forward without something sticking to you.

I once thought about trading for an old brokedown ranch, a remote place back in the hills with a decent house and a useable barn and with plenty of water and pasture. It needed work but more than anything it needed someone to be responsible for it. I think I liked its location best. Set on a flat between two rocky ridges three days northwest of the dead city and Aurora, it had fine views of the flats in the east and the hills and forest to the south. I couldve set on my own porch sipping whiskey and retracing old journeys.

But I aint a stationary type, and I like the going more than the arriving. Thinking about owning that old scrap of a ranch was just as good as owing it. For a couple months I took possession of it in my head and enjoyed it the same as if it was mine. I thought about all of the improvements I could make and the serene times I would have porchsetting. I stuffed my head with reckoning the costs of the cattle and horses and all I would need for the house and barn.

But I backed off from the actual possession. What I liked best about that old ranch were its remoteness and fine views, and they were free. I can climb any of the high hills, set on a rock, and have all the fine views I wanted without having to fret over leaky roofs and broken fences, or hauling hay and hunting strays. Or worry about wackers swarming over the ridge. I stay light enough to travel, and I aint always been responsible.

I kept my silver and bought whiskey and high times instead, and I aint come close to taking up responsibility since then. I get enough of that helping Joe with all his wives and kin back in Aurora. I tried to imagine what the old man was feeling. Losing so much so suddenly.

We were back again on the porch, but the old man was crusty with me for having booted the roosterboy in the head and for having exchanged unkind words with the beaverfaced district manager. I had tried to explain to old man that a little beaverfaced district manager with three blond clownboys all decked out in gray needed to be poked a little, and sometimes I cant help but poke.

"Him and me, we got business together. Thats all you need to know. You dont need to get in his way."

"Whats this National Recovery Alliance?"

He shook off my question.

"Nothing but foolishness. Just a bunch of men down south giving themselves a fancy name. But you dont worry much over names, do you?"

That was as much as he would tell me about the district manager. He had waved off my complaints about having been threatened with knives, chains, guns, prisons, and eradication. All he wanted to know were my thoughts on the lost boys. Yet he knew what I was going to say.

"They were taken, and it wasnt no random snatch. Someone, several someones, waited on them. They had been watching for a while, maybe a long while. They came for the boys, and they had the grab set up so they could slide out without being seen."

The old man nodded. He knew all this, and he had thought it out long before I came along. He had plotted out the rest too, the hard part he needed me to say. Someone close to the family had helped, someone close enough to know who was who, and who the old man doted on.

"Me and Joe will hunt around for a trail. Probably wont find anything. Theres a lot of wackers and slavers around, a whole tangle of them up and down the front ranges stealing children for ransom or sale. Somebody somewhere knows something. There might be a trail to follow."

I waited before finishing the obvious. But the old man looked off towards the redrocked spine. I couldnt tell what he was thinking.

"Eventually the going is going to bend back into returning here. Those that took them boys had help doing it. Aint much chance in snatching two little boys and disappearing without sight or sound without inside help."

The old man looked back at me and nodded. He was tightlipped and grim, but then he turned back toward to look out on his land. The sun was starting to slip behind a thin series of wispy clouds to the west, and a band of golden afternoon light was had spilled over the plains to the east. It was a pretty view.

"This is the biggest ranch around. Aint no one come close to doing what Ive done. But Ive grown old, and lately Ive thought a lot about letting go of all the lookingafter and the worryingover. I got a big family, and Ive been planning on dividing things up and letting my sons and daughters do all that lookingafter and the worryingover. I wanted to play with them little boys, ride horses, mess with little projects that Ive always been meaning to."

"When were you going to do all this?"

"It was being talked up a bit. Nothing was settled."

It was my turn to nod. I thought about a story I had once heard about another rich man who wanted to divide up his property and retire. As far as I could recall, that one hadnt turned out too well. I started to pull myself up.

"You got all you need?" he asked. "You can take a couple of horses, what gear you need."

"Got more horses, guns, food, and truck than we need. Well probably stash most of what we got."

"I want to send one of the boys out with you."

The thought stopped me. Except for a wild boy who once attached himself to us, me and Joe always travel alone.

"Why?"

He shrugged. "Help. Be good for him, and hes a tough kid. He can shoot and ride like the devil. Be good for him and good for you. He can help."

"Me and Joe dont need help."

"You take him with you. You doin my business, and hes part of my business." He swept an arm toward of knot of young men back towards the barn. "Besides, itll be a favor to me, and I will make it worthwhile for you."

I didnt like the idea, but I thought I would ask anyway.

"Who?"

"Sid." He waved towards the knot.

"Whos Sid?"

I looked towards the figures knotted up. There in the middle was the roosterfool staring back at us, still muddiedup and sullen.

"You had a bad start with him, but hes a good hand."

"Cant do it. Wont do it. Dont want to do it. Cant take a fool of a roosterboy out on the trail."

"What rooster?"

I pointed to the figures. "The fool in the middle. He struts and squawks like hes king of the barnyard."

The old man frowned and shook his head. "Hes alright. I spoke to him about about what happened, and hes sorry. And hes ready to go. Hes their oldest brother. Their father wants him to go. You take him with you, and he can help hunt up my little grandsons. You take him, and then bring him and them boys back, and Ill double my reward."

It was a tasty offer, but I wondered.

"What if you aint got so much to give by the time me and Joe get back? How you going to give away something youve already given away?"

The old man waved my thought away like he was tailswapping flies with his horses. But then I had a thought. Or rather I saw the thought standing by the side of the house.

"Me and Joe will take the kicking girl instead of the roosterfool."

"What kicking girl?"

I pointed. The girl looked up then and turned away.

"She kicks rocks."

"What do you want her for. Shes only a girl. Her mother would have a fit."

"She already came between me and three cutters."

The old man sighed and looked off again.

"I dont care. Take them both then."

"I dont want the rooster. He already tried to slit me open. I would be afraid to sleep around him. He aint practical with knives."

"I heard you werent afraid of anything."

"Im afraid of most everything, especially roosterfools with sharp knives and disagreeable attitudes."

"You take them both, and Ill square things with you."

Chapter 6

I was waiting on the kicking girl when the parents come up to me. I didnt know them as the parents, not at first. The old man had gone inside, done with me, leaving me with his view and an empty cup. The man was tallish, whiplashthin, and had a head of curly dark hair. He was a smiley sort, and when he looked towards me he opened up with a happy grin. Stepping slowly, he had the woman propped on his arm and was helping her up the steps. The woman was small and frail. She looked like a sudden gust would knock her down and roll her away.

They came up, the smiler husband making quiet introductions while he eased his wife into a chair.

"Are you going after my boys? I heard youre a finder." Her voice was whispery, and she stared at me.

"Ill look around. My partners already out in the hills, looking around. But it aint likely we can do more than what all the others have already done. Theres a lot of people out looking for your boys."

"But I heard youre good at finding things. Daddy said you and your partner have luck. You take my Sid and share your luck. You bring my little boys back to me. I heard stories about you." She balled her hands into small, gnarly fists.

I have felt lucky at times, but I never thought I had luck. I never thought of it as something that you got, kept, and carried along. And I never thought of it as something that could be shared. I didnt know what to tell her.

"Once or twice me and my partner Joe have been lucky to find something that was missing, and once or twice we found some lost people."

"People?" she asked.

"Once or twice. But there have been lots of times when we werent so lucky."

I let it go, not wanting to match up the lucky against the notsolucky times.

"Why would anyone want to take your boys?"

"Evilness." She spat quickly. "Just plain evilness. Somebody wanted to hurt us. Theres evil in this world. Theres devils at work. Corruption pours out of the pits."

"What my wife means," the smiler added, "is that we have thought about this constantly since they vanished, and we have no other way of explaining our boys disappearance."

"Evil always has a face. I dont think demons came snarling out of the ground and grabbed your boys. Or bloodyjawed monsters gobbled them up. People more or less like us took them. I just dont know why. They wanted something, and I dont know what they wanted. If we knew the why, we could figure out the where."

The woman nodded, and the man smiled. I wondered if I should mention what they feared the most.

"If we find something, it might not be a good thing. Sometimes bad things happen to little children. The Fires burned kindness and mercy out of most people."

They both looked at me, and I saw sorrow in their eyes. We paused awkwardly until the curlyheaded smiler broke the silence.

"Im sorry you had problems with Sid and then the district manager. I know Sids wild at times. But hes good on the inside. With Daddy hes got a lot to prove. He wants to help find the boys. Youd be helping us by taking him with you."

I looked at the husband and wondered why he was sorry. I thought maybe he was the type that felt sorry about most everything. I try to cap my sorrying.

"The district managers just trying to help us all. Hes the only authority we got, and hes just trying to help us get things built back up. He does some business with Daddy, and ever since Jemmy and Ben went away hes been out here near every day." He smiled helpfully.

I looked at the wife. She was staring at the floorboards, looking at something only she could see, maybe waiting on the evilness to ooze out.

"Most times you cant build anything up till all thats rotten gets torn away."

Not smiling so helpfully, the husband looked at me.

"Im not sure I follow what you mean. The district manager is restoring peace and order. Hes helping to rebuild a civilized society."

I studied on the redrocked spine. I wasnt sure what I meant either. I didnt think the littlebeaverfaced fool was interested in building anything up except himself."

"I aint sure what things should get built up and civilized. Seems to me lots of things before the Fires got built up in shoddy wobbly ways. The Fires aint flaming whitehot anymore, but theres plenty of smoldering and cindering, and until its all ashed up and blown away I wouldnt rush to get it all built up again. There ought to be ways of doing without so many puffedup peacocks ordering other people around. I once heard a crazy man ranting that the best government was no government, but he got dragged off and locked up. I sometimes have a problem with authority."

"I dont know what you mean. We need civil order. Youve got to have people in authority."

He spoke politely. I think he wanted to be respectful while encouraging me to consider that I was talking nonsense, which maybe I was. His wife looked up once at us both and then moved her gaze down the way, looking at the barn and corral. Maybe she suspected evilness had crept into the hayloft.

"The district manager is only trying to get things organized and lawful. We need his authority to control the peace and help get things regulated and orderly. Hes helped a lot of people with the distributions, and we aint had the raiding and killing like we used to."

"Who decides whats lawful, and who elected this little fool?"

He looked off for a moment to examine what his wife was examining. There wasnt much to see except a clump of the clan down by the barn. Off a ways the kickinggirl stared back at us, hugging a pack and saddlebag.

"He was appointed by the new governors down in New-Pueblo.

"Appointed? How did a little baldheaded beaverfaced puffer get appointed? And how did these governors get to be governors. Were they appointed too. Up north we got the Prince, and he came in after his father went out."

"All Im trying to say is that things have gotten better since the district manager organized this territory. We dont to turn out every night to guard against those godforsaken raiders like we used to. The district managers a good man with a tough job."

He smiled at his own conclusion and patted his wife on the shoulder, but she was too busy keeping vigil over evilness to acknowledge him.

"Look, we just come up here to offer our help. My names Henry. You need anything, anything at all, you send word back to me. We are sending our son Sid out to help you look for Jemmy and Ben."

I returned his smile. I believed he wanted to be helpful.

Chapter 7

As soon as I saw the four brutes watching us I knew I had made terrible mistake. We had got up on an old chunkedup highway running north and south, and we were slowly making our way around the breaks and cracks when I saw them up on a hill to the west of us. They was just setting on their horses with the sun behind their backs, and I couldnt see much except their outlines in the glare. They just set and watched, making it so obvious that I thought they shouldve held up a bloodsoaked sign announcing their bloody intent.

Old roads can be dangerous, and I had been hoping that Joe would find us along the old road before we ran into trouble, but no luck. Before the Fires thousands of people had traveled up and down the old highway for hundreds of miles, never imagining that their gaspumps would ever run dry, or that they might have to arm themselves for all the wackers, raiders, and crazies the scorchings let loose.

Roosterboy Sid wasnt happy with me, especially since I made him ride ahead of me while I cradled my carbine. But Nell the kicking girl was between us, and she seemed okay with the arrangements. She had actually perked up when the old man asked her if she wanted to go hunting for the lost boys, and had been all in a flutter to pack and get out of there. But as soon as I saw the four brutes I regretted bringing her out.

The old man gave us three extra horses, and they were horses good too, and the thought had crossed my mind that if nothing else me and Joe could lose the kin and trade the horses. I was aiming to lose RoosterSid no matter what, as I suspected he was waiting to take aim at me. Right before we rode off he had been huddled with the little beaver and his grayboys, and for all I knew he mightve been expecting four brutes to come after us.

Evening had settled in, and we passed the riders and slowly headed on. They stayed atop their hill a quarter mile above the road, and I tried not to keep looking back. I suppose RoosterSid had seen them. But he remained silent and sullen when I had poked him about the four riders. Nell saw them and looked back at me, but I just nodded and smiled and acted like everything was splendid. Which it wasnt.

There were a couple of hours of light left, but I pulled up around the next bend and started to make camp on a small rise above a woodcovered ravine. It seemed as good a place as any. Sometimes when you know troubles coming its best to turn around and confront it.

I asked Nell real nice to gather a lot of wood for a big fire. Most times when me and Joe we are between beds we never bother with a fire except during the icy months, but tonight I wanted a fire big enough to sparkup the night. She wasnt thrilled about the fetching wood but shrugged and went off, and as soon she was gone I got in front of RoosterSid, but he still wouldnt hold my gaze.

"Your friends back up on the ridge are going to come into

camp and do their best to ruin my day and all my tomorrows."

He looked back towards the stretch of empty, broken road we have just come. "What friends? What the hell you talkin about?"

"Those four wackers atop that last ridge. They might as well have held up a sign, though they probably couldnt spell enough words to make a sign. Now I got to kill them or theyll kill me. And if they aint acquaintances of yours, then maybe theyll go after you and the girl too."

He looked back at me and scowled. "I aint got any idea what youre talking about. I seen them four, and I aint got the slightest idea who they were. If anyone comes at us, Ill kill them." He looked back up the road. "Theys probably cattlestealers lookin to pick off some strays. Theres lost stock all around these hills. Every month or so Grandaddy will send a pack of us out to run them off."

"It aint cattle theyre after. If they were peaceable, they wouldve come down to swap words and whiskey. They were waiting for us, and now theyre waiting for us to settle down. Theyll come at us tonight."

He gave me his best toughguy look, and if there werent for more important considerations I mightve shaken that look out of him.

"We got some issues to settle between us. Ill give you whatever chance you want. But I need you to get Nell away from here. Take whatever gear you want and go down that old drybed in the cut and get across the road into the flats and scrub where you can circle back to your ranch. Theyll come after dark. You get Nell out before they come. Shes your kin. Get her back home."

"I aint afraid of any thieving wackers." He looked at me steadily for once, and I thought he probably wasnt afraid. But he shouldve been.

"I didnt say you were. I just need your help. I shouldntve brought Nell out here, and now I am obliged to get her back home alive and well. I cant take these wackers on with her still here. You keep her safe, and me and you can settle up any way you want afterwards."

He looked back up the road as if he was waiting for four riders to come into view and then shrugged.

"You want to shoot it up with four riders you aint even exchanged words with?"

He acted like he didnt get it, but I knew he did. He probably didnt become so roosterlike being a brainless fool.

"I dont want to shoot it up with anyone, but I aint got a choice. Those brutes aint got no other work but killing."

"How can you be so sure? They were just sitting up there. Maybe they were out hunting antelope or wolves. The district manager pays a bounty for wolf skins and skinner scalps."

I was sorry to hear about scalp bounties. Skinners were people gone wild who wanted shut of everything and everyone but themselves. They will steal, and when confronted they will kill, but for the most part they just want to be left alone. I was sorry to hear that the little muckbrained beaverman was paying scalp bounties, but then I realized it likely that the four wackers wanted to cart back a piece of me for a beaverbounty.

"Theyre hunters alright, but they aint hunting antelope or wolves. I know you know that. Im asking you for help. Take Nell down yonder and stay out of sight."

He weighed his decision and then nodded. "I didnt want to make camp with you anyways."

Chapter 8

A large fire burned thirty yards or so below where I was setting. Only a fool would have built such a fire, but I figured it was okay if the four rotbrained rateaters thought me a fool.

I was waiting, and the longer I waited the angrier I got. Sometimes when I know bloodwork is coming I get edgy and wished I was someplace else, and most times this happens when Joes not around and theres more of them than there is of me. But now I had no idea where Joe was or when he was going to show up, and I was dumb enough to sit there and not be scared. I might as well have been a rotbrained rateater myself.

But I was thinking back to the barn and RoosterSid and the whitelight of blindrage. Sometimes I get too angry to have enough sense to slink off out of the way. I dont mean for it to happen, and I dont like for it to happen, but sometimes when some dimwitted brute comes at me my heart starts thumping and my blood racing, and my head gets squeezedup into one bad thought, and the next thing I know Im into something I ought to be out of. It doesnt happen often, and I was surprised and sorry it happened today. I couldve done better with both the roosterfool and the little beaverman.

I sat there staring off into the dark waiting for the blackhearts to swarm, feeling myself getting angry all over again. I couldve slunk off, and shouldve, but I didnt want to leave Nell. I was hoping she was down tucked away in the drybed with the Rooster, but I didnt know, and the notknowing and the waiting were picking at me, pushing me somewhere I shouldnt go. I sat on a rock ledge in the dark listening to the fire crackle and spark, waiting for four muck-suckers, and I was not feeling tolerant.

I didnt wait long. Two of them came on before the last of the days light left the sky. They didnt try to hide their coming, making no effort to keep quiet or out of sight. They just rode up the road and then tied up their horses near where I had built the big fire. They stood on the edge of the fires circle, each resting a hand near on a handgun stuck into their belts. One was tall and dark and younger than the other, who was shorter, thicker, and graybearded. Both were wildhaired, dirty, and tattery, wearing mudcrusty old clothes, and both had cutters slung over their backs. They laughed and whispered something to each other.

"Hey you firebuilders, where you at?"

Their laughter and casualness scratched at me, and I waited a little before I stood up and pointed my carbine at them. When they saw me they did not flinch or step back. They looked me over and then the darkhair spoke.

"What you holding that gun on us for? We aint done nothing

to you."

"Just being careful."

"Wheres your partner?" the graybeard asked.

"Yeah, and the female? We seen you come up the road."

I took a few steps towards them, feeling the rage build. I felt in control but out of control at the same time. I hadnt mistaken the four.

"They went on ahead while I made camp. Where are your other two friends?"

The darkhair started to move away from the graybeard. I stepped closer until I was close enough not to miss.

"No you dont. Stand together until we get all the whos and wheres sorted out."

"What sorted out? And what two friends?" the darkhair asked.

"We dont want no trouble. We just came up thinking you had some food or something to drink you wouldnt mind sharin," the graybeard added.

I didnt move my gaze or the carbine. "Theres a bag with a couple cans and some biscuit by the fire. Youre welcome to it. Take it and clear out."

"You aint being friendly to strangers. We dont mean you no harm. Tell the other two to come out. We aint talked to no one other than ourselves in a long time. We been a long ways off in the high country hunting." The darkhair smiled. Neither he nor the graybeard moved a step towards the foodsack.

"Hunting what?"

I felt my anger begin to boil, and I was foolish enough to think I could kill a hundred wackers if I had to, and yet the little reason I had left reminded me it was fatal to feel that way. I knew that the other two more were coming up on me, probably behind me, and I knew all of them probably felt equally stoked and killready. But I didnt stop myself.

"What I want to know is, can you make a sign? Between the two of you, do you know enough letters and words to make a sign that says something like, maybe, "Dangerous Curves Ahead" or "Proceed with Caution?"

The darkhair got beadyeyed, and after a moment the graybeard spoke. "What in hell you talkin about?"

"Literacy. Im talking about literacy. I want to know if youre literate. I want to know if you can read or spell? Can you make a sign that says, "Danger! rotbrained wackers. Slippery when wet."

I never got my answer. The instant I spoke someone below us tripped or slid on some loose rock, and the second I stepped back shots exploded the night, chipping the rocks behind me. I fell to the side and began firing the carbine at the two in front of me. The darkhair rolled away from the fire, but I caught the graybeard so that he suddenly shrieked and a leg crumbled. More shots were fired from below, hitting the rocks and dirt to the left of me, and then someone else opened up to my right, trying to pin me down in a crossfire. Not caring enough to duck, I ran to my left after the darkhair. I came around some scraggly mesquite to find him pulling on his cutter, bringing it up to me. We both fired at once, but his burst hit the ground in front of me, kicking up dirt and rock. I hit him in the chest with two shots, and knocked him down. I plucked his cutter and beat it back up the slope toward the dark and the rock ledge. I wanted to get behind it and then try to come down behind the two trying to cut me down in a crossfire.

But they were moving too, firing wild bursts above and behind me. I was hoping they would run out of bullets and have to change clips. But as soon as I got to the rocks they leveled their fire enough to shatter chips all around me, and all I could do was hunker down and then pop up with a couple of shots when they paused. All of a sudden I did not feel so strong or fearless. I began to worm my way up toward another series of boulders when I heard someone running towards me.

Then more shots were fired, but not a cutter. Big bangs of pistol fire. But I couldnt tell what it was or who was firing. I thought maybe Joe mightve turned up.

The running man had stopped, so I worked my way back

around the rocks. I saw him, or rather saw his shape, creeping back down the slope, slinking his way to the left. I didnt know what he had seen or where the fourth wacker was.

The fire was still burning bright, and I didnt want to risk a glance at it and lose my night vision. I went left after the creeping man. I wasnt sure how many shots I had left, so I switched to darkhairs cutter, thinking at this point he wouldnt mind. But before I got to the creeper he stood up. Ahead of him was Nell. It was dark, but there was enough light to see her looking grim as she steadied a big old army pistol with her two hands. Not thinking or caring about the other crossfire I rushed toward her. I hadnt taken more than a step before the creeper dove and Nells hands exploded. She screamed and the creeper was on his feet again holding a cutter on her. I yelled and ran and just as he turned back towards me his body jerked and twisted up with a sudden burst from a cutter, and he dropped. I thought maybe Joe until I saw RoosterSid step up next to the girl, cradling a cutter against his belly.

I yelled at them to get down, but they just stood looking at me and looking around in the murky light. I yelled that there was one more lurking around, but the Sid just shook his head.

"Theres one more down yonder, but hes done."

"Done," I asked.

"Done," he nodded.

I went over to them, peering around, expecting to see a muzzle burst everywhere I looked. But there werent any, so maybe the Sid was right. But I moved them back out of the way. Nell had a bruise on her temple that was already starting to swell up.

"Howd you get that?"

She shrugged. "I aint sure. I shot at the other one down the slope. He was coming around to get behind you, but I got behind him. Next thing I know the pistol bucked up and hit me. You got anything smaller than this old thing?"

Sid moved closer and patted Nell on the shoulder.

"You shouldve seen it. The one she shot went down like a rock and didnt roll an inch."

I didnt want to see it, and I was sorry they had seen it. It wasnt a good thing, and yet I couldnt help but feel better him than me.

I made them squat down low just the same. I had questions, and maybe a warning, but I wanted to listen some. There wasnt much to hear except the fire and fat graybeard moaning and cursing. He was up a ways close to the fire. I thought I would go around his dark side and shoot him to get him to stop moaning.

"You gonna go kill him? You want me to shoot him."

I couldnt tell if the Sid was smiling, but I thought he might have been.

"No, I would rather talk to him. Theres two I know of that aint got much talk left in them, this one here and one back up a ways, and I am assuming your doneman aint talking either.

"Hes done talking."

"Then maybe the moaner will talk to me if Im real nice. I better see to him before he bleeds out."

But I paused.

"I appreciate your shooting, but I asked both of you to stay out of sight."

"They was gonna bust you wide open. You was done for." then Sid paused. "Nells the one that done it anyway. I give her that big old pistol for protection, thinking you wasnt gonna make it, and as soon as the shooting started she took off runnin up the hill. Only thing I could do was come after her, but before I got to her she come up to that first wacker and blew him away. Boom, and he was done."

"Done?"

"Believe it."

I looked at Nell, feeling both sorry and grateful.

"At least you didnt kick him."

Chapter 9

I didnt have to come up behind the moaning graybeard and shoot him. He was far more concerned with his wounds than he was in wounding us. But I nudged away all guns, rocks, and sharp objects just the same before I settled down with him. I had sprayed him twice in the leg and once in the foot. He was rocking back and forth and cursing up a storm.

"You bastard, you shot me."

I nodded, seeing no reason to deny the fact. "Seemed like a good idea at the time."

He snarled some and gave me his meanest look, but seeing that he was rolling on the ground bleeding out didnt make him look so mean.

"Just freakin shoot me then. Do it quick. Finish it. I feel like my whole legs on fire."

"I dont think your wounds are mortal. An infection probably will kill you, but not my bullets." Which in truth I believed. He didnt seem to be bleeding too much. One shot had scraped a long gouge on the upper thigh while another had taken out a bigger chunk a few inches below. The third shot had crumbled his ankle. Considering he had been shot three times, he was lucky.

"Shoot me, you bastard. Im dead one way or another. If I dont freakin give out tonight I pus up and die in a week. Just get it over with. Do it quick. Im freaked out."

Now, to be honest, this fat greasygray moaner didnt actually say freaking and freak. He probably didnt have more than a hundred words in his vocabulary, and fiftyone of them would make most people blush, even in these wild times. But I get tired of the same wornout words. Being an admirer of a higher level of malediction, I do what I can with what I have.

"You want me to shoot you some more?"

"Just freakin do it."

I shook my head and stared off toward the dark below us. The fire had died down some, but I had Nell the pistolshot girl gathering more wood. The Sid was out gathering guns and whatever else struck his fancy.

"No, I think Ive shot you enough for one night. I dont think Ill shoot you anymore."

"Freakin shoot, finish me off. You aint so cruel to leave a man to suffer so."

"I aint sure yet, you and your friends were going to . . . What was it you were going to do?"

"Freak me, its a freaking hard world."

My whitehot rage had ebbed out, and I was getting tired of all his freakings.

"You didnt answer my question."

The old fool just rocked and moaned. I was trying to press on his leg wounds to stop the flow, but he kept twitching away.

"Hey, I got an idea. Theres a bunch of heavy rocks around. You want me to go get a big pointy one and bash on your head? I bet I could put you out of your misery in two or three good wacks."

The moaner rocked back at me and looked at me for a moment.

"No, I dont believe I would like that. Why wont you just freakin shoot me?"

"Im tired of shooting. I got a big knife in my pack. How about I go get it and cut you open so you finish bleeding out?"

"No, I dont believe I would like that either. Are you some kind of crazy person? Aint no one that cruel to play with a dyin man. Cept maybe a couple crazymen Ive known along the way."

"There aint no shortage of people that think Im crazy, and sometimes I believe them. But Ill be honest with you here. Though you aint got much to offer, Ill make you a sweet trade. You answer a few questions, and Ill hunt up some things and take care of your wounds. Ive done some doctoring and I can clean you and patch you, even stitch you. Hows that? A fair trade? If I treat you, you aint going to die."

"What the freak you want to do that for? You done shot me in the first place."

The old fool got quiet for a moment. He seemed to be considering.

"Naw, just put me out. I aint gonna last long gimping around, and I aint got no retirement plan. Oh hell, go get a freakin rock then. Just do it quick."

I gave him credit for knowing what a retirement plan was. Since the Fires there aint been a lot of retirement plans around, or places to retire to. Nell the pistolshot girl dropped a load of wood near the fire and sat off a ways. But close enough to hear.

"No, I dont think Ill use a rock. Too much trouble. But Ill offer you another trade. You answer a few questions, and Ill give you a pill that will do precisely what you want, something that will put out of your misery and carry you beyond."

"You got a pill thatll do that?"

"Sure. I trade leftovers. I got lots of old medicines and pills. I got these fatblack capsules that will put you to sleep so that you never wake up. You just swallow one, close your eyes, and its over. But youre sure you dont want me to work on your wounds? You can live, if you want. Once you take the pill, its all over for you. Its a bona fide killpill. "

He wheezed some and coughed. It was a hard choice for him. It would be a hard choice for anyone. Nell had been breaking branches and throwing them on the fire, but she stopped and got real quiet.

"Ill take the freakin pill. I aint lived but one life, and it aint been all that great. Freak, I known all along that it would end this way, and Ive lived longer than most those Ive run with. Give me the pill and ask your questions."

It wasnt much of a trade. I asked questions but didnt not get much in return. I asked why he and his friends came after us, but he didnt seem to know much more than the other one I shot, formerly known as Scratch, had told him and the other two, which was little. The old moaner had been soaking in a whiskeyshack back up a few miles on the old road when Scratch had gathered him and the other two up in a hurry and had come out hunting for us. He said someone had given Scratch a handful of silver to put us down, but he didnt know who that was. They were splitting the silver plus all our horses and truck. I didnt think he knew much more, and I couldnt get more out of him. Nor did I get anything out of him about the lost boys. He had heard of them, of course, being so close to the old mans ranch, but he claimed he didnt know anything about them. This part I tended to believe. An old cutthroat like him would have jumped at the chance to get the old mans reward.

Sid had come up and offered to shoot the graybeard, but now the old moaner now seemed inclined to take my pill.

"You got my killpill."

"In a second, in a second. I want to ask a couple more things. Then Ill give you your killpill." I held up a fat round black capsule. It might have been for stomach pains, or a stuffed nose. But it wasnt. Back when the dead city was still blazing me and Joe had come across an old pillstore full of meds in a little mountain town that hadnt yet been raided or burned. Food was scarce and most of the people there had either left or shuttered themselves up, so no one minded two strangers. While Joe picked over the leftovers, I had spent a week inside the pillstore sorting through every jar and container. I had come away with two mules worth of pills, rubs, lotions, bandages, and gauze. It had been a prime haul, and I still had a nearly full jar of fatblack capsules.

"How come you got them kill pills anyway?"

I shrugged. It was a fair question to ask. But I did not want to waste a lot of time trying to describe how long it took me to figure out what pills were good for what. For a while, I would just give out any sort of pill when someone was sick. I dont think it mattered what the pills were really for. Someone hurt or sick would grab and gobble up whatever pill I gave them. People are generally mad for leftover medicines, thinking theyre magical and powerful. So maybe a pill for a stuffed nose was as good as a pain pill. But then I picked up this old leftover fat paperback that was some sort of pill dictionary, and I figured out most of what I had. The fatblacks were some of my best pills.

"I picked them up along the way. Traded for them. This is a tough world, and you never know when you might come across someone like yourself in need of a merciful end, someone in need of being eased out of their suffering. People will trade most anything for quick relief."

"Ease me the freak out then," he said, and reached over towards my hand. As he reached he moaned. He wasnt doing well, and I still couldnt get close enough to see how much he was bleeding.

"Hold on. I want to know what your name is. What is your name?

He rolled back to where he had been lying on his side. "You are some kind of crazy. What do you want to know my name for?"

"I collect names. You can ask Joe when he shows up. I am a collector of names. I have a prodigious collection of names."

"A what kind of collection?"

"A freakin collection, a big freakin collection. Now add to it. Whats your name?

"Why did I have to get shot by some freakin crazy person?

I held up the capsule in my fingers where he could see it.

"Bear. They always called me Bear."

"Well, Mister Bear. Pleased to make your acquaintance. But that aint your real name. Dont matter though. Names aint always that important. Over there thats Nell the Colt girl, and back yonder is Mister Sid."

He looked at me expecting something else, but I just smiled and gave him the pill. He rolled it around in his hand for a moment.

"Aint a big thing, is it? You sure it will do it?"

I nodded. "Itll do it just fine. Itll take you out right easy. Youll get sleepy and slip off easy."

He looked around the hill. The fire had died down some but was still bright enough to raise silver patterns that danced across a circle of bushes and rocks. The stars had started to come out. Except for the wind and the fire, everything was quiet.

"Aw hell, its as good a place as any." He popped the pill and coughed. I gave him some water and he washed it down.

"Is that all there is to it?"

I nodded.

"How long will it take?"

I shrugged. "Less than a half hour. You just relax and let yourself drift off."

"Just drift off, huh? Aw freakin hell. Dont freakin matter. I always thought I get shot to hell or stretched up anyway. Might be better to drift off."

"Tell me one more thing, though. Whats your profession?

"My freaking profession?" he snorted.

"Your work?"

"My work?"

"Your living? What do you do with yourself when you aint thieving and murdering innocent folk?"

He eased himself back and crossed his hands over his chest. "I aint got no work. Do I look like the type that grows freakin vegetables in the mud? I done a little ranchin and farmin, and I worked down south in NewPueblo a few times doin odd jobs, tearing down houses and rippin out piping and nails and whatnot. But I aint exactly got what you call a line of work. Regular stuff just didnt take."

He sat back up, groaning a little as he moved.

"What you want to ask me that for?

I shrugged. "Like to get to know people."

"Know people you done shot and then killpilled? Ill tell you what I done?"

He eased himself further down and yawned, again crossing his arms. "Its a hard life, and I done the best I could. I fell into some hard times, and then I fell in with some bad people, and the badness stuck. But I aint never shot anyone in the back, and I aint never shot at anyone who wasnt shootin at me, or about to."

"So what did you do?"

"Will you freakin go away? Im getting sleepy and I dont want to bother with you. Lemme just look at the fire and drift off."

"Just tell me a couple more things. You probably robbed, stole, and killed your whole freakin life, but what I want to know is if you ever done any slaving?"

"What?"

"Slaving, kidnapping, child snatching, kid stealing. Come on now. You aint got a lot of time. You ever truck with people?"

"I done told you I aint involved in them two boys, nor were any of those I ran with."

"That aint what Im asking. You stole horses, you stole cattle, you stole leftovers. Did you ever steal any people?"

He yawned and closed his eyes.

"I aint directly done that, but theres some around thatll buy and sell anything, no questions asked, people included. Little kids, little girls or boys, it dont matter. Now lemme be."

"Last question, old man, and you last words, make them count. Who around here buys and sells people? If I had two little boys to sell quick, where would I go? Who would I see?"

He opened his eyes and looked at me. "Aint no secret. Morrisons place. A few miles west above NewPueblo, up a road that snakes out of town. Morrison will buy anything stole or stripped and move it along. He likes to snatch women and children.

"Wheres he move it all to?"

But the old moaner rocked his head slightly, closed his eyes, and drifted off.

I sat for a moment and thought about the old man and his life. I thought he probably had done the best he could in a hard world. Nell moved close to us and leaned over. Mister Sid started over from where he had been sitting.

"Is he dead? Did you really kill him with a pill?"

"No. He killed himself a long time ago and was just walking around not knowing he was dead. Lets build the fire back up some and boil some water."

Chapter 10

"Theres another one of them comin at us."

Sid went to give me shake, but I was already awake, just resting in the warmth of the early light. I hadnt figured on another one of them, but I knew that theres always another one of them, since theres more of them than there is of me.

"Whos them?"

"Another one of them wackers from yesterday. Hes down on the road coming around the bend."

"Whats he doing?"

"Nothin. Just ridin along. Hes leading some horses. Lets go up behind them rocks and shoot him."

I stretched, rolled, and sat up. Seemed unfair and too early for blooding.

"Seems early for backshooting. Maybe we can trade away the Deadman. He aint doing us much good."

I went over to the hills crest and looked. There were still long shadows in the dips, but there was plenty of the early mornings goldenlight. I looked all around at the prettiness. I always thought it was the most satisfying time of day, just when the sun breaks over the east, and the soft goldenlight slips over the hills. Usually, when there werent wackers, crazies, or militias around, early mornings are calm, quiet, and peaceful. I looked back down the road at the rider.

"He dont appear to be too homicidal this early. Why dont we just let him ride up?"

"And then shoot?"

Sid seemed a little too anxious, but then I figured he was still worked up over the nights shooting. Despite the bluff and boast, I doubt he had much experience killing someone who was intent on killing him.

"No, lets take him captive. Let him ride up and you creep around him and come up behind him. Maybe he can tell us more than that nasty old stinking Deadman did last night. But be real quiet and stay hidden and you can take him by surprise."

Sid seemed to like this. He grabbed one of several cutters he had gathered and scrambled up the ridge. In a few minutes the sun would rise high enough to wash away the shadows and the golden-light.

By the time the rider had come up to the road below us Nell had appeared. Since the shooting and the killpilling she had been quiet and standoffish all night. The right side of her face was lumpy and red.

"Should I hide?"

I tried to give her a smile big enough to reassure her. I could see the Sid skulking behind some rocks about fifty yards or so over, angling down behind the rider.

"No, he dont look like he wants to shoot us. Lets go down and talk to him."

By the time we reached the old road the rider had tied up his horses and was sitting on a rock facing the drybed below. He must have heard us crunching on the loose rock but he didnt turn around.

"I have come for chewing gum, chocolate, and canned peaches," he announced.

I looked over the horses. He had strung them together and tied them up. A dozen horses, and half were carrying heavy trail packs.

"Hell, Joe, we aint seen peaches or chocolate in a year or more, and youre hoarding all the bubblegum. Break out something eatable for breakfast. We done heavy lifting last night. This is Nell, who decided yesterday that I was in dire need of her protection. She shot a miserable wretch who was trying to shoot me."

Joe turned around and held out his right hand. He shook his big shaggy head and grinned.

"Nell, this is Joe Cruz, my partner. Hes the craziest man this side of the divide, maybe on both sides, and each one of his six wives will attest to that."

Nell went forward and slowly held out her hand, which disappeared when Joe gripped it.

"Do you really have six wives?" she asked.

"Pleased to meet you, Nell. Thank you for protecting this old horsethief. He is in desperate need of help. I do have a big family back up beyond Aurora, but a half dozen wives might be too generous a count."

Joe turned to me, still grinning.

"What about the other one down a ways hiding behind those rocks?"

"Oh him? Thats Sid the Killer. He wanted to backshoot you, but I persuaded him to come up behind you and take you captive."

"Take me captive?"

"Thats right. Take you by surprise and then force you to tell us what you done with those two little boys."

Joe turned back to me.

"Aint much to tell there. You have some surprises last night?"

I nodded. "Four of them. I got a Deadman up a ways and I dragged off three others to get chewedup by deadeaters. Nell shot one, Sid another. I helped the third out of his misery."

Joe stood up and stretched his long frame. "I found four horses tied up around the bend down yonder. I watered and grazed them some, and they decided to follow me and our bunch. Ill hunt around in the packs. Maybe we got some little fruity cans, maybe applesauce that aint yet rancid. And maybe you can tell your friend Sid not to shoot me in the back when he takes me captive."

Chapter 11

"This your Deadman?" Joe nodded towards the graybeard.

I had pulled him aside and crossed his arms. He looked peaceful enough.

"May he rest in peace," I said.

Sid was off with the horses. He was not real happy with me when he found out all his stalking had been for nothing. I tried to explain to him that there were not a lot of people who could creep Joe. But Nell was delighted with him, as most are. She followed him around, watching him. He probably was the biggest and the strongest man she had ever seen. And the strangest. I tried to explain to her that when I first met Joe he was a scrawny runt stealing whatever he could find to stay alive, that I had to save him from two men who were beating on him. She didnt believe me, though, and looking at Joe sometimes made me skeptical of my own memories.

But back then things were different. The whole world was burning and raging. The Fires were hellhot, and just about everyone was shooting and stealing in order to stay alive. When I first met Joe I did shoot a couple of men who were trying to shoot me, but what had started it all was a starving scavboy trying to steal their packs. They had bloodied him up and were about to do a lot worse when I got involved. It just happened the way it did. I had seen a lot of little throwaways come up short, but something pushed me into the middle of Joe and the two men battering him. I stepped into it because I didnt want to see another starvy kid bashed, cut, and gouged for sport, not because I thought Joe would grow into some kind of monsterman that all the whiskeysoakers would talk about.

Me and Joe were lucky to survive those times. A lot of people just as good or better didnt make it through. One way or another, the Fires got them, all burning and starving and raiding, every moment a struggle to stay alive in a world that didnt much value life. Lots of people just crawled off and gave up. We seen plenty of people like that, alive but already dead.

Joe sat down next to the Deadman and slapped him a couple of times. The Deadman groaned but didnt wake.

"So you shot him, give him a killpill, and then spent half the night trying to keep him alive?"

"Nell helped once she figured out he was still breathing."

"Why?"

"Why what?"

"Why spend half the night fixing someone you just shot, especially when he had been trying to shoot you."

There were several answers, and some of them more or less

true. I shrugged, and Nell shrugged.

"Because he was bleeding, and because when he was awake he was all twitchy and snappish and wouldnt let me get near him."

It wasnt much. I cleaned him up, took out one bullet that was still in him, and then bandaged him up. If he was careful, if he kept his bandages clean, he would probably make out okay. If he wasnt careful with himself, he would fever up with infection and die.

Joe rocked the Deadman some, who groaned and tried to push his hand away.

"He wanted me to shoot him to end his misery, but I didnt feel like shooting him or sticking him with a knife. I offered to bash in his head with a rock, but he didnt want to get bashed in the head. I could have strangled him, but I didnt think of that. So I give him a killpill."

"A killpill?"

"One of those old fatblacks Ive been carry around forever. You know the ones. He took it and slept the whole night. Hes going to be groggy for a while after he wakes. He wanted me to ease him out of his pain and suffering."

"Aint he going to have considerable pain and suffering when he wakes up?"

"You want to shoot him?"

"No."

"You want to bash in his head with a rock?"

"No, and I dont want to stick him or strangle him neither, so dont ask me that. I think we should ride on out of here before he wakes up. Leave him with his friends down yonder for the buzzards to peck on. Hes gonna wake up wishing you had shot him."

Which is what happened.

We had been fixing to leave, gathering and packing. Sid had taken it upon himself to deck himself out with nearly every gun and bullet in his personal arsenal, which had grown to a sizable stack since last night. I thought about telling him that guns aint all that valuable, that there are plenty enough guns and bullets around, tons of guns in fact, but he was excited. Nells bruise had turned black-bluey where that old pistol bucked and cracked her cheek. I had her soak it for a while with a cold wet rag, but she didnt want me to mess with it. Yet I did trade for that old ArmyColt, giving her a small automatic with half the kick and, since she claimed she could read some, a small fat dictionary I had been lugging around. She didnt seem to care much for the wordbook but was happy enough to trade away that old handgun.

I gave the fortyfive to Joe, but it wasnt a weapon he was fond of. All those old heavy pistols tend to buck even in the strongest hands, but I was afraid Nell wouldve done more damage to herself with it.

To make up for not getting backshot, Joe had given the darn thing back to Sid, who was happy to increase his arsenal. He strapped it on, the largest of three handguns he was carrying. He had given it to Nell in case I got knocked down, but he hadnt figured that she would run off to shoot a wacker. I would have given her a small automatic if I had known she was intent on shooting, or that I would need saving. I had been trying to get her adjusted to going back home, but she was not of a mind to be adjusted.

"Hes stirring," she said, ignoring my latest offer of adjust-ment.

Which was true. The Deadman groaned some more and then coughed. Joe came over and peered at him.

"What are you going to do with him?" he asked.

"I dont know. Maybe shoot him. Bang him on the head with a rock."

The Deadman opened his eyes and looked straight up at Joe. He moaned some and closed his eyes again.

"Who the freak are you?"

"Hes the archangel Elijah, son of Abraham and Delilah, and hes about to pass eternal judgment on your sorry self. Confess your sins and beg for mercy."

The Deadman turned to my voice and reopened his eyes.

"You shot me, you freakin bastard."

51

"Thats a fact." I agreed with him.

"What happened? I thought I was gonna die. You give me that killpill."

"You did die, only Elijah here brought you back to life to confess your sins. You got one final chance to make amends for your miserable life."

The Deadman raised his head slightly and looked around. He raised himself a little higher and looked down at his leg and side.

"What the freak you talking about? And what the freak did you do to me. Im freakin hurting. We had a deal. You was gonna help me."

I looked around and appreciated the view. The ridges flattened out further to the east, but for a long stretch the land rippled, a wide distance of rolling hills and gullies. The grass and scrub were still green from the rains and washoff.

"He did help you. He saved your life fixing you up last night. We helped him. He pulled a bullet out you," the notshy Nell said. "You ought to thank him." She gave him a fierce look from her notbruised side and pestered a rock with her foot. Then she looked out east at the hills.

"I didnt need no help. I didnt ask for that kind of help. A oneleggy life aint worth savin, and thats the freakin truth."

Joe started laughing. "Maybe you ought to shoot him. You shot him yesterday, bandaged him up last night, and now you can shoot him again today."

Sid laughed along with Joe. The whole time we worked on the Deadman Sid hadnt been all that excited with the doctoring. He was splitting the world into us and them, and he would have been content to leave the Deadman to die. But these days I aint content to leave those hurt and damaged, even those crazy and mean.

Back when the Fires were the hottest me and Joe hardly had any interest in anyone except for ourselves and Joes family and kin. We swapped, traded, stole, and scavenged, but we never had much connection with anyone. Back then when the world was blazing hot people looked out for themselves and never bothered with strangers.

A lot of people fastened themselves to clans or communities and lived in fortified towns, or got swept up by raiders or militias, and made it through the Fires as part of a larger group.

But me and Joe stayed away from the groupings, and we never got involved with people. Except for trading. But that was business and there wasnt any real involvement. Lots of times when we were out trading or scavenging we would come upon a moaner or a crawler who was in misery, and most times we would just ride by, maybe throwing a biscuit to those starving, or an old raggy blanket to those freezing, but some times we couldnt do more than offer a silent wish for better times.

Aside from Joes tribe, the closest connection we have is with the Prince up in Aurora, but we aint on backslapping harddrinking terms. I knew his mother long before she knew the Princes father, which makes me and Joe tolerable but not altogether acceptable. We aint invited into the Princes reception hall on feast days, but there are a couple of side entrances. These days we transact a little business for the Prince, grubbing around in the dead city, picking and trading, dodging the scavenger laws and taxmen, giving the Prince a percentage of whatever. Times are still loose, and its good to be shifty.

But an unconnected life aint possible. Part of being human is being connected, and now that everyone aint always pointing a gun at everyone else connections are likelier. People aint so liable to shoot every time a stranger wanders up.

Lately me and Joe have stumbled into people that stuck to us since we come down from the Magic Mountain, and now theres a couple around Aurora and the dead city that I aint kin to but am still connected to, and the woman way up in the high country who seems to tolerate me some. Getting connected happened before I realized it was happening.

I sat there wondering what I would have done with the Deadman a decade earlier. I probably would have left him to rot.

"No, I dont want to shoot him again, maybe tomorrow."

The morning was cloudedup and I thought it might storm later. I thought it might be a good day to lay up in a whiskeyshack swapping lies. I turned back towards the Deadman.

"Listen to me, you old fool. Deads just dead. There aint no advantage in it. There aint no profits, hopes, or chances , and there certainly aint no whiskeydrinking and wild times. Nothing. And nothing aint ever coming out of nothing. As long as theres life theres a chance thingsll get better. You got a chance now. We will leave you water, clean bandages, and a horse, even a cutter, and you can choose what you want to do. Your leg and ankle will heal in a couple months. Youll hurt, but youll heal. Your ankle will probably leave you limpy, but youll get around ok. You can roll around in the muck and rot up and die in a week if you want. You can shoot yourself if you want. Its too late for the bloodyminded fools you rode up here with. Theyre gone, theyre just stinking meat for the buzzards and night creepers, but youre still here, and you still have a chance. You dont want that chance, thats up to you. But deads just dead, and it aint no release."

The Deadman groaned. "Im hurting. You got to do something. You freakin owe me."

"Ill trade you something for the hurting if you tell us more about this Morrison and his snatchers."

Chapter 12

I rode up slowly, stringing three horses behind me, giving the watchers a good long look at me. I intended no surprises. There were three men stretched out on the porch, two others off to the right skulking around the side of a brokenroofed garage, and at least a couple of others slunk off where I couldnt see them

To get the horses, I had to fight with the Deadman. He was fixed on taking a sturdy sorrel, the best of the four horses Joe had picked up, arguing that it was his horse when any fool could see that the old grey favored him. I finally got the Deadman to take his own horse by giving him a sack of food and a couple extra full clips for his cutter. Its hard to trade with a man whos got no reasonable expectation of values.

The Deadman had gone off grumbling that I still owed him, even after I gave him some painpills. So, I had one good horse and two pretty good horses behind me, thinking I would see what I could get for them, thinking maybe I could get Morrison to trade something I wanted.

Morrisons place was a distance up a twisty road above NewPueblo. Before the Fires it had been a pretty place, a big house set on hill with a pleasant view of the town and valley below. It had a big garage, a fancy barn and corral, and sturdy fencing surrounding a mountain pasture. A pretty place, but it was a getaway place, not a real ranch. Probably the owners were just rich people who drove up through the ridges in a big car with sacks full of groceries and bottles of whiskey and who sat on their big porch looking down at everything, thinking they had it all. Now Morrison and his slugs had it all.

There were a couple of horses in the corral, but neither as good as the sorrel, and I was hopeful I could strike a good deal. When I first came round the last curve I couldnt see the three porch loungers too closely, or they me, but as I rode closer we sized each other up. I had no doubts about their work. They didnt seem in any hurry to run off to fix a fence or watch over stock. Probably none of them had ever bothered with fences or stock. Mid morning, and they were gunned up with nothing to do but stare down a stranger.

We had spent the night in NewPueblo below, a cinder-blackened crust of what had been a goodsized town before the Fires. Not much was left of it except for scattered buildings and houses and a whole lot of rubble and wreckage. Whole blocks were filled with little more than broken bricks, splintery boards, and patches of roof shingles, and all of it ashy and sooty. There wasnt anything new about NewPueblo. But then many of the old towns were still like this. I hadnt ever lived anywhere that wasnt all broken and splintery.

When I was real small the old couple who took me in lived in a building more or less whole and unbroken. Living in their old

55

apartment was as much of childhood as I had, or can remember. I was just a gutterboy, a throwaway begging and stealing but mostly starving, and they picked me out of the muck, though I dont much remember that early part. I do remember them teaching me to read, reading to me out of old books and making me read back to them, and then making me write letters and numbers, giving me mouthfuls of sugarwater when I did well. They gave me stacks of old magazines, and I used to turn those old creasy pages for hours, staring at pictures, reading strange stories I couldnt quite make out about a world that hadnt been scorched. I would make my own stories, imagining beautiful peaceful cities with stores filled with endless aisles of fruit, candy, and canned foods, where you could buy anything you wanted with little plastic cards, and the government gave everybody little plastic cards. Those were golden times, and I dreamed they would come back. I dreamed of endless grocery bins overflowing with bananas and oranges. I aint ever eaten a banana or orange that wasnt rank oily in a can or dry withery in a package.

Which was why I was surprised when we wandered into the NewPueblo Central Grocery and found a small mountain of melons stacked on a table. They were a bit wrinkly and worn, having been off the vine for a while, but they had definitely been plucked off vines by someone somewheres close enough to haul them to market. I wondered how far they had traveled and where they had come from. These days most people who aint bloodyminded keep patch gardens, but most dont grow enough to sell or trade.

The NewPueblo Central Grocery was like a lot of open stores in burnedout towns. A few scavs had enough guns, brains, and enterprise to band together and plunder whatever they thought they could sell or trade. Most of the store was a fencedoff concrete lot filled with all kinds of junk gathered up from the broken buildings and houses. There were piles of scavvy lumber and brick, rusty old bicycles, loose stacks of old books and magazines, boxes of leftover household junk that might or might not be useful, and piles of old pots, pans, bottles, and cups. There were rows of raggy old clothes, and of course there was a jumble of guns, mostly old handguns and beatup military cutters with clips and sacks of ammunition. There were a few of old hunting rifles with scopes that Joe pawed over a little. There wasnt a lot of eatables except for a row of four glass cabinets filled with cans of leftovers, watched over by a large woman with wild grey hair and a surly look. She had an old small caliber revolver strapped around her fatself.

Then there were the melons. Since it was still early in the hot season, we had not seen anything fresh grown in a long while. Which made me wonder over the melons. The old woman poured herself out of her chair and came over to me, probably to growl at me not to touch her melons.

"Them melons tasty. I can let you have a few real cheap. You got any silver?"

"Whats a few and whats real cheap?"

"Ill give you three melons for a cutter with a full clip. Ill take a horse for six melons, seven if you got a saddle with it."

The old womans expectations were unreasonable, falling way short of a fair trade, but most bartering starts out unreasonable.

"Your melons wandered off the edge of ripe some time ago, and in another week wont fetch horseshoe."

We finally settled on a flashlight and a couple of batteries that generally functioned, and two cans of leftover beans to add to her precious glasscased collection. Maybe she guessed the batteries would fade in a day or two, and maybe she guessed the beans were spoiled, but she probably figured she could move them. Some fool would stumble in and get fixed on the idea of seeing in the dark, or on the idea of eating beans out of can. Leftovers always carry a high price. Most times its the idea of something that people want the more than the object. Leftovers are links to lost times.

But the old woman knew she wasnt going to get a better deal. So we got six melons, one apiece for three of us and three for one of us. But before we got the melons and tumbled out I started itching.

"Whered these melons come from? You grow them around

here?"

The old woman paused before her glasscases and shook her scraggly grey head. "Naw, not me, I dont mess with growin stuff. A couple guys came by with a wagon filled with them melons, and I swapped for the mess of them."

"What did you swap? Get a good deal? I would like to meet those guys. They still around? They ever get any bananas or oranges?"

The old woman eyed me closely. I spooked her with questions. She turned away to lock the beans away with the rest of her collection. With her back to me she offered the usual response. I wish I had a can of beans every time I heard it.

"Times are hard. We do the best we can."

Without elaborating on the we or the best, she locked the glasscase and settled herself back down in her rippy chair.

Before we had made it into the street, Joe had got out a spoon and commenced work on his three melons. Nell and Sid didnt waste any time either, even though they didnt carry around their own spoons. They cut them up with Sids knife, the one he had intended to use on me, and slurped them up almost as fast as Joe. Sitting on some old cement steps leading nowhere I ate mine with unrushed dignity. Though wrinkly and dimply, the melons were savory.

Chapter 13

I was still thinking about melons the next day as we snaked up the twisty road to Morrisons. But the watchers and loungers gave me new thoughts to consider. As soon as I come up the last stretch of hill the three on the porch pulled themselves off an old ratty couch and casually picked up their cutters. They were also holstered with handguns, and it all seemed like more than enough arsenal for a stranger stringing three horses

Before I came within seventyfive yards a fourth came out of the house to receive me. Casual and unhurried, he came down off the porch waited for my approach. Morrison, I supposed. Nothing too remarkable about him except that he was dressed clean, wore his dark hair long and loose, and sported a pair of bright blue leftover running shoes that looked unsmudged and new. The shoes and an automatic caught my attention.

I smiled and nodded hello.

"Down below they said I might come up here to trade some horses. I got three horses here Ill swap for whiskey, silver, or guns. You Morrison?" I didnt really care about the guns, but theyre a standard currency.

The man a stepped a bit closer. He shook his black hair back while keeping one hand near his holster.

"Whos it told you to come up here?"

I slowly dismounted and turned to him. "Hope you dont mind me getting down. I dont like to talk down to a man. Mostly this big old woman with wild hair who didnt want me handling her leftovers. She had a table of melons, though, still sweet too. You know where she got them melons?"

Morrison shook off my question along with his hair. "Aint got no idea about melons. Whered you get these horses." He turned back to the porch. "Hey Earl, you come down here and look at these horses. You recognize them?"

Earl was the biggest of the loungers, a large towheaded smiley man with a big belly, but he jumped lightly down the steps. He circled me and the horses and went back to take a place alongside Morrison. "I recognize these horses."

Morrison nodded. "Stranger, I dont know you, but Im guessing you aint nothing but a backshootin horsethief. I thought I recognized these horses, and I know the men that rode them. They was friends of mine."

"The horses or the men?" I asked mildly.

He stepped back like he was going to pull up a gun or swing down a fist. I just smiled. Better to be a fool sometimes.

"You tryin to be funny or what?"

"Mostly or what. Ive known a lot of horses I liked better than some people. Had a dog once, and that old dog was a better friend than most Ive known. You sure you never heard where them melons come from? I believe Im partial to the fruit. Someone must have a big glassy greenhouse somewhere around here."

Morrison scowled at me. "You quit on them melons, and you tell me where you got these horses, or youre gonna wish you choked on a damn melon."

I smiled and then shrugged. "Me and my partner were camped over a days ride from here on a little rise above the old chunked up highway running north and south. At dusk four men come up and we fell out."

"What the hell does that mean, you fell out?"

"We had a disagreement."

"We gonna have a disagreement if you dont tell me what happened to the men who rode these horse." Morrison swung his hair around and pointed at the three horses I had. He was heating up, but his Earl just kept smiling like he was enjoying the show. The two other loungers came down the steps and spread out. And a couple of others slipped around from the back of the house. If we stumbled into disagreement, I wouldnt have had much chance. I needed to give Morrison something he wanted.

"Well, the three who rode these horses aint having any more disagreements. They started shooting, and we shot back, and my partners a fair shot. The fourth, an old shaggy greayhead, rode off. Hes a bit limpy, but he might make it if he doesnt feverup."

"Wheres your partner now?" Morrison asked, and stepped back to the side. He was either trying to get a better angle on me, or give the Earl and the others a better line.

I pointed back a ways.

"Hes covering me from that clump of trees. Hes a fair shot, and for distance he favors this fancy old hunting rifle with a big scope. Hes probably got us crosshaired right now."

I was certain about the crosshairing, but I lied about the where. Joe was across the road, further back, in some rocks. Sid and Nell were, I dearly hoped, even further back where we planted them out of the way.

"Me and the boys will take our chances with your damn crosshairs. Aint no one around here who can shoot so accurate at that distance. We are gonna kill you and take the damn horses, and then we are gonna kill your friend."

"Me and Joe aint from around here, and Im trying to be honest with you. Joes a fair shot. Ive seen him hit a nailhead at over 2000 yards, which is a lot further than what we got here. How many yards you figure its to that clump of pines?"

Morrison smiled and started to pull on me. Then suddenly he eased up. "You ride around with a shooter named Joe? Joe who?"

"Weve been stuck with a few names, and some aint too polite, least the ones I get. Joes got a dozen or more wives and they all have their own pet names for him, except when hes inattentive, and then they aint so lovey. But most people around the ranges know him as Joe Cruz."

The Earl snorted. "Hell, hes dead, if he was ever alive. I heard them stories years ago. I once heard he carried two barrels of whiskey for ten miles, one under each arm. And then when he got to where he was goin he drunk both."

"You go on up there and tell Joe hes dead, if he ever existed. Then come on back and let me know his response."

Morrison waved the Earl back and came back closer to me. "Aint we all had different names one time or another? Ive had several. What name you favor?"

I looked around a little. A string of long wispy clouds had drifted over the high ridges across the valley. With the days heat I thought they would probably burn off. The whole ridge was dry, and I wondered when it rained last and if his scummy pond and stream ever shriveled up in the heat. Morrison gave a hairshake and waited.

"I dont favor any name, but Ill tell about that old Joestory. It was a keg of beer, a leftover keg of king of beers if I remember correctly, and he carried it all night. We were being tracked by some sotty fools who believed they had a prior claim to that keg. Didnt matter none for anyone. By the time we got it tapped the next morning it was so shook up that it exploded in a geyser that went up half a mile and when it come back down it rained beer on both sides of the Divide. Surely was a high time."

People generally think a name is a good way to know who a person is. Back when the world was a small place they mightve mattered, but not anymore. Sometimes Ill toss a name to those pestering me for a name. Most times people will call me what they like.

I imagine I had parents and a birthname. Back when the Fires were blazing hot everything got muddled and blurred, and whatever I started out with got misplaced. I have often attempted unmuddling by making things up, and some favorite stories I spun so often that I got to believing them. My parents got killed saving me from murderous raiders. I was misplaced in some stinking camp over-flowing with lost people.

I dont really know the real what or why. What I remember best is the old couple, and what little I remember before them are the endless streams of people moving along the old roads, never getting anywhere, just moving away from what was behind them, that and a lot of acrid smoke blackening the air. I dont know much else, so when I need something for someone, I make it up. I imagine Morrison always did the same.

But Morrison didnt need a name or a story. Thinking we were just a couple of old horse thieves, he decided he knew who we were. He probably had heard some old worndown story of something we might have done that set somebody chasing us. Once he fitted us into a narrative, he didnt seem too agitated about me showing up with three horses he was acquainted with, or the sudden absence of the wacking fools that had ridden them.

Morrison seemed more interested in me bringing Joe up to the house, but I kept explaining that I dont bring Joe anywhere, that he goes where he goes. The one thing Morrison didnt ask about was what we were doing there. He seemed satisfied that we were on the run from somewheres and trying to unload three horses to get somewhere else.

"I give you a crate of them melons you like so much for them horses."

We were up on the porch with several of his loungers. Earl and another, a tall skinny stick of a man, had slipped off towards the barn, and I caught a glimpse of them moving into the trees down below the pond. I figured they were setting off to circle in back of Joe, but I knew Joe was smart enough to keep them circling till their breath give out. I just hoped Sid and Nell were smart enough to stay hid.

"Well, you want them melons or not? You said you liked them."

Morrison had brought out whiskey and coffee, or rather he had poured after a young woman came out with a tray and set it all before him. She was young yet old, and she was raggy, darkskinned, and had long black hair tied in back. She came out silently and served stonefaced and unsighted, like she was seeing without seeing anything. She wouldve been pretty if she had smiled. I wondered what her story was.

"I might take a couple, but Im already pretty meloned up from getting some down below. I just was wondering where they came from. Someone must have a nice farm somewheres. I aint seen so many melons like these before. Whered you get your melons?"

Morrison just waved me away, looking irritated.

"You want to trade for them old horses or not?"

"Ill take two little boys for three horses. Youll come out ahead, getting three for two."

Morrison tensed up and again seemed like he was about to pull or swing.

"What boys you talking about? You like little boys. I aint heard that about you."

"A rich old rancher up the front range a ways lost a couple of little boys, and I hear hes offering a big reward."

"You accusing me of havin them boys around here?"

63

He swelled up and made an angry show, but I figured it was bluff.

"No, I was just thinking that this rich old rancher might settle for any two little boys. I was just thinking you might have heard something, you being a prominent businessman around these parts. I heard down below you sometimes help people move about, buying and selling."

"I aint no slaver. You accusin me of slaving?"

I shook a no and then looked off to the tree line, wondering where Joe was, watching for movement of Earl and the Stickman.

"No sir, not me. Sometimes I have been wrongly accused, so I tend not to accuse anyone of anything. But people get moved around from time to time, and a man ought to get rewarded for helping people get relocated. I was hoping for a tip or two about where to look for them two boys, or maybe to find a couple others to replace them. The old man up a ways is offering near half of everything he got. And I hear hes got a lot. You know anyone buying and selling little boys?"

Morrison laughed. And the porch chorus snickered along with him.

"Maybe Ive helped people relocate now and then. I am just a poor businessman doing the best I can in these hard times. I am a relocater, but I aint no slaver."

The dark woman came out again and set a bowl of bread on a little table next to Morrison. She was still expressionless, her eyes as blank as her face, seeing but not seeing. I noticed that, as she bent down, that one side of her forehead was scarry. I again wondered where she had got relocated from.

"But I know what youre talking about. We heard about that reward and them little boys. If I had a couple little boys around, I would claim that reward. Every sumbitch for two hundred miles has been out looking for them boys. We looked around some, but didnt find a trace of them two. I heard that old rancher got lots of problems with his family. Them little boys probably got piled under some rocks a couple a miles from where they started."

I nodded.

"Maybe so. Cant ever tell. But since weve been moving south away from the Prince and his Rangers we thought we might look around, ask around. I thought you might have heard something. Lots of stories get told."

Chapter 14

I didnt learn much about the lost boys or the buying and selling of people. Morrison was tight on both subjects. But we talked about the hard times, and I drank his coffee, sipped his whiskey, and nibbled on his bread. I never saw any movement in the distant pines, nor much else. He asked about what we were doing so far south of the dead city, and I let him know what he thought he already knew, that we got chased out.

I was about to get back to the three horses when Earl and the Stickman sauntered around from the side of the house, Earl all smiley and casual, the Stickman stony and serious. They were good creepers, as I hadnt seen or heard them come back, though I had been watching for them. They ambled up and joined the other loungers. Earl grabbed a whiskeycup out of another loungers hand and drained it, still smiling like he was the happiest of men, while the Stickman disappeared inside. Almost immediately the dark woman come out with another bottle and started filling whiskeycups. She moved around without causing notice or response. I watched her, but she didnt watch back, and when she came to me I nothanked her and tried to catch her glance, but I missed. Earl reached over and grabbed the bottle, letting the dark woman vanish back into the house.

"Say, what kind of guns and weaponry you got around here? I might trade a horse for a couple cutters or maybe something larger like a spittergun. You got anything that makes a big bang?"

I rode off with a couple more things than I had when I rode in, but less than I had wanted. I was less one good horse and two generally acceptable horses, and less the information I needed. But

I rode off certain Morrison and his bunch were snatchers, slavers, and probably a lot worse, and I suspected he knew a more than he let on. If the lost boys were still alive, if they werent piled under rocks somewhere, someone had to know something.

Just to keep Morrisons story spinning about who he thought I was, I offered for the dark woman, offering the three horses for her. But Morrison shook me off.

"Hell no, we just got her broken and comfortable. I wouldnt take six horses for her. But Ill tell you what, if you want a whore thatll fetch, carry, and do your pleasure, I know where you might find one or two. You go back down to NewPueblo to that goodfornuthin aunt of mine at the Central Grocery and tell her I sent you down there to get a young woman. She will set you up if the price is right. She always keeps a couple girls around to rent or sell."

I hadnt really wanted the dark woman, but I felt tugged to hear by Morrisons words. Her breaking could not have been easy.

I settled on a sack of six melons, three cutters and clips, an old tin lantern that still had kerosene sloshing around in it, a couple rolls of leftover tolietpaper, and rustytopped jar of honey. I dickered for more, and probably could have gotten more, but I was getting itchy to get out of there. I didnt particularly want the melons, or the lantern, though tolietpaper and honey are always welcome. But I had gone there to trade, so I traded, and it didnt hurt to let Morrison think he had gotten an edge on me.

I also rode off thinking Morrison and his loungers were going to take a run at us and that a couple more cutters around might not be a bad idea. I had pulled for something else that boomed or banged, but Morrison wasnt trading anything beyond old military cutters. I guessed he and his pack would try to take back all that he had traded away, that and whatever else we had. Taking was their business, and killing was their practice. All the whiskey, coffee, and bread, and all the smiley porch talk were just the preliminaries of transacting their business.

Joe had showed himself once, coming out of the rocks and

then melting into the trees, just a flash of man and rifle so Morrison and the others knew someone was out there waiting on me. Maybe Joe Cruz, or maybe not. I figured that, with a dozen or so against two, Morrison was calculating his profit potential was high.

We set up on a small rise not too far from the NewPueblo gates, me and Joe, Nell and Sid. Anyone coming at us would have to scramble over jaggy wreckage and debris cluttered near the road and then come up the slope with little cover. We tied up and hid away most everything, and me and Joe stayed awake most of the dark hours, waiting and watching, keeping the cutters stacked and ready.

But it was quiet night with nothing but the wind and worries to stir things up. After a couple of hours Joe went off into the dark to watch over our camp, and Sid took his place. He was a bit raw that he didnt get to go up to the porch and stare down the loungers, but I had told him how important it was to protect Nell, a job he seemed to take seriously. He sat with me for a while, wrapped in a blanket, his arms wrapped around a cutter, until the long day pushed him off.

The next days direction was uncertain. Joe was of a mind to circle back up the ridge and watch over Morrison and his loungers, since they were known slavers. I thought we might go back to the NewPueblo Central Grocery and push the old woman a little. Morrison mightve sent word down to her that we were in the market for a young girl, so it wouldnt hurt to show up and confirm what others suspected. But I also wondered if it might be best to angle south and get out of Morrisons territory.

Most journeys end up moving away from something rather than to something. Most times I never know where we are going till we get there, so every treks a discovery, and you learn by going where you have to go. But I sat there waiting, starwatching, and wishing that we had a direction. But then no one ever knows that. I dropped off thinking I should quit worrying and just wait till the morning moved us away and towards.

Chapter15

"Shes gone. Nell, shes gone."

I had been feeling tired and fogbrained but suddenly shotup, wide awake.

"What the hell do you mean shes gone?"

Sid had come tearing up the slope, redflushed and fretful. I didnt want his words.

"Just that. We went off a ways down towards the river to wash. She was with me, and then she climbed the bank into the trees down a ways, and she didnt come back. I waited a while and then I called her, and then I went after her."

"Show me."

A few years ago I had been scavenging in the dead city, scrounging leftovers, and I came across some boxes full of books tucked away in a closet. People dont trade books much, and most get burned up or wiped away, but I always keep a stack or two around. I remember picking one up because it had a funnylooking cover. It was written by a little smileyfaced bald man wrapped in an orange blanket whose name I couldnt even begin to pronounce. It was a little thin paperback about breathing, and I couldnt make much sense of it, but the general idea was that people could control their lives by controlling their breathing. I picked up the habit. Late at night, and sometimes during the day, when my mind gets snagged, I keep that little book in mind, and I start to count my breaths. One in, two out. Three in, four out. Its supposed to be a way of calming and releasing. But sometimes there just aint no way to calm and release. After Sid came running up I could feel my blood boiling.

I hurried after Sid down toward the riversedge, up a steep slope, and into the pines, all the time clutching a cutter fully bolted and clipped, ready to spray the first thing that moved. Above the embankment there was a seam of rock that trailed off into the trees. Sid pointed off a ways.

"Is this where she went?"

"I guess. I didnt follow her or nothing. She got up sayin she would be back in a minute. I thought she was just going to, you know, go off a ways for some privacy."

I was having problems calming and releasing. Had that little smileyfaced bald man with the unpronounceable name been in front of me, I would have shot him. I couldnt imagine how I would feel if something grim happened to Nell. I didnt want to think that. I thought maybe she was hiding, or maybe she twisted an ankle and was hobbled up somewhere.

I followed the rocks into the trees and tried to find her tracks, but it was still too early for the sun to have scattered all the dark, and I cursed myself for not having better eyes and for being old and dumb and for everything else I could dump on myself. I cursed myself double for having brought her along.

I screamed her name several times, but the only thing I heard back was the sound of the wind brushing the pines and the rivers current. I fired off three shots, and then three more, to bring Joe back to camp, and then I plunged off in what I thought was a likely direction for a stonekicking girl, or the vile pusfilled snatchers that took her.

Sid had already repeated his story to Joe by the time I got back, girlless, scratched, and out of breath. I had gone wide and then circled back in what I thought was a wide arc, stopping to listen every so often. I hadnt heard anything like a lost girl or a band of thieving snatchfiends.

Joe watched as I ran the last stretch down the hill. He was seated on a blanket eating something out of a can. He spoke calmly between bites while I caught my breath.

"Sid here thinks she was gone for maybe ten or fifteen minutes before he went lookin for her. Thats plenty enough time for a quick grab and dodge. Whoever took her had been close by, watching for a chance at her. Im guessing someone watched over us all night waiting for a chance."

I went up and stood near Joe. I wanted to run back into the pines.

"We could try to track her."

Joe shook his head and swallowed. The suns light was just beginning to spill over the landscape, but there were still plenty of dark pockets left from the night.

"We still wouldnt see much for a while yet, and with the noise and commotion we would be easy targets for whoever was out there."

I knew he was right, but I also knew I couldnt wait around an hour waiting for full light.

"Nell didnt disappear by herself. Someone came for her. You figure theres any question about who?" I asked, but I knew the answer. Joe shook his head.

"Nope. The only question is which direction. You and Sid get saddled and head out. Take that twisty road up the high ridge like yesterday and wait for me to catch up on top of that last ridgeline before the road drops back down Morrisons. But dont push the horses too hard. Dont get reckless going up that road. Theyll be expecting us. Ill take care of the packs and all, and then Ill look around some more to be sure. Dont go charging into Morrisons. I wont be far behind. We can all ride in for brunch."

I nodded, already gathering up gear and guns.

"Did they take her, them guys yesterday?" Sid asked.

I stopped and turned back to him. He already knew the answer. He just wanted it confirmed. Sometimes knowing aint fully knowing until you hear somebody else say it.

"Aint but a few miscreants around here in the people-snatching business. Or maybe you figure that old frazzly melon-woman followed us out here and stole Nell for her rental business? She probably couldnt navigate her way up that first hill. Its Morrison, or some of his bunch. Im guessing that Stickman scouted you both out yesterday and that those bloody stonehearts were planning to come after her before I had stepped off the porch. Nell didnt just disappear, just like them two boys didnt just disappear. The ground just dont crack open and swallow people. People just dont vanish."

"What are we going to do when we get to Morrisons?" Sid asked.

I suspected he knew this answer too. I didnt hesitate to respond.

"Shoot those sonsofbitches and take her back."

Chapter 16

The Deadman was the first to greet me.

"You sumbitch, you done this to me."

He was boxed up in an old rusty cage and looking a lot worse than when I had left him on the old road. Someone had beat on him, leaving his face mashed and swollen. I doubted he could see much, and his words were slow and slurry. Not content with the beating, some bloodyminded brute had picked at his leg and ankle, tearing off the bandages and opening up his wounds. The Deadman was lying on his side, holding himself still to keep the pain from streaking.

"Just kill me, you sumbitch, just shoot me. I cant stand anymore of this. You owe me. You done this to me."

The cage was set near the barn, and knowing I was being watched I was careful to dismount with two cutters and a couple handguns. I probably looked like I could shoot a few dozen deadmen, and then some. I looked around but didnt see anyone porchlounging or skulking about. But I knew they were around.

"Aint we already been down this road? Cant you ask me for something else. How about some water? Wipe some of that blood off your face?"

"Shoot me quick, you sumbitch. You done this to me. I aint got nuthin else left."

The Deadman was probably right. Unless he got a lot of help and a new life, he didnt have much else left. I wasnt sure I had either.

"No, I dont feel like shooting you just now. Maybe later. I got some more of them fatblack killpills. Take a few of those and youll really slip out. You got something to trade?"

"Freak you and your killpills. I aint had nuthin but pain and misery since you shot me."

"I left you clean, bandaged, and medicated for pain. Howd you get back here in such a mess?"

One cutter was slung over my back while I cradled the other, expecting Morrison or some of his loungers to pop out. The Deadman groaned but ignored my question, which didnt really need an answer. He made his way back to the only place he knew and the only life he knew.

"You would have made out better if you had picked another direction, maybe headed into the peaks. Found yourself some old splintery cabin somewheres and healed up. Guess you didnt think your friends would beat on you and then use you for bait."

I leaned down close to whisper, turning back outward to catch sight of whatever was coming.

"You got anything to trade. Ill get you out of here, clean and fix your wounds again, and give you something good for the pain if you tell me where the girl is. Your best trade since you aint got much of future around here locked in a rusty cage waiting to die a slow death."

But before I could get an exchange going Earl came out of the barn with two other loungers while a fourth came around the far side by the corral. All of them had me pointed. Smiling like he was the happiest of men, Earl motioned towards the Deadman.

"Yall shouldnt be messin with him. He got himself in a heap of trouble. Morrison set him out here to think about his . . ." Then Earl paused to consider his words, ". . . "his inefficiencies.""

"Whats he done?"

He heaved his shoulders in an Idontknow.

"Its more like what he aint got done. Morrison cant tolerate inefficiency and stupidity. Hes out on a trade with a few of the crew, but he wants to deal with Bear when he gets back, thats if the old fool lives that long. He dont look too good, does he?"

"Just the four of you left?" I asked but expected there were several others.

Earl moved out a few steps and planted himself next to the hulk of an old pickup, and with his best smileyface spoke to me like we were on the best of terms.

"Nice to see you again. Were all friends here. Put down your guns and come on up to the porch. Tell your partner out yonder to come on in and set with us."

He pointed back towards where Joe had shown himself the day before.

"I came here alone today, and I came back alone to do some more trading. I got a bottle of leftover whiskey and a couple cans of candy yams and apricots. You know what yams and apricots are? Theyre real good eating. And that whiskey? Well, it mightve been up north in one of the Princes storehouses. By the way, wheres the Stickman you went creeping through the woods with yesterday. He about? He dont seem half so happy smiley as you. He out with Morrison. Hes a tracker, aint he?"

Pointing his cutter at me, Earl headshaked and smiled.

"You best understand. Im like Morrison. I dont tolerate inefficiency and stupidity either. I invited you up to the porch to set and youre talkin to me about damn yams and apricots while pointing a weapon at me. That aint good. You talk a lot, but you dont say much. Put down your weapon."

Before I could say much of anything Joe came around the barn behind and stuck a cutter in back of the fourth loungers head. He stripped the mans cutter and pushed him a few steps towards the rest of us.

"How yall doing? Trader offering you a fair price? Ill trade this here friend of yours for a young girl."

Earl shifted towards Joe and looked his happiest.

"Well damn me. Are you really Joe Cruz? Youre big enough. Ive always wanted to meet you. Ive heard stories about you. I was just trying to get your partner to put down his weapons. Id sure like to set with you and talk some. Why dont you let that man go and come on to the porch. We dont have any young girls around, but Morrison keeps plenty of food and whiskey around."

Earl stepped back and turned like he was headed towards house but suddenly pulled around the rusty hulk and steadied his rifle against it, aiming directly at me.

"Lets all be friendly. Yall put down your weapons. Id surely hate to have to kill anyone this morning."

"Shoot him if you want. Im tired of him losing things." Joe shifted an arm around his lounger, pulling him tighter. "Yall sure you dont have a young girl around here?"

"Lets all do a little trading," I said, hoping to get Earl to relax his aim. "Im sure theres lots we can exchange other than cutterfire. This is going to get real bloody real fast unless you do the smart thing."

But Earl held his aim steady and kept smiling like he was enjoying himself. The fifteen feet between us felt more like five. I thought he had a good chance of ruining me. Stopping by the Deadman didnt seem like such a good idea.

There was a time way back before Joe when I was young and foolish and whiskeywrecked in an old building in the dead city. It was one of the few old bigbuildings left standing, though considerable parts of it had been scorched in the Fires, and the rest of it had been fought over dozens of times, so that it was chipped and damaged. The main floor had become a gathering place for wackers and crazies, who would drink themselves until they were brainfried and then run out and go after anything or anyone. It was all loose, wild, and ravy, sort of like a bloody storm tide that rolled in and out on an irregular unpredictable pattern. I shouldnt have been there. It was a bad place and liable to get murderous in an eyeblink. But one of the bloody tides had rolled in with an unusually large amount of leftovers, and I thought I could slink in, collect a few things left lying around, and slink out before things got too savage.

But the whiskey was flowing, and I jumped in headfirst, and soon I was corneredup in big square room with only high windows on one side and only one door on the other. There were a couple dozen others stretched and sprawled about, all hard types loaded with weapons and whiskey, but everything was fine and peaceful until two men who had been sitting at a table together suddenly went at each.

I had no idea what the disagreement was about, and I suspect those mushbrained killers didnt either. One moment they were laughing, and the next moment they were rolling around the floor tearing at each other, trying to rip each others head off. And then suddenly one idiot rolls away and pulls out a handgun, one of those blocky automatics that were so popular before the Fires, and started blasting away at the other idiot, who despite being bloodiedup, pulls out another handgun and starts firing back.

Then it all got killcrazy in seconds, but I vividly remember the scene as if it the moments were stretched into hours. As soon as the blasting started, nearly every other blind drunken idiot fool pulled out a gun and started firing at every other idiot fool. It wasnt like the friends of one idiot were peppering at the friends of the other idiot. There were no sides, it was too insane and brutish for anyone to take time to choose sides. A hot, wild, and bloody freeforall fight, and every whiskeysoaked fool was firing at every other whiskeysoaked fool.

In an instant the room was filled with chaos, smoke, and headsplitting gunracket. I backed up as much as I could and went low. I crawled under a long table against the wall and tried to look invisible in all the clang and clutter. But just as I thought I might wait out the bloodwork one of the idiotfools drops a half dozen feet away from me. He had been holepunched a couple of times in the chest and was done for. Groaning in pain and coughing blood, he had only a couple minutes until life seaped out of him. Not a big man, or memorable in any special way, he was tattered and greasy and hadnt shaved or cut his hair in years, and I watched how every time he heaved his blood reddened his beard. But then he rolled his eyes over my way and noticed me.

And the strangest stupidest thing happened. This stupid deadman who could have enjoyed a few last moments of peace starts to grab at the handgun he dropped, one of those bigheavy longbarrelled revolvers. He could barely pick it up and had to draw it up against his bloodybelly for support. I watched in amazement for half a century, or maybe less than half a minute. That foolish stupid deadman wanted to kill me, a man he didnt know, a man he hadnt even seen before until he had dropped to the floor to die.

Much later after me and Joe got hookedup I told him about this crazybloody moment, and he said the deadman had probably just wanted to take me along with him for company. But I dont think so. He was a crazykiller, and I think all he knew was killing, and even in his last painful moments he wanted to kill.

I shook my head to tell him no, and then I called for him not to do it, to drop his gun, but he kept his bloody eyes on me and struggled with that crazybig revolver until he could prop it up on his bloodyholed chest and aim at me. His fingers were slick and slippery, and he fumbled with the gun. I kept telling him not to do it, but when he finally had that pistol proppedup and his bloodyfingers locked on the trigger, I quit trying to be reasonable and shot him.

I hadnt wanted to and had hoped not to, hoping that he would bleed out before he could aim and fire. But I couldnt wait. There just aint no use in waiting on crazies to get reasonable. It was a bad crazy time. I stumbled out of there with the other survivors feeling shocked and in a strange way embarrassed, as if we all had fallen in some nasty muck and didnt want anyone else to notice.

Chapter 17

I get that sick dontdoit feeling every time some crazyfool has a weapon aimed at me, and I was feeling it with that idiot Earl smiling at me while intending to shoot me. There just aint no use in trying to be reasonable when times get crazy.

"Hey Earl, you always smile at people you kill."

The dangfool broke out a big bellylaugh and shook his head. He appeared to be enjoying the thought as much he did holding an automatic weapon aimed at me.

"No, I just like you, is all."

I aint sure what happened next, and there aint a lucid way to describe it even if I knew it. Suddenly the whole world exploded, and there was chaos and confusion and all that was rational and reasonable disappeared in a savage instant. Suddenly I was wrapped in a crazywild world of cutterfire, smoke, dust, the clatter and clang of empty shells, and above all the deafening mindnumbing noise of gunfire and screaming. It would have been nice to keep a cool head and calculate a reasonable course of action, but savagery and killing are a noxious contagion for which there aint no antidote.

I dropped and rolled at the first fire and knocked against the Deadmans cage. He squinted back at me out of one swollen bloody eye.

"Shoot me, you bastard."

I was feeling such madcrazy rage that I suddenly wanted to kill him, and if three more loungers hadnt come tearing around the other side of the barn I would have shot him. Instead I threw a small caliber pocket pistol into his cage and encouraged him to shoot himself while rolling forward towards the Earls pickup, firing off bursts at the barn loungers, hoping to stay under the line of fire coming at me from two different directions.

Time gets confused in such wildness, and what took moments seemed to last for hours, and I suddenly felt tired and thirsty and worndown, my head pounding and my ears ringing, and the pounding and ringing kept on after the firing slowedup and then stopped.

But that was good, since the pounding and ringing reminded me I was still alive. I was crouched by the front of the pickup while Joe had scrunched down by the barn door, peering around inside. From what I could tell most of the loungers were down or had bolted. But I didnt really know who was left standing and was worried that Earl would pop around beside me wanting to punch holes in me. I flattened out to look for his big feet and then saw an amazing sight. There was the Earl all bloodiedup and crumpled, lying on his side, smiling at me. I went around the pickup to find the dark woman standing over him with a pump shotgun. She had shot him in the lower back at close enough range to tear open a big bloody hole. She looked once at me but showed no sign of recognizing me.

I am not sure why, since for all I knew there couldve been a host of Morrisons killers coming down on me, but I bent down close to Earl. He was still alive, still smiling.

"She got me good, didnt she?" His voice was whispery and hoarse.

I nodded. There wasnt anything to say.

"I got a twin brother, his name is Burl."

With that his breath give out and he stopped. Joe stepped behind me, startling me enough so that I twisted around sharply.

"Scared you, huh?"

I shook my head and stood. "No, not me, I knew it was you."

"Yeah, that so?" Joe smiled and then pointed at the dead Earl. "What about him? He gone?"

I nodded and looked at the dark woman.

"We aint exactly met. Whats your name?"

The dark woman looked back at me and raised her shotgun until it was pointed at me. I felt a sudden cold shudder.

"She dont like that question anymore than you do." Joe laughed and moved off toward the Deadmans cage.

I straightened and tried to look agreeable.

"Thats all right. I aint much on names either."

She stared for a moment and then lowered her weapon. She turned away and started towards the house.

"Marena. My name is Marena." She called back.

Chapter 18

I wasnt happy. Twice in one week was two times too many to have some slopbrained wormeating wacker trying to kill me.

But Sid and the Deadman were even less happy than me, although now neither was feeling much of anything. Sid had been cut up by two rounds, one had shot through his right shoulder while the other had gouged his right thigh. I had cleaned and bandaged him as best as I could, using what I could find. But Sid was weak from bloodloss, and I could only hope that he wouldnt bleed away internally or get infected. He needed to gain strength for the long journey home. I was less concerned about the Deadman, who had taken a couple of my painpills and then guzzled himself dopeydrunk on a whiskey jug he pulled out of the house. I was considering dumping him into the deadpile of recently departed Joe had made down at the barn.

"You ought to be extra nice to him. He saved your life. Him and Sid kept you among the living. And the woman too."

Joe seemed almost cheerful. He had arranged two surviving loungers on the edge of the porch and then settled himself in an old creaky porchrocker. The loungers were ductaped and unhappy. One was taller, scraggy, and gaunt, and he wore his hair long, while the other was a bit shorter and thicker and kept his hair cut short. He had both arms tatted murky blueandpurple with an odd assortment of mushy designs, including a bigtoothed wolf. Neither wanted my help or conversation.

I wasnt really sure who had saved who, and I thought perhaps I mightve contributed to my survival, but I let it go. Joe wanted to poke at me about what had happened, but I didnt know all that much about what had happened. What I had seen and what I remembered was partial and disagreeable.

Sorting out always comes later, and often its all madeup anyway. Sometimes all the crazy jagged pieces dont fit together, but someone whos still standing will start jamming things together to tell a story.

Joe maintained that the Deadman had shot one of the barn loungers with that little pocket pistol I had thrown at him, dropping him before he could drop me. Shot the fool wacker in the kneecap and then shot him again when he fell. Maybe so. Sids work was undisputable. He had gotten behind the last three loungers and had knocked them down before they did much damage, and if he hadnt taken two rounds of return fire he would have kept on knocking down all those who remained standing.

"He couldve taken that little pocketgun and shot you. I think he holds a grudge against you."

"Maybe Ill shoot him when hes sober."

"That could be sometime tomorrow. You better shoot him now. He aint likely to feel too good tomorrow. He drank most of that jug. Go ahead, one little pop in the head, and he can rest in peace. He saved your life. Its only right to give him what he wants."

I ignored Joe and stared off down the slopes toward New-Pueblo. It was a pretty view, and I wondered some more about the people who had built the house. They had built the house and porch for the view, and they mustve spent considerable contentment enjoying the scene. I wondered what they had done when the Fires got lit. I imagined they would have held out as long as they could, thinking the blazing inferno down below along front ranges would never reach them. But eventually everyone got scorched.

"What are you intending for these two?" I pointed to the two survivors. Joe yawned and rocked, making that old rocker creak as much as he could.

"I dont know. I thought we could all be friends and hangout. Maybe ride around eating melons and drinking whiskey, having a fine time. But they aint being friendly. Maybe you should shoot them too."

"Seems like a lot of trouble to drag them up here and then have to drag them back to the deadpile."

"Yep, living is a hard journey." Joe creaked some more and then leaned forward. "What do you boys think, is life a burden?"

He looked back at me, and I knew he was enjoying himself.

"Trader, what was that you threw at me the other day, that booky thing you dragged out, something about a valley of tears or something?"

I had no idea what he was talking about and struggled to recall, but then I remembered. "A vale of tears. It comes out of the old book."

"Thats it, a vale of tears. Im going to remember that one. You boys think life is a vale of tears? You ready to depart? Try out the next world?"

Neither fool responded, though the inky one glanced sideways at the other. I imagined they probably believed me and Joe were both crazy and cold enough to poke a cutter in the back of their heads and knock them off the porch.

I heard a stirring inside the house

"Why dont you ask the woman to shoot them? She hasnt let go of that shotgun since dispatching Earl. I dont believe she holds much affection for any of Morrisons bunch. She certainly didnt like that smiley fool Earl. I bet . . ."

The door behind us slammed open and the dark woman came out. She had wrapped herself in a big shapeless graysweater and was still carrying the shothgun. I looked at her and tried to look amiable, but I got her cold Idontseeyou stare in return. I was afraid she would shoot the fools before we could drain them of what we needed. But before either me or Joe could say a word or raise a finger she quickstepped behind them and kicked the scraggy longhair in the lower back. He screamed and fell off the porch. Before he could roll himself up Joe was standing over him with a cutter.

"Dont be thinking of running."

The fool looked at Joe and then back at the dark woman. Her coldblank expression had not changed.

"You keep that bitch away from me. If youre going to kill me, then kill me, but keep that scuzzy bitch away from."

The dark woman raised the shotgun and fired before I could stop her, but I jostled her enough to deflect the shot off the side, where she punched a rather large hole into the porchfloor. She gave me a savage look and tried to jerk the gun out of my grip. I think she wouldve shot me if I had let go.

"Hold up. Quit fighting me. I aint done you any harm. Me and Joe and Sid mightve even done you some good."

She looked back at me and slowly gave up trying to jerk the shotgun away. But I kept my grip. I wondered if she was totally brainfuddled. Sometimes people get so lost inside their heads they cant ever come back out.

"Joe, you better take that fool down to the deadpile and shoot him. Shes not going to give us any peace with him around."

Joe nodded. "I suppose thats best. Come on, you. She dont like you, thats a fact. Lifes a vale of tears, but maybe theres peace on the other side."

He half dragged and half carried the scraggy man down the hill towards the barn. We watched them go, and when they were far enough away I let go of the shotgun. She stepped far enough away from me where I could not grab it again, but she didnt raise it, and she didnt point it at me. I settled back where I had been sitting. Nearby the Deadman was stretched out and snoring.

"Sure is a pretty view here. Wish I had a big house and big porch and a pretty view."

The dark woman refused to respond. She kept staring off towards the barn. In another minute there was a short burst of cutter fire behind the barn. Then she turned and went back into the house, slamming the door.

After that, it wasnt too hard to get Inky to start talking. Joe came back from the barn alone and set back down in the rocker behind the last lounger. I waited a moment and went inside the house to find the woman. She was sitting in the kitchen with the shotgun on a table in front of her.

I pulled a few cupboards open. There were jars of pickly stuff but not much else.

"There much to eat around here? Hows Morrison feed all his crew? Well be heading out soon. Got plenty of guns and horses but not much food."

The dark woman shook her head and kept staring at a spot on the far wall. I looked with her but had not the slightest chance of seeing what she was seeing.

"You should come with us a ways. Get away from this place before more of Morrisons miscreants show up. You can go with Sid back to the old mans ranch. Theres people up there who would be grateful to get Sid back. Theyd take care of you. Good people. Not like these killers. Not everyones nasty and brutish."

The dark woman shook her head again and continued her wall vigil. I opened a few drawers but found little that was takeaway value. I wondered how long Morrison had kept her and thought she had probably suffered all sorts of misery.

"Think about it. We could use your help. Youve had a bad time, but that dont have to continue. Let it all go. Theres always the chance of something better around the bend. Me and Joe aint predatory."

I got nothing back from the woman, not even a nod or a glance. Back out on the porch I checked on Sid. He was breathing fine, still in the deep sleep. I settled next to Joe and waited.

"Joe, you ought to shoot the Deadman so he dont wake Sid up with all the snoring. He does sound like a bear."

"Maybe after I deal with this one." Joe pointed towards the shorthair. "He dont seem too happy or helpful. You see hes got a wolf on one arm and a naked woman on the other. What about the woman inside? Was she helpful?"

"Yeah, sure. She was right helpful. Told us all that we need to go after Nell."

Joe smiled back at me and then poked shorthair in the back with his cutter.

"That right? You hear that, you bloody rateater? That poor woman youve been abusing told us what we needed to know. That means we dont need you. You are . . . Whats a good word? Trader give me another good word."

I knew Joe was enjoying himself. He didnt care much for old useless words, and he never wasted three words when one would do.

"I dont know, Joe. Theres plenty of words for this bloodstained rotbrained inky fool. What kind of word you want? Unneeded. Unnecessary." I thought for a moment and then threw out another. "Wait, how about dispensable? Thats a fancy way of saying you can get rid of him. You can take him down around the barn and dispense him with the others."

"Dispensable, thats a good word. Come on you, youre dispensable. Shame to waste all your artwork, but it cant be helped. Ill make quick work of it. Lifes a vale of tears, and youre dispensable."

Joe got up to grab Inky, but before he could get a hold of him he rolled off the porch. I got to my feet thinking we would have to run the wacker down, but he only rolled over a ways in the dirt and then struggled to his feet until he stood swaying before us.

"Yous let me go. Ill tell you where Morrisons gone. That damn bitch dont know. She dont have no idea where Morrisons gone. I do, and if yous let me go and Ill tell you."

Chapter 19

Stretches of the old highway was cracked and broken and rather useless in the lonely stretches. There wasnt much out there except for weeds, rock, and scrub, and every so often a few clumps of houses that got splintered in the snows. The only human activity we found was a ratsnest. Theres always rats slinking around.

Before the Fires broke out, streams of people had raced up and down the old highway going thousands of places on thousands of errands, and probably none of them ever thought the gas would run out, or that the world would get scorched, or that going out for bread or sodypop could get murderous.

During the hottest times, traveling any distance anywhere was hazardous. Even going down the block to visit a neighbor could lead to savagery. Nearly everywhere around the dead city there were roadblocks, walls, and barricades, and packs of damnfool idiots with too many guns and too little humanity stomped around whatever patch of bloody ground they called their own, ready to slog it out with every pack of damnfool idiots that came through. The Fires were a hard time for travelers and strangers.

And after the Fires began to burn out, after most of the damnfools had used each other up, there wasnt much purpose in traveling the old roads, even when there was still some gas around to fuel a few cars and trucks. Anyone crazy enough to drive on those old interstates was sure to attract a handful of devils who savored a good bloodsoak.

Most of those who came through the Fires stayed locked and hidden away someplace they considered safe, and there wasnt much purpose in traveling any distance, except to hunt and gather. Other than the bonafide crazies, all the wackers, skinners, trolls who got wildeyed and ravy, there werent many who wandered far from their safeground. The Fires squeezed the world together, contracting boundaries, limiting contacts, and blotting out destinations. Distance got measured in miles, half miles, and even quarter miles. Most lived in tiny nutshell worlds of barricaded blocks of boarded up houses.

Me and Joe never cared much for boundaries, and over the years we traced a lot of the old roads into the mountains, going a little farther each time we went trading, dragging the mules and packs up with us. After a while we got to know the different ranges and valleys and those remainers that clung to the high country. That was how we eventually ended up in Nineveh and stumbled into the Magic Mountain. Every journey we ever took ended up someplace unexpected.

We never spent much time wandering south and east into the dry country, following the old highway that curves between the mountains and the flats. NewPueblo was about as far south as we had ever been, and now me and Joe were a few days past it. The mountains were off to the west, their white peaks misty in the heat and haze, while the land east was arid and scrubby, and rough with parched hills and drybeds. We didnt exactly know where we were going. Just some place unexpected.

Sid was a sight. We had loaded him into the back of creaky flatbed wagon that had been converted from an old truck, and the last I saw of him he was sitting up cradling a cutter with a couple others nearby and a box loaded with twentyround clips, ready to defend himself from hordes of wackers. There were plenty of horses about to pull the wagon, but Sid had been grumbly the whole time, and the only way we could get him loaded and headed home was to agree that he could come hunting after us in a month or so if we didnt make it back. That and telling him he had to protect the old mans ranch from Morrisons snatchers, who might turn up looking for more children.

The Deadman had been easier to manage. He didnt have much choice but to take to the road and scout out a different life. To carry Sid back to the old mans ranch, we motivated him with horses, silver, and agreeable possibilities of ranch women and whiskey. I gave him a note for the old man, which the useless fool couldnt read. I couldve written that he was an old scoundrel who should be hanged on arrival, but I didnt. My little scrawl listed the horses and silver, though not the agreeable possibilities. I couldnt be sure that the fool wouldnt guzzle himself deaddrunk again and run off the first chance he got.

We rode with Sid and the Deadman down through New-Pueblo and then out to the old road. We were hot to go south after Nell, and we couldnt take a wagonload of Sid and the Deadman with us, and so we did the best we could for them. They turned north, and we watched them slowly make their way till they disappeared over a rise.

Once someone rides off, you let go of them. You cant be sure where theyll end up or what theyll find. Hopings all thats possible. I hoped I would see Sid again. But the worlds an uncertain place, and every goodbye deserves a mindful thought.

I had hoped the dark woman would go with them, and I had tried to persuade her with the agreeable possibilities of a new direction. I told her more about the old mans ranch and then about Aurora and the dead city up north, and I offered to write her a note like I did for the Deadman. But though she heard, she never listened, and she never said more than a few words at a time. She sat stonefaced and unmoving in the kitchen, the shotgun on the table in front of her, a load of anguish in her head. Once she looked at me eye to eye for a few moments.

"Ill think on it," she finally said.

The next morning she gathered a sack of shells and rode off with her shotgun and a second horse and without saying another word. I hoped she would get to a better place.

I had no hope for Inky and the few snatchers who remained. While we were loading up, a couple more had came out of the woods, surly and raggy, and not much older than Sid. They didnt seem surprised that we were there and that Earl wasnt. They lurked like buzzards, perching themselves above the house, watching us, waiting for us to leave, not bothering with the deadpile, or the bleeders we laid out in the barn. I had pressed them to consider new work, but there aint much chance of killers letting go of killing.

But we had hope that down south somewhere along the old road was a melon farm. Inky had given us that much. Somewhere down south was a big farm that bought children. Inky claimed he didnt know about Nell, and neither threats nor duct tape could get him to say more.

"I dont know nuthin about no girl. Morrison went off with two little boys he picked up west of the Pueblos the other week. Yous can kill me, but thats all I know."

The only other thing we squeezed out of him was a name. We were headed to a place called NewHarmony.

Chapter 20

We were ratwatching. Joe had pulled out an old pair of binoculars so we could keep watch them slink about. We were tucked away on a small hill a little north of the nest, ratwatching, trying to figure out how many were nesting inside an old ramshackle motel. We watched while a couple rats wandered in and out and then while another, an old whitebeareded fat rat, set himself up to sun in a lounge chair in front. We thought that there were a dozen or more hidden about. When you see a couple, theres usually a couple dozen about.

Off to the west a string of patchy dark clouds had gathered over the peaks, and by late afternoon the sky would likely storm. Finding shelter wasnt a bad idea. But a ratsnest aint a grand choice. We were two men and four horses and had sufficient weapons and ammunition, but as soon as we rode up the rats would scurry out excitedly, sniffing us out like we were old friends, and then inviting us inside to enjoy their hospitality, where they would backshoot us as soon as we turned away. Theres no lack of rats nesting along the old highways, waiting to gnaw on whatever comes along. Rats are wackers too lazy to go out and find somebody to hunt down.

Joe had discovered the rats. We had ridden south for a couple of days and had not come across much of anything except splinters and rust and a few burnedout crossroads. But when we judged that we were coming up to what was once a middlingsized town, Joe had gone ahead before light and had found the nest in a line of broken buildings. Most of the other buildings had been burned out or fallen in, but the motel was not in too bad shape considering it had endured years of misuse and decay. There was no mistaking its infestation.

There were a couple horses hobbled out front, and even a couple rusted carhulks parked as if some rusty travelers had pulled up and spent the night and were just about to check out and continue their journey. The old fat rat sat in front on wide brick veranda, sunning himself. We couldnt see the sign from our hillperch, but Joe had given it a look before circling back. Someone had added to the original sign. Someone had crudely painted Baileys above the original lettering, and then underneath had added, Harry Bailey, Host.

"You think thats Harry Bailey Host out there warming himself? Maybe hes digesting that full holidayinn breakfast of eggs, bacon, pancakes, and fried potatoes." Joe was squinting with the binoculars, playing with both the little focus knob and me.

"I cant quite see him as well as you can. Maybe hes feeding on some fried leg of man. Ive heard rats will eat anything, even their own young."

Joe squinted back at me. "Whered you hear that?"

"I dont know. Theres lots of stories about people eating people, cannibals and zombies and the like."

Joe went back to squinting at old chair rat. "You think that old rat feeds on people?"

"I dont know, Joe. I cant see him as well as you can."

"Maybe if you ride up he will hop out of that chair and bite you on the leg. Personally, I dont think youd be good eating. Too old and gristly. You think Harry Bailey Host is serving something else for breakfast besides leg of man?"

"I dont know, Joe. I cant see—"

Joe swatted me with the binoculars and I looked. But there wasnt much to see beyond what I had already seen. No other rats were around except the old fat rat, and he was probably asleep.

"He dont appear armed and dangerous. Maybe hes got a mess more of those melons weve been eating. You like those melons so much, why dont you ride up and see whats for breakfast?

Joe ripped the binoculars out of my hands and fiddled with the focus knob.

"Why dont you ride up and ask what Harry Bailey Host is all about? Im the backdoor man in this outfit. You go at them head on with guns blazing, and Ill sneak around from behind. We will trap those rats in a deadly crossfire."

I tried to rip the binoculars back, but Joe turned away.

"Or you can just ride up and politely ask how much Harry Bailey Host wants for a clean room and hot bath."

I rode up slowly to give the old rat plenty of time to look me over. Joe had outfitted me like a wacker, so I had two cutters, one over the saddle and the other over my back, and a little boxy automatic machine pistol hanging in front. I thought I looked more foolish than deadly and hoped the old rat would not require demonstrations of my marksmanship.

He pulled himself out of his chair slowly and took a step towards me. He had gone graywhite and grizzly with red watery eyes. His beard and hair were both long and snarly, and the rest of his appearance was generally grimy and saggy. Except for a couple knobby turquoise rings and a chunk of turquoise strung around his neck. Vanity is such a random thing.

"How you doing? You looking for a room?"

"Maybe. Looks like it might storm later. You Harry Bailey?"

"Yep. Thats me. Been welcoming travelers and giving refuge to the weary ever since everything went to hell." He paused and scanned me over. "You passing through somewheres or just wandering?"

I dismounted slowly, banging cutters and pistol, and tied off next to the two nags.

"Passing through, heading south. Me and my partner are hoping to catch up with some friends. You know Morrison from NewPueblo? He come through yet? He told us to catch him at NewHarmony."

The old rat looked blinky and redeyed at me and then shook his head.

"Morrison, from up in NewPueblo? No, dont believe I do. You say hes a friend of yours? Whats your name? If this Morrison comes through, Ill tell him you stopped by."

"I aint sure what my name is today. I am a trader and a scavenger, do some doctoring, preaching, fortunetelling, and gambling. During the freezings I generally lay up and drink whiskey, though sometimes I go out into the weather. I kept a school once, but the students were too wild for me. Mostly I scavenge and trade. Me and my partner have been all through the ranges up north and west of the dead city, but we aint been down this way much before."

He nodded and eased himself back down into his chair.

"Then how do you know this Morrison fellow from New-Pueblo?"

I skipped over his question and watched while a younger rat emerged. He looked a bit like the old fat rat with long beard and wild

90

hair, but younger, stronger, and darker. Smiling, the younger rat stepped off to the side, and I thought it likely he had a handgun hidden under his baggy sweater.

"Maybe Ill take a room and wait on my partner. Hes about a day behind. How much you charge for a room and a bottle? You got anything worth drinking?"

The old rat smiled and showed me his teeth. I was surprised he still had his teeth.

"Me and the boys aint particular. We take most anything in trade. People give us what they can. We are here to help those worn out from traveling and needing a safe place to stay. Seems like you got plenty of firepower. Ill take those assault rifles of yours for a room."

I smiled back at him. Two cutters and a couple clips were worth about a weeks lodging up in Aurora. But values are relative.

"No, cant trade it. These old highways are dangerous to travel. You never know when some howlers or screamers are going to come at you."

I patted the cutter strapped across my front, but as soon as I did the younger rat stepped back and stuck a ratty hand underneath his sweater.

"I got a couple of the Princes silver coins. If you dont like silver I got some gear thats tradable. How about a fancy mapreader compass in case you ever get lost and cant find your way?"

"We aint got no use for a compass, but silvers good. I heard about something about a heathen up north in the dead country calling himself a Prince of Aurora. He minting his own coins now? Lets see some this silver."

"The Prince is a man of vision. Hes pretty much rebuilt Aurora and now hes set on bringing back the dead city. Pretty soon hes going to unite the states and bring back bubble gum, chocolate, bananas, and canned beer."

Both rats snorted and the old rat showed me his teeth and redeyes.

"Ive heard others say the same, but the good Lord dont

tolerate those that swagger and swell. Theres a couple down in these parts struttin around and making claims theyre recovering whats been lost."

We looked at each other for a moment, measuring and sorting. I get edgy when the good Lord gets suddenly dropped into a conversation. But then the old rat broke off his stare and smiled some more.

"Come on, you trader and scavenger, Ill show you a nice room, and you can give us what you think its worth. We are here to be charitable and help those needing rest, and not take more than anyone can afford."

Chapter 21

"We killed your partner, and now were gonna kill you."

I was laid back hoping that the old fat rat would show himself so I could do the killing. But he wasnt obliging.

"Thats charitable of you, Mister Harry Bailey Host. Final rest for the weary. And I only thought you were only an old ratty thief. Transporting weary travelers to the beyond is generous."

I was at the top of the stairs at the end of the north wing, and the old fat rat and a couple more of his brood were below me out of sight around the lower steps. For the moment, we were in an acceptable standoff. I had all my guns and clips and a good line of vision along the hallway in front of me and down the steps below me. There wasnt much light in either, but enough to see a rat or two. I had bloodied one rat who had stupidly attempted scrambling up the stairs.

The old fat rat was being more cautious now, but I knew more rats would come scooting along the hallway and up the stairs. I wasnt in an ideal situation.

For an old moldy room in an old shabby motel, my room had been passable, but I hadnt stayed there. As soon as I thought the rats had gone I relocated to down the hall, since they were plenty of vacancies, but as soon I was out a little lurker rat saw me and raised the alarm. My attempts to negotiate a passage out had been refused, and I was left at the top of the stairs with little alternatives.

"Lets do a trade. All you rats clear out, and let me out of this ratsnest, and me and my partner wont have to exterminate. Ill even throw in a horse and a genuine jar of leftover penutbutter. All you rats like sweet stuff, dont you? Think about how good it would taste. Sweet and creamy just like it was before the scorchings."

"We already have your horses, and now were gonna kill you and take what you got. No need to trade with the dead, and thats what you are. You think youre so clever. Were gonna cut you into pieces and feed you to real rats."

As a show, one of the rats stuck a bony arm around the staircase and fired off a cutter burst. The shots went high and wide and I didnt bother to return fire.

"If you keep wasting rounds like that, youre going to riddle your lovely motel with splintery holes. Morrison aint going to be happy with you when he learns you been hassling me."

The old fat rat laughed, and his broody kin snorted after him.

"You aint no friend of Morrisons. You think youre so smart, but you aint. He told us when he come through to watch out for some fancy talker who claimed he was with Joe Cruz. Kill you slow is what he said."

"So Morrison did stop by. I am in a hurry to catch up with him at NewHarmony. I hear hes got a couple little kids and an older girl with him."

The bony rat fired off another burst, peppering more of the ceiling. In the limited space of the stairs the shots were especially loud. My ears were pounding, and I waited for the sound and ceiling scraps to settle.

"I didnt say where he was headin or what he was totin. Youre all kinds of confused, aint you?"

His words sounded hollow in the ear pounding. I wondered how my words sounded to him.

"You rats been eating any melons lately? I thought you were

fleshgobbling cannibals. You eat people, or you just drag the dead off to rot up and get picked over? Melons would be good for your bloody diet."

The old fat rat didnt bother to respond. I could hear whispering but couldnt make out any words, and I thought my time was probably running out. The hallway was empty, and I wondered whether I could creep my way along to get to the other stairs. I felt like a possum up a tree with a pack of snarling hounds below me.

Only I had more than enough firepower to scatter the pack. I fired off a burst and followed it by jumping three steps at a time till I got to the bottom step and turned to fire off another burst down the next flight.

Only I was practically ratless. I saw the back of a young rat, maybe the little lurker rat, as he raced down the next flight and ran out of sight. I could hear him thumping down towards the ground floor. No one else seemed to be around, and I wondered where the rattrap was set.

But then I smelled smoke and eased up. Joe liked a good fire. I sat on the steps and waited, only there wasnt much waiting. I heard some heavy steps come out of the hallway down the next flight of stairs and called out.

"You aint going shoot me, are you? I am just a poor weary soul in need of rest."

Joe came around the corner and looked up at me. He was loaded with more weapons than me.

"I dont feel like shooting any weary souls tonight. Maybe in the morning. I get irritable in the morning."

"Theres plenty of beds around you. You need a good nights rest. You want to find a nice comfortable room? Harry Bailey Host would be happy to have another guest."

Joe came up and sat next to me.

"Too many rats nesting around here."

"Then I guess we ought to slip out of here while the rats are trying to put out your fire."

"Thats a good plan. Which way you want to go? Down or

down?"

"We should go down."

"Good. Down it is." Joe got up and arranged his cutters and started down. "Only one thing. I didnt start the fire."

"Then maybe its spontaneous rat combustion. Or maybe a fiery thunderbolt from the good Lord took vengeance on the wicked. What do you think?

Joe threw back an arm, cautioning me to hush up. Then he turned back to me.

"I think its a decent fire, and I think you ought to quit talking nonsense till we get out of here. Theres more rats running around than we thought."

Chapter 22

Joe was right both ways. It was a decent fire, and rats were plentiful. But we slunk out without getting singed or shot and went back up a ways to watch. We could still see the fire sparking upward while a commotion of rats scrambled around. Some had started hunting after us, circling the motel, while a few more headed out towards the old road, but a fair number seemed intent on hauling themselves and their ratty junk out of the fire.

We hadnt learned a lot except that Morrison had come through and was still headed south. Joe had cornered the young rat I had startled at the top of the stairs, but he was sullen and unsociable, even when prodded with a cutter behind the ear. The only thing he added, after threatening our imminent destruction, was that Morrison often came through.

"He always stops here doin business with Pap. You want him so bad, you jus wait aroun and hell come back."

I am not much of an age guesser, but I supposed our trapped rat was closer to ten than twenty. He looked a lot like the others, all tattery and shaggy with long hair and yellow teeth. He seemed on the sickly side of rathood, and I didnt figure he had much of a future giving comfort to weary travelers.

"What business?"

The rat refused to answer me, and since we were in a hurry Joe attached him to iron stair rail with his own ropey belt and we left him. But I wished we had squeezed more out of him.

"Maybe we should have dragged that sullen rat out with us. He might have come around with a little petting, feeding, and encouragement."

"What do you want a pet rat for? Aint you got enough things to worry about with a missing girl you lost?"

I ignored the lost part.

"We aint never had a pet rat before. Maybe they make cuddly companions."

"Maybe you want a couple snakes too. A couple big old rattlers as thick as a mans arm. I hear down in the hot country they got big hairy spiders the size of a mans fist."

We both watched the motel for a few moments.

"No snakes or spiders, but a baby rat might be ok. You want to get em young, before they get too ratty and nasty. Its all in the training. To get socialized and agreeable you got to get em when theyre young."

"Youve gone firecrazy. You inhaled too much smoke. You shut up about rats and think on Nell."

I turned away from the rat fire and leaned back, looking at the night sky.

"That young rat you cornered knew a lot more than what he told us. Theres a story around here we needed to hear."

Joe kept his watch but nodded.

"Probably, but weve got other things to worry over than handling baby rats. When theres light enough we can slide alongside the highway. Morrison left a trail of some kind.

We tried to find a trail, but it wasnt much use. In the early light a disagreeable noise suddenly shattered the quiet, a sound I hadnt heard in years. There was nothing but the wind washing over the scrub and grass, and a few morning birds, and then suddenly down below us some rat started up an old sputtery motorbike. It spitted and popped in several bursts before catching, and we watched in amazement as a stringy rat on top of the whiny motorbike tore out of the Harry Bailey Host motel and headed south on the old highway. We watched and listened as the old bike jittered its way around some broken chunks and a couple old rusty hulks till it got to a straight stretch, and then the rat rider opened it up. The sound was screechy and jarring, but in less than a minute it faded to a waspy buzz as the rat got away.

"I dont believe I have ever witnessed a nasty rat riding an internal combustion motorbike before."

Joe nodded. "I didnt know rats could do anything besides scratchy ratty stuff."

"This one seemed proficient in motorbiking. Which means he and bike have had some experience in the business."

"That and enough gas to go places. Where you think they got gas? I thought all these old road stations had been sucked dry years ago. Where you think hes headed?"

I considered gas, rats, and directions for a few moments. The sound had all but died away except for distant buzzing.

"The direction aint the hard part since this old road goes but one way. The question is, is he running from or going to? Best guess hes is scurrying someplace down the road. Maybe a melon breakfast. You best hurry yourself if you want to follow him. Youll need to run him down before he starts spreading stories that Joe Cruz burned down his nest."

"Not me. I think its your turn to chase down motorbiking rats that are several miles ahead. Youre a faster runner."

I looked back towards the motel. The fire had burned out, leaving one side black and cindery. There were probably hot places still smoldering.

"Sure was a nice fire. Lets watch the nest to see if any more rats slip out. Maybe we can borrow a motorbike. I bet I could ride one."

We got to the old womans house a little after middday. We crested a hill and saw the house off a ways. We werent really heading towards it, but the closer we got we saw it was inhabited. Off to the side there was a large garden that someone had to be tending. We had been angling back towards the highway, but veered off to the house, thinking maybe there might be someone knowledgeable about slavers, rats, and farms. Maybe we could trade for some information.

There had been more rat activity back at the nest. Not long after the whine and sputter faded a small pack of four rats had mounted up on some scrawny horses and had ridden off south after the motorbiking rat. We figured we would trail them a while to see where they would go, but it was rough work with the hills and cuts. It wasnt long before we had gone too wide and lost sight of the rat riders, who seemed to be in a skulky hurry, and we came across a stream cutting southwest towards the old road. To keep out of the drainages and gullies, and to find an easy crossing, we had picked our way further east until we saw the old womans house.

Strangers aint often welcome. Once the Fires had scrunched boundaries and snapped connections, the pockets of people left got wary of anything unexpected beyond their fences and barricades, and the sudden appearance of strangers was always a cause for concern. Wackers often rode up with big friendly smiles.

Over the years me and Joe had developed a routine of taking a slow approach, setting up where we could be seen but not shot, giving people a chance to look us over, maybe hauling out some sort of leftover for show. But we didnt have much time to be slow, or much to flash. So we rode up near the front and each of us held up an empty hand.

The old woman surprised us by coming around the side of the house. She was tall, thin, raggy, and gray, but despite the gray she had a firm purpose about her. She pointed a cutter at us, and with a steady hand pulled back the bolt.

"Ive killed plenty who rode up here."

I raised other my hand and tried to look friendly.

"We aint plenty. Me and partner are just passing through trailing some rats out on the old highway. We might harm them when we catch up with them, but we aint generally harmful. Aint that so, Joe?"

Joe nodded, but I knew he would pull that little machine pistol out in half a second.

She looked us over and stepped closer. She was old, but not all wrinkly and weary, and she kept her hair long and tied back.

"What rats? Who you talkin about?"

I could not think of a reason to lie to her. Sometimes the truth is the safer route.

"You know an old rat named Harry Bailey? Calls himself Host? Got himself a ratsnest back north a few miles on the old highway? We didnt get on too well with him or any of his brood last night, and things heated up. This morning several of his rats took off heading south on the highway. We thought we would follow them a ways."

She stared back at us, holding the cutter steady. I nudged my horse a step forward and reigned her to the side, giving Joe cover to pull if he had to.

"Why?" She waited a moment, and then asked again. "Why follow them murderous bastards?"

She spat out her words as if they were distasteful. I eased up, hoping we had common ground.

"Something valuable was taken from us, and we need it back. We think them screechy rats might be a link to where we need to go. You ever hear of some place called NewHarmony Farm?"

I started to dismount, but she instantly pulled her cutter in and aimed at me. Less than twenty paces away, she had a good chance of knocking me down.

"Stay where you are. Or Ill shoot."

At that moment three more cutter barrels poked out of the front windows. I couldnt see much except for a small hand gripping one of the barrels. I slowly sat back in the saddle. I knew Joe was tensed and ready.

"We aint murderous bastards. I can guarantee you that. We lost something dear to us, and we aim to get it back and balance our account with those that stole from us. Thats all."

"What is it that was taken?"

She held steady, but the small hand moved around the cutter barrel for a better grip and then finally rested it on the window edge. I started hoping we had a lot of common ground.

"Wasnt an it. It was a youngish girl who was traveling with us, someone under our protection. We were camped back near New-Pueblo gates, and one morning she disappeared. Me and Joe took off after a weasely slaver named Morrison. You ever hear of him. We squeezed one of Morrisons bunch until he told us to head south and find this NewHarmony place, and last night we squeezed a Bailey rat until he told us Morrison comes through regularly. Thats all we got, and it aint much. If you can add to it, we would be obliged and get on our way. Seems youre looking out for some young ones. You understand our responsibility.

She looked at us hard. There was no softening.

"Get on your way, then. I got nothing for you."

"We were hoping to trade for a little help and direction. Thats all. We trade along the front ranges and into the high country up north around the dead city. Cant you give us back a little something to help us on our way. You know about Morrison or this farm?"

"I dont know you. Theres nothing I got for you. Theres liars, spies, and murderers, and thieves swarming loose around the country, smiling one minute and shooting the next. You ride on. I got no trust for you."

I kept trying to appear friendly, but she was an icy woman. I knew Joe could take her down if I dropped to the side. Yet it seemed best to ride on. But just then an older boy came around the other side of the house. Sids age or a bit younger maybe. I didnt see his face too well, but one side looked mashed and scarred, as if he had taken a beating that never healed. I did see he had another cutter leveled at me. I nodded to the old woman.

"Well be moving on. No offense intended. But give us this

much. If you had a young girl under your protection taken from you, would you be heading towards this NewHarmony Farm?"

"You get out of here now," the older boy screamed at us.

Both the woman and I looked over at him. He poked his good side at us and gave us an angry look.

The old woman softened. "Thats alright, Joshua. Theyre on their way."

She looked back me. "This place youre looking for, we got no love for it. They call it an orphanage, but it aint."

"Who they?"

"A bunch of murderous bastards that aint got no right to be moving around upright and breathing. Theres packs of them roaming around claiming they got legal authority, but they aint got no more authority than a pack of coyotes." She stared a moment, and then added, "no more than cutthroats like old Bailey and that devil Morrison. If they got something of yours, you best get it back real quick. Head south till you get to the next crossroads on the old highway, and then head west. There aint but one road heading that way."

"Much obliged."

I pulled off a few steps and Joe fell in with me, but then I stopped and called back.

"You take in throwaways, little kids thats been tossed away?"

She looked at me without expression. Joshua took a couple steps towards us, still holding his cutter. The little hand in the window pulled back, and for a moment I saw a small figure.

"I was just wondering. Me and Joe were throwaways back in the Fires, street trash slung out and left to rot. We know what starvings like."

I waited, but she offered nothing in response.

"Yall got a nice garden. Hope the vermin dont get to it before you harvest."

The old woman shook her head, and after a moment she waved us on with her cutter.

Chapter 23

We stopped to admire the sign for several minutes:

No Trespassing!

Do Not Enter!
Violators Will Be Prosecuted!

New Harmony Farm
A Residential Agricultural Collective
Independence County
Union Territory
National Recovery Alliance

"Its a nice sign. Somebody had a steady hand and put some time and effort into it. It aint sloppy or smeary, its well spaced, and for a sign hanging on some rusty barbedwire its downright informative. In the world of signmaking, I think its respectable."

Joe ignored my critical judgments and continued to stare.

"I aint cultivated like you and dont care for signs telling me not to go someplace. Aint there been enough counties, territories, and alliances? Aint we had enough NoTrespass signs."

"People are boundarymaking animals. People love to draw lines and set out signs. If there were two starving wormeaters about to expire, one of them would scratch a line in the dirt and dare the other to cross it. Its a weakness of the species."

After a few more moments Joe quit the sign and turned back towards the road. Passing the sign, he rode on for a few paces before calling back. "What species?"

I followed after him. To the left and right the barbed wire stretched for miles.

"Maybe theyll forgive our trespasses?"

"Whos they?"

We had followed the crabby womans advice and took the only road heading west, and we had climbed a series of hills until we finally reached a high point where the road began to drop. Going up the road had twisted and threaded its way through a few burnedout settlements and crossroads but mostly through rock and pine. The country seemed deserted and wild, so we were surprised when we finally got to the top of the last ridgeline and started down.

Ahead of us was a pretty picturebook sight. For almost limitless miles before us the land stretched out south, west, and north into open rolling country, a rich green of grassland and patches of wood that extended till the high peaks tipped the clouds. The land was rolly, and we could see several streams that snaked the low areas. Off to the south there was a series of wooded ridges. Though the morning had been blustery, the afternoon hadnt cloudedup, and the sky was a bright blue dotted with white clouds. The only scars we could see were the charred remains of a few burnedout ranchhouses and a couple old barns that had fallen in. Them and the sign and the barbed wire.

Aside from a few dry gulches, patches of cottonwood along the streams, and crusts of rock scattered around, the land was so open that there wasnt much in the way of cover along the road, so we rode along not thinking too much about getting prosecuted for trespass, but we should have.

We had started around a bend and crossed a bridge over one of the streams, when half a dozen riders tumbled out of the streambed after us, firing off cutter bursts into the air to scare us into panic. The road dropped off on both sides, so we spurred ahead, but we hadnt got more than a few strides when another half dozen clambered up to the road a fifty yards ahead of us. On foot, the ones ahead of us spread out across the road and pointed their cutters at us. There wasnt much to do except pull up. Those behind got to us first.

For a few moments of surprise, we just stared back and forth. "Look, Joe. Grabies!"

Three of the behind riders were young boys, and a fourth only slightly older, not hardly Sidaged. All four were dressed in similar gray shirts. But before we could react further two more riders came out from under the bridge. I waved hello at Morrison and Stickman.

"Hey, how you doing?. Surely a pleasure to reunite. Me and Joe have been hoping to catch up with you and ask for your help to hunt down a young girl we lost back up around NewPueblo. You seen any lost girls down this way?"

Morrison smiled back at me, while the Stickman offered an empty stare.

"First you want lost boys, and now a lost girl. Youre never satisfied, are you?"

The older gray boy whistled sharply, and the ones ahead of us came running. They were all a bit muddied from jostling around in the drainage below the road, and except for the cutters and grim looks they might have been a pack of boys out on an afternoons adventure. I turned to the whistler.

"We started out looking for a couple lost boys taken from a ranch up north a ways. You seem to have plenty. Can I trade you for a couple? What will you take for a couple about five and seven years old? You got any that age?"

Except for raising his cutter towards my head, the whistler ignored me. In what seemed a curious parody, his grabies did the same. I edged my horse a step towards them and slanted sideways, giving Joe room to pull behind me.

"Never satisfied, and damn persistent. What happened back in NewPueblo? Whats this about a lost girl? You aint accusing us of something, are you?"

I looked towards Morrison and shrugged.

"We had a girl with us, kin to the lost boys. She was going to identify them if we ever caught up with them. But the morning after we traded at your place she disappeared. I thought maybe your Stickman here borrowed her."

Morrison glanced at Stickman.

"Whered you get that strange notion?"

Sometimes the truth is so plain it never gets spoken. Morrison had all the answers before he asked his questions.

"Actually, we went back to your place and we wheedled it out of one of your porchloungers, a young inky fellow. Traded him a little bag of silver for some directions, and he told us you headed south with a few young ones, including a girl who sounded like our girl, headed for some place called NewHarmony."

Morrison laughed amiably.

"Sounds like you traded away silver for nothing. Whatd Earl have to say about it."

I looked off a ways towards the west. A few more clouds had gathered, darkening the eastern slopes, but the rest of the grasslands were still brightly sunlit.

"He was friendly and helpful, but this one inky fellow was particularly obliging. But you say he fed us lies?"

Morrison nodded. A couple of the younger grabies wobbled their cutters. With all their clips, straps, and trail clutter, it was hard to see the boys behind their weapons. The wind was pushing southeast and off a ways a couple buzzards started circling in the sky, riding the high wind.

"Me and Joe have made worse mistakes. Guess we will leave off looking down here in this happy valley and head back where we came from. We might have to go find the Prince and get him to help us."

Morrison shook his head.

"That wont be possible. Yall have trespassed on restricted land. These here Roamers are sanctioned to prosecute all who ignore the signs." Morrison laughed, enjoying himself. "Hell, they knew you were coming the minute you passed the boundary. Their job is to prosecute you. We came along to help. Theres been a lot of raiders lately."

"Prosecute?"

"Execute."

"How come you dont get prosecuted? Yall dont look much like the grabies."

"We are authorized agents of the National Recovery Alliance. You see, NewHarmony is a NRA orphanage. We bring lost children down here all the time. We are rescuers of orphans."

Morrison seemed to be enjoying our exchange a lot more than I was. I wondered when we would get to something useful

"How much does rescuing throwaways pay these days? Me and Joe might have to give it a try."

Morrison smiled a silent response, and Stickman kept up his stonyfaced stare. The grabies were crowded around with their cutters close enough to poke us to death. They were packed so close together that, if I dropped, Joe could probably knock them all down at once. He had pulled the machine pistol and had edged back a couple of steps. I didnt want him to shoot the littlest grabies and hoped we could trade words instead of bullets.

"Say, you got any little baldheaded, beaverfaced district managers around here. I met one back at the old mans ranch, named Ungar, and he had a couple gray boys with him, only they were older and had nicer uniforms with black stripes. I had assumed they were special district manager protectors, but maybe they were from around here. They looked a bit like these boys."

I nodded towards the grabies.

"You see, after meeting this beaverfaced district manager, we told the Prince about him claiming to be some kind of territorial official, and the Prince sent us back out looking for him. Thats what we are really doing down here. We are authorized agents of the Prince of Aurora to negotiate a treaty. Take us to your leader."

Stickman nudged himself a step until he had angled to the side behind the grabies on foot. Off to the south a couple more buzzards had joined the circling. Morrison turned toward the older gray boy.

"So what you want to do, Lieutenant? Take them back to the big house, or do what you were sent out here to do?"

Without a moments pause, the older gray boy barked at us.

"Dismount, and surrender your weapons. I am arresting you by the laws of the National Recovery Alliance."

Chapter 24

Me and Joe have been arrested a few times, but most times it didnt amount to much. We would get roughed up and locked up, but generally we were turned loose after a while, and most times after exchanging something someone wanted. There were times after the Fires started to cool when everyone got arrested by somebody. Until the Princes father got things organized around the hills and dead city, there were armed groups popping up everywhere, claiming the authority to arrest anyone who approached their roadblocks. But lines kept getting shifted around, and half the time you never knew who was claiming what area. Most times being arrested wasnt much more than a dog marking its territory. And most times to get yourself unarrested by handing over something that somebody was eyeing. It wasnt much different than a pack of greasy trolls stopping travelers out on a mountain road. You pay as you go.

That was about the time me and Joe got into the trading business. Every group was hunkered down over some patch of nothingmuch, and nearly every group was set on clobbering the next group down the road for its patch of nothingmuch. But a lot of the meanness and madness in people started to burn out with the Fires, and aside from the most heartless wackers, most people found trading easier than the constant bloodletting. Even the cruelest stonehearts will offer something for whiskey and tobacco. Me and Joe never cared much for one patch over another, and we kept moving around.

But once or twice we got pushed into tight places. Ever since I was a starving throwaway grubbing in the wreck of the dead city I have hated darkness, and there have been a couple of times when some swaggering halfwit scumsucker locked me away in a dark place and left me to die. Me and Joe take such things personally.

Years back the Princes father had a mind to do away with us but then, as a show of kindness, offered us a slower death, locking us away in the dregs of an old courthouse until we rotted and starved.

He had set up his own markers around the dead city, claiming all of it for his own domain and butchering anyone who claimed otherwise. Some of his raiders had caught us hauling leftovers out of the ruins of what had once been a big apartment house. We had crawled our way through the broken building, digging out bits and pieces of lost lives , and were packing it all up when we were arrested and dragged off. Though the king of looters, the Princes father made a spectacle of summoning us before a crowd of his bootlickers and condemned us. He sat elevated at the top of a big old judges bench like he was some exalted lord of creation, decreeing that the law was the law and had to be obeyed, that nothing could be restored without obeying the law.

The old man had style, making up his own laws, and decreeing who lived and who died. But they were his laws and his words and his melodrama, and without that murderous bunch of bloodspillers he bribed into following him, he wasnt much more than a squeaky mouse. But the old robber granted us an unmerciful reprieve, and with a straight face told us that, though our lives would be spared, our liberty would be forfeited. We were beaten, starved, and abandoned behind a heavy steel door in the basement.

Had it not been for the Princes mother, we would have rotted away in that nasty basement. Like me and Joe, she was another lost child of the Fires, and she was a smart, kind, and generous woman. I had known her long before the Princes father ever encountered her. Though it took a couple of hard months before she found out where we were, she had us released, paying far more than we were worth. Me and Joe have always been exceptionally grateful towards her, and loyal. We also swore we would never again get locked up and left to starve and rot.

Chapter 25

I looked at Lieutenant GrayBoy and then asked, "What exactly does being arrested by the laws of the National Recovery Alliance mean in practical terms? I mean, in terms of actions and outcomes, what are you specifically intending?"

The young man ignored my questions and barked again. "Dismount and surrender your weapons."

The grabies pressing around us shifted a step or two and gave us their meanest grim looks. I thought it was more spectacle.

"Hold on a moment. Youre asking us to give something up, but whats getting traded? What are you willing to give in order to get? Me and Joe are always open to a fair exchange. We will let you arrest us for a little while in return for a couple of your youngest gray boys and some information about our lost girl. That seem fair? We will give you two hours of being arrested in return for two of your boys and some information. Hows that?"

Lieutenant GrayBoy hesitated a moment and looked back at Morrison, who offered a quick reply.

"Just shoot them."

"Hold on. That dont seem fair. Theres two of us and only a dozen of you. Maybe you should all go off and come back with a dozen more grabies. Joe here is whats called a dead shot. Hes lethal, and back in Aurora and all along the front range people tell stories about Joe Cruz, and those with any sense are skittish about stepping in front of him when hes holding a gun. Maybe we can come to an agreement before we got grabies bleeding on the ground."

No one made a motion to fire, so I blundered ahead, talking more nonsense. Sometimes if I talk enough nonsense someone will think there is some sense.

"Besides, like I said, we are authorized agents of the Prince, and it aint good to shoot the Princes envoys. Yall aint so far from the dead city that he cant reach into this happy valley. Hes a formidable man of considerable vision and a large army. He sent us down here to negotiate a treaty recognizing whats yours as yours and whats his as his, and then setting up trade agreements. You got any of those melons left? We can set up a regular trade and call it the Melon Road."

"Shoot them, Lieutenant, just shoot them. You have your orders."

We didnt get a chance to lay out the Melon Road. There was a splash and some quicksteps off to the side of us, and suddenly there was a loud crack and Stickmans chest exploded. Morrison pulled his cutter towards me when there was a second loud crack and the side of his head exploded, splattering blood mist, bone splinters, and brain mush on both Lieutenant Grayboy and me. His halfhead looked stunned as he slumped and dropped, jostling the startled horses off a few steps. Before he could raise his cutter I lunged at Grayboy.

"Enough," I screamed, "theres been enough killing. You dont want to see any of these boys cut apart too." I grabbed his cutter barrel and he jerked back, looking at me fiercely, but I was hoping he wasnt feeling murderous.

"Hey Trader, look who it is."

I turned back towards Joe and then looked at the muddy figure who had come up next to him.

"Hello Marena. Nice to see you. You also looking for something in this happy valley?"

The darkhaired woman looked once and then ignored me. She walked through a wad of grabies and went over to what was left of Stickman. She pumped and fired a shot into the deadmans head, splattering the nearest boys. We all watched in amazed silence as she went over to the ruined Morrison and repeated the process.

"You know, Marena, dead is dead, and the dead dont get any deader."

I tried again to get her to stay, but she went off again without revealing much.

"I aint got anything left. Them bastards used me up. Theres nothing left of me," she said.

We were standing by the bridge, having gone down to the creek to wash off the mud and mess, feeling a bit awkward. The grabies were shuffling around, gathering and arranging, with Lieutenant Grayboy whispering at them. They were getting ready to ride off, ten boys on six horses, with the smallest grabies riding double.

Lieutenant Grayboy was hostile, but there was no fight in him. He was set on going back and hauling out an army of grabies. He turned back towards us just before they went off.

"Yall better turn back and ride out. Theyll be more of us coming after you."

With that the graby squad ambled off, the smallest grabies bouncing on the back of horses, looking like they were wearing large gray kites. They were a mixed bunch. Most tried to ignore the spoiled meat lying in the road, with a couple looking retchy and pasty, but a couple others were way too interested in the gore and mess of what had once been living people. They stood over the remains, and one poked with a stick until Joe cleared them out. I took their interest as an unhealthy sign. No one that young needs that kind of lesson in biology.

But the woman was set on going off. She had recovered her horses, the same she had taken from Morrisons, and had loadedup her shotgun. We watched as the grabies made their way west on the old road.

"I did what I had to do, and now Im done. I came down here to do it. Thats all I got."

I had given her another dose of the old mans ranch. I had even thrown hopeful times with the Prince in Aurora, but she showed no interest.

"There aint nothing left of me exept getting after those that hurt me."

"Theres always a new day, and each day offers a hope for something better to come along."

"You got to have something to hope for, and I aint got nothing hopeful left." She pointed to bloody meat. "Everything I had they took from me."

As a last resort, I gave her directions to the crabby womans place.

"Its on your way if youre headed north. Shes taking care of a handful of small children, got a small place and big garden. Didnt seem like she had any help other than a disfigured older boy. She could use your help. You tell her that me and Joe told you to stop by her place. Shes got no love for child slavers like Morrison, or this NewHarmony place. I suspect shes had hard times."

I wasnt sure Marena was listening or not. She got on her horse and turned back towards the east. We watched her back a few moments.

"Hey Marena," I called after her, "you light any fires back out on the old road?"

She didnt respond. I looked at Joe.

"After ruining these two authorized agents, I guess she wouldnt have an easy time riding into NewHarmony."

Joe shrugged and saddled up.

"Fine with me. I aint sure I would be comfortable with her behind me carrying that shotgun. How many more shells you think shes got? I hope not too many. Lets go find Nell and get out of here."

Chapter 26

We saw the boys herding their flock a long ways off, and for a while could not really make out what they were, just a splotch of browngray moving slowly down one of the ridges to the south.

"Whats that off a ways? You see it?"

Joe was staring off, shading his eyes. I knew he was just trying to poke a reaction out of me. Years ago I gave up trying to see what he saw. I started to pull out the binoculars, but he made a grab at them.

"Give me those. Your eyes are so feeble you can barely see your toes."

I gripped the binoculars tighter and peered.

"Oh yeah, I see it. Way out yonder. Theres a big sign that says, "Heres Nell." I handed Joe the binoculars. "Here, you look."

"Dont see your imaginary sign, but I do see two boys herding sheep. Look out there yonder down the north slope of that last ridge. You see them about halfway down?"

Joe handed me back the binoculars, but I saw nothing more

than a browngray splotch.

"Oh yeah, I see them. Boys and sheep. One of those boys just yawned and reached into his pocket for some peppermint candy. Theyre probably aching for a couple strangers to ride up. Lets go talk with them."

We started down slowly, letting the horses set the pace, wanting the boys to see us long before we got close to them. The road curved around a bit but then extended in a straight line for miles. We rode in silence, but then Joe couldnt resist.

"Youre a feeblesighted man. I bet if I had said there was a fat raccoon dancing a jig on its hind legs you would have said you seen it too. I bet its reading all them musty books that made you so feeblesighted."

I let it go for a few more minutes but then I couldnt keep from throwing something back.

"People see what they want to see. Sometimes I prefer to see things differently."

"Sometimes you dont see whats poking you in the nose, and other times you see things that aint there."

"I didnt see any dancing raccoons, but I did see one of those boys yawn and stretch while the other thumped at something in the grass with a big stick. I would say ones older and ones younger. Maybe your hawkeye vision aint all that hawkeyed after all. Sometimes you need to see things with your eyes shut."

"We aint allowed to talk to no one."

The older boy, a few years younger than Sid, looked at us glumly. He had some blueblack bruising around an eye, which made him look all the more glum. The younger one, maybe half his age, nodded. Both were scruffy, dirtclumpy, and raggy. The older boy clutched an old hunters rifle, while the younger wrapped his hands around a shepherds staff twice as big as he was. They wore old boots that were globbed with mud. Off a ways behind them their sheep chewed silently, ignoring us.

"I aint no one. And this heres Joe Cruz, and he aint no one

either."

"Yous better ride back up to pass. Strangers aint allowed around here, no matter what yous call yourselves. The Roamers will be coming through, and you dont want to mess with any of them."

The older boy raised the rifle a few inches, halfway between pointing at us and pointing at the ground.

"You best lower that rifle." Joe snapped, but I didnt think he was too worried.

"No, I dont suppose we want to mess with any more Roamers. We already ran into a few, and they gave us a hard time until we convinced them we aint a threat. We are just a couple of harmless traders from the dead city. Aint that right, Joe?"

Joe stared at the rifleboy. I looked toward the staffboy.

"How you doing today? Were just passing through looking for something we lost. You ever have to hunt any lost sheep? You seen a bunch of disagreeable slavers come through with a couple boys and a young girl? How about a skinnylooking rat riding an old sputtery motorbike that sounds like a nest of angry hornets? You two from the NewHarmony Farm?"

"There aint no dead city. Thats just a story people tell to scare the littlest kids." The staffboy raised himself up a notch to make sure that we recognized he was not a littlest little kid. "You got any food?"

The rifleboy swatted at him for asking, which led to a couple pushes and shoves between the two.

"Sure, we got some food we can share, but theres no telling whats in the food sack, maybe some leftover peanut butter. Joes always carrying something sweet too. Maybe hes got some chocolate bars. Joe you got any chocolate bars?"

No chocolate bars, but Joe did pull out the some fruity hardcandy I knew he was hoarding, which the boys cracked and chewed enthusiastically. We gave them a pocketful of crackers, and after some more chewing they treated us with some information and hazy directions.

"We didnt see no riders, or no rat, but we heard that whiney motorbike come through day before yesterday," Rifleboy said, and Staffboy nodded.

"Where was he headed? The Farm? He go to buy some melons?"

Rifleboy looked at me and shrugged. Staffboy took up the conversation.

"All them melons is gone. We didnt get none of them. We dont get a lot of stuff."

"Thats too bad. Joe here thought those melons were particularly tasty." I looked off a ways toward the road. "You say more grayshirts will come through this way? How come you boys aint grayshirted?"

"Cause you got to win twelve fights at the sortings to get chosen. Im gonna win my next fight. Im gonna be a Roamer when I get bigger. They get to eat first and eat as much as they want." Staffboy puffed up his chest and hammered the ground with his staff, giving us a fierce look to let us know he was set on his own grayshirt.

Rifleboy poked at him with his rifle, but the younger boy stepped away. Joe threw him a bag of appleslices one of his wives had sucked dry before we left. Staffboy tore the bag open and grabbed a small handful. Rifleboy quit poking at him and reached in for a share. I didnt like the sound of sortings.

"So you all got a pecking order based on sortings and fighting? Is that the arrangement of personnel at the farm?

Rifleboy nodded.

"How come you talk funny?" Staffboy asked.

"Ive been asking that question for years, and he aint never answered me yet," Joe responded.

They had nearly finished the appleslices. I let them chew and swallow some more. But I was itching with questions.

"Who arranges these sortings, and who decides who wins. Yall have to fight each other? Do girls get sorted too?"

"The Guardians, theyre the older guys. They make the fights and decide who wins. Most times they dont stop a fight till someone gets beat on and then kicked around. Like Jeb here."

Staffboy started to point at the older boy, but he didnt let him finish. He dropped his rifle and launched himself at Staffboy, knocking him down.

"I got jumped before it started. It wasnt a fair fight. It wasnt fair. Say it wasnt fair or Ill mash you." He screamed. He had climbed on top of Staffboy and held a raised fist over him.

Before any damage was done Joe reached in and grabbed both boys, pulling them apart. I reached into the food sack and pulled out another bag of appleslices.

"So those that beat on other kids get to have gray shirts, eat a lot, and run around with automatic weapons. What do the other kids get to do, herd sheep and cart melons?"

NewHarmony Farm was larger than I had imagined. The main house might once have been normalsized, but now it was a sprawling thing of wings tacked on to each side, and there were a dozen other buildings scattered around, including a couple large barns and two long greenhouses, which seemed to have enough glass to rewindow the dead city. Surrounding the buildings were several acresized gardens fenced off, and further off larger fields that were already tipped with green sprouts. Shuffling through the gardens and nearly every field were little raggy people carrying buckets and poking at the ground with rakes and hoes. I wasnt feeling too teaseful, so I handed the binoculars to Joe without the usual banter.

"Take a close look at those people mucking in the fields and around the barns. Tell me what you see."

He looked for a moment and then looked away.

"Children. Lots of children."

Chapter 27

There wasnt much elevation around the farm, so we had backed up a ways to a small bluff above the creek and tied up behind a stand of knobbly pine. We had been watching for a while, trying to gauge the ebb and flow of the farm. We hadnt seen much except little people scratching dirt and hauling water, them and a couple dozen older grabies scattered among them carrying cutters strapped to their backs. A couple were on horses. We didnt see any Guardians or big people. But there were four watch towers anchoring the far corners.

"Just another day in the happy valley, huh Joe? You ever see a farm with guard towers before?"

Joe ignored me and pointed the binoculars at the big house.

"I believe we should take them by surprise. We can surround them. You take the front, and Ill take the rear, and on my shout well rush them. With our surprise attack, we might only have to shoot a couple hundred Guardians and grayshirts before they surrender. Keep the carnage down to a minimum."

Joe was smiling. It was an old joke, which I ignored. I looked off a ways. If I squinted just right the whole farm looked pretty. But it wasnt. I couldnt squint out all the little people or the thought of how they got there.

"I read about places like this. Long ago they had big farms that raised tons of stuff to sell. All the hard work got done by people stolen from across an ocean while the thieves that stole them sat back on their porches and balconies and watched over them, thinking they deserved what they plundered."

"That right? What happened to all them places? They still around someplace?"

I couldnt think of anything clever to say.

"The got burned down in their own fires."

"Maybe we should light some fires around here. Maybe this place needs a good scorching."

Joe was right. Sometimes a fire aint such a bad thing. But fires are hard to control.

"Where do you think everything from the fields and gardens around here goes? I cant get much sense out of this place. Whats all this growing for?"

Joe moved the binoculars around, looking for something.

"What do you mean? Whatre you picking at?"

"This is a big place, more than three or four times the size I thought it would be. Gardens and fields everywhere, and who knows whats sprouting in those glassy buildings. Theres probably tons of stuff that gets picked and collected. Where does it all go? Those sheepboys were starving."

"Theres lots of ratty people to feed around here. Maybe most stuff gets carted back to NewPueblo."

"That bloated pimpy old woman back at the Grocery said they hadnt ever had melons before. She said only one wagonload came through. There could have been a dozen more wagonloads hauled out of this happy valley. Whered it all go?"

Joe looked back at me. Then he shook his head and yawned.

"You dont know how much gets pulled up and carted off. Youre just picking at something for the sake of picking at something. Maybe all the poor orphans aint starving like them shepherd boys. Maybe all the poor orphans get gorged on melons and corn and," Joe thought for a moment, "and cabbage."

"The grabies eat first and eat all they want, and then whats left goes to the field muckers and stock herders. Those sheepboys were starving. Im betting a lot of those little people we been watching scratching and hauling are hungry too."

Joe pulled up the binoculars and resumed his scan.

"Im telling you, you cant see the ground in front of you, but you think you can see stuff miles off, and stuff that aint even seeable. Theres only one way to get at whats itching you. If you dont like my surprise attack strategy, you best go up to that big house and knock on the front door."

I didnt have to knock on any doors. We waited until somebody came knocking at us. We set there watching a while more when suddenly there was activity up at the big house. A group of a dozen blacksuited men emerged from one of the wings and headed off towards a low rectangular building.

"What do you think, Joe? Guardians or grownup Grabies?"

Joe followed them with the binoculars while I squinted and blinked.

"They aint little people. And Im guessing they aint going to stay in the building for too long. Theyre carrying packs and long rifles. Maybe theyre manstalkers sent out to hunt after us."

Joe was right. Soon a pair of oversized doors in the front of the building began to slide back, and in another moment half a dozen little green fourwheelers pulled out and parked in front. The vehicles had a double seat in front and a little flatbed in back, looking like little trucks. The men gathered in tight circle around the vehicles. Joe watched them and then handed the binoculars to me.

"You might as well see what you can see."

I couldnt see much detail, but one thing obvious.

"They sure aint grabies. Maybe theyre nightstalkers after wolves."

The group dispersed to their little trucks, and I handed the binoculars back to Joe. He watched and I squinted as they started to head off. Three of the fourwheelers headed towards the front road, which I imagined would lead out to the old pass road we had traveled down. Another turned around and went off towards the back, while the other two turned toward our general direction. We watched as they disappeared down into a gully and then came back out on the other side, which of course was our side. But as soon as they came out of the gully one of the little trucks veered off to the south, following a line parallel to the creek, but the last little truck kept heading in our direction. I looked at Joe.

"We going to surround them and take them by surprise?"

Joe nodded. "Good strategy. You take the front, and Ill take the rear."

We watched them follow a trail as it went around some rock and scrub. The little truck kept coming towards us.

"One thing, though, if our surprise attack gets messy, and them blacksuits start shooting, dont hesitate. You knock at least one down. You hear me? Dont start fooling with them with any of your blather. Theyre out here to kill you, not talk to you."

Chapter 28

We didnt have to shoot them, though Joe yanked the rider to the ground and stomped his right hand when the fool reached for a cutter.

The trail they were following came over the bluff a couple hundred yards south of us, and we had waited on top, me standing a dozen paces in front and Joe tucked away in back and off to the side. It was easy enough, since they werent expecting any sort of savage wildman that close to their compound, or to be standing in the middle of their track. They came over the top and lurched to a sudden stop, and while the rider raised his cutter Joe jerked him out and threw him to the ground. When he tried to raise his weapon, Joe clomped down on his hand hard enough to get a yelp out of him. The driver thought for a long moment and then raised his hands. I tried to talk with them.

"I drove a gopher in some tunnels once. Up way north in the Magic Mountain. It looked a lot like your little truck only it was gray and hauled dishwashers and lightbulbs back and forth. It had a go pedal and a stop pedal and you just pointed it where you wanted to go with a steering bar. I bet I could drive your little truck. Want to give me a go at it? What will you take in trade for your little truck?"

I looked inside the little truck, but it didnt look familiar. I turned back to the two blacksuits.

"I was a good driver too and only scraped the walls a couple of times until some damn fool stepped on my gopedal foot and made us all have an accident. After that Joe got mad and wouldnt let me drive any more. It aint pleasant when Joe gets mad. You ever have any accidents?"

The two looked back at me, silent and sullen. Joe had dragged them over to the side and belted their hands together in back. Then he had found a couple little stretchy cords in the truck and added that to his manwrap. The blacksuits werent going to get unwrapped without help. Once he had wrapped them, Joe had started playing with a fancyscoped rifle he pulled from a case that had been strapped behind the rider. It had a long barrel and a little twoleggy stand that folded out in the front. There was no mistaking its purpose.

One of the men was older, squatter, and grayer, a bit wrinkly but had a hard look about him, while the other was younger, taller, and thinner. Both were clean and cleanshaven, which meant they were bedsleepers and daily washers. Since we had left the old mans ranch, me and Joe hadnt had much chance for either cleaning or clean beds, and compared to the blacksuits we were wild savages, which is what they took us for. They werent happy, especially the older blacksuit with the footstomped fingers. But I kept working at them.

"Whatll you take for one of your blacksuits? I might have a bottle of leftover whiskey and a handy pocket gadget with a couple dozen little foldout tools. You never know when you might need a corkscrew or tiny saw. You got any bottles to open? Where do you get all those blacksuits? Me and Joe are traders from up around Aurora and the dead city and came down here to swap for some melons. But I will barter for a blacksuit. Do they all come with all those little pockets, flaps, and zippers?"

The younger blacksuit looked at me once and then went back to studying something on the horizon. I couldnt get the older one to even look at me. Joe had quit playing with the rifle and had pulled out some fancy binoculars that were twice as long and twice as heavy as ours. I went back at the two blacksuits.

"What are you out here hunting after? Bear, snipes, wolves, maybe a panther? We heard a lot of wolves howling at night while on the road coming down here. Which one of you is the shooter and which is the spotter anyway? Or maybe you switch off and take turns. Joe doesnt like to take turns, though hes got a hundred wives and nearly as many weapons. I am a humble man myself, and dont take up what cant be traded away. Yall aint come here hunting a couple wild savages like us? Where do yall get your gas for the little trucks? Most of that old commercial gas that didnt get burned up in the Fires went bad after a while."

I got more silence. There were a few small birds chattering as they darted around the scrub, but not much else to listen to.

"Hey Joe, they dont want to talk to me. You think theyre mad at us? Maybe you shouldnt have stomped on the older ones hand."

Joe had set the big binoculars up on a tripod and was studying the farm buildings. He looked over once and resumed his vigil.

"Try torturing them, try fire, knives, sharp sticks, burning splinters. Strip some flesh, break some bones. Or maybe you better just pick up a rock and crack their skulls. Lets pack up and go after that other little truck that went south of us. Theres plenty of blacksuits skittering around. Maybe we can take a load of fancy rifles and big binoculars back to the Prince."

"You want to skin them first before we get to skullcracking?"

Joe held up one Idontknow hand. I went over to the older blacksuit and squatted in front of him.

"We are just fooling with you. We aint never skinned anyone before, though Joe mightve cracked some skulls along the way. But neither one of us are bloodyminded brutes. All we are here to do is find a girl a damn childsnatcher and slaver named Morrison took from us. You know of Morrison? We get the girl back, we let you go, and we are gone from your happy valley, never to return. The girls name is Nell, and she was brought here less than a week ago. Can you help us find her?"

The blacksuit offered nothing.

"What? No help? This here is a humanitarian undertaking."

I felt more agitation than I showed, and I wondered if anything short of burning splinters would get him or the other to talk. But suddenly his top shoulder pocket launched our dialogue.

Chapter 29

"Hey Joe, this blacksuits buzzing at us."

Joe leaned in next to me.

"Maybe you better step back. He might be contagious. Got

some kind of happy valley bug eating away at his insides. Maybe you better crack his skull and ease him out of his misery?"

I reached over and pressed against a little shoulder pocket. It was vibrating.

"He aint contagious. Someones trying to communicate with him. Maybe this person will talk to us."

I pulled a slim rectangular phone out and for a moment just stared.

"Look Joe, its just like the little phones we played with up in Nineveh."

I pressed a button and the buzzing stopped. For a moment there was nothing but a little hissy noise. Then I heard a voice.

"Team Six, report your status?"

I took a deep breath and then straightened up.

"Hello, you got any generals? I like generals. I would like to talk to the general in charge."

I waited a few seconds before the voice responded.

"Who is this? This communication line is restricted. Where is Team Six?"

I waited a few seconds before responding.

"Im just a poor trader passing through. Me and my partner stopped to have a conversation with these two blacksuits here, but they aint saying much. You aint a general, are you? I met a general once, but he was a fiery stubborn fellow hellbent a glorious death. Which he got. You aint hellbent, are you?"

This time there was no pause.

"This is Captain James Franklin of the National Recovery Alliance. Let me speak to Team Leader Six Captain Leo Sadler this instant."

I liked the pauses, so I kept at it. I looked back at Joe, and he was smiling.

"Hello, yall still there Captain James Franklin? Is Captain Leo Sadler the older one with the stony look? He aint said a word since we met. How far are captains down the ladder from generals? If you aint got any generals strutting around the barnyard, I would be happy to speak to a president, commander, overseer, or emperor. You aint got any kings hanging around, do you? Whos in charge of this National Recovery Alliance? Up in Aurora we got a Prince."

The voice screamed back at me.

"Let me speak to Captain Sadler, now!"

I gave him back a bit of a pause.

"Yall dont have to scream into these little phones. They work just fine."

The voice didnt respond. I could hear some talking in the background, but I couldnt make out the words.

"Listen, Captain James Franklin. Me and my partner just want to strike a fair deal. Are you a dealer? If not, give us to someone who deals. We just want to get what was taken from us and then get out of this happy valley. Can you help us or not?"

There was a pause, and then a different voice opened up.

"This is Colonel Alfred Elliot Stevens of the National Recovery Alliance. Who am I speaking with?"

I returned his pause.

"Hello there, Colonel Alfred Eliot Stevens. That sure is a nice name, and you got three to go into one. I aint never met any Alfreds or Elliots before, though once I knew sneakthief named Stevey. Me, I aint so particular about names. I am just a poor trader from up around Aurora and the dead city. Me and my partner came down here looking for what was taken from us. Can you help us recover what was taken from us, seeing how youre in the recovery business?"

"Let me speak to Captain Sadler. Before anything else, I need to talk with Captain Sadler. I need to know that Team Six is ok."

I didnt bother pausing.

"You mean the blacksuits. Theyre fine. There just setting here admiring the view. They didnt want to talk to us, so we quit fooling with them. Do you all really run at each other with all those titles? I thought all that military claptrap got scorched in the Fires. Yall been down in this happy valley ever since things got hot? That was a long time ago."

"Who am I speaking with. Tell me your name."

Joe laughed, watching to see how I would respond. He always enjoyed it when someone pressed me for a name.

"I aint particular. Call me whatevers handy. Most people call me whatever they want, so I go by whatever."

There was a slight pause.

"Do you have a birth name? What did your parents call you?"

I gave it a pause and looked over at Joe. I noticed the leggy blacksuit looking back at me. I thought that might be progress.

"I dont know about birthnames and parents. Ever since I was a little throwaway kid getting blistered in the Fires Ive been bumping around looking for answers to your questions, and I aint found none yet. Can we move on to more important questions, like can you help us?"

"Let me speak to Captain Sadler first before there is any further discussion."

"I told you, he aint being communicative. I can hold this little phone by his head, and you can speak to him. But I aint guaranteeing youll get an answer."

I held the phone by Captain Blacksuits head, and Colonel Alfred Eliot Stevens began a series of questions about Team Sixs status, but I didnt think the Captain wanted to say much about his current status. Finally the Colonel asked directly if he and the other blacksuit were captives, and got a whsipery "Yes Sir" in response. Then the Colonel started in about birds and some numbers and did the Captain understand?

"Yes Sir. Acknowledged, Sir." This time the Captain barked.

I pulled the phone up, but before I could get started talking the Colonel started in with a syrupysweet voice.

"Well, Mister Whatever, I would be happy to talk with you about negotiating the release of our men. Please tell me what it is exactly thats been taken from you and why you think the National Recovery Alliance can help you? Our mission is to protect and serve."

But before I could even begin with the exactlys the leggy blacksuit started screaming.

"Get rid of that phone. Get rid of it. Throw it off the bluff.

They know exactly where we are. Theyre tracking you. Theyre sending a drone to kill us all. Get rid of it."

Suddenly Captain Blacksuit exploded.

"Shut up, shut up, damn you."

Despite the manwrap he squirmed around trying to knock heads with his partner. Joe reached in and swatted him with little effect. He swatted again, harder, and still the man was wild in rage. Joe gave me a quick shrug, balled his fist, and swung, catching the Captain on the side of the head, who slumped and slackened.

"Is that right, Colonel Alfred Eliot Lying Murderous Scum Stevens? You trying to kill us all?"

Having caught some of the screaming urge, I shouted at the little phone. I took off running up toward a high point on the bluff and flung the thing as far as I could.

By the time I got back to Joe had unwrapped his manwrap enough to get Leggy loose and the Captain rewrapped and attached to a ring in the back of the little truck. We loaded up with Leggy driving, and Joe for some peculiar reason hopped into the front with his new fancy rifle sticking out like a flagpole, leaving me to heave myself onto the back with the Captain Headknocker and the big binoculars. I was not happy with the arrangements and thought, as soon we as scooted off someplace safe, I would trade for a front ride.

I didnt get a chance to frontride. Leggy, whose name we later learned was Sergeant Adam Locklan, ditched the little truck a quick halfmile or so west of the bluff and then ditched us, wanting no further part of the National Recovery Alliance nor any part of our Nell Recovery Project. Getting rid of the little truck and most of everything it carried made sense, since there was a passable chance that it also carried some sort tracking device, and getting blasted by something we could not see or shoot at did not seem a favorable option.

I would have had the entire Cruz clan after me if I let Joe get blown to pieces by a baby bomber plane, though he deserved some rough use for taking the front seat.

After getting jolted and jerked along for the quick ride, we dumped both the truck and Captain Leo Headknocker and humped over a crust of rocks and down the backside, taking only a couple blacksuit packs, the fancy rifle, and a belt of fancyrifle bullets. Even Joe had no desire to lug twenty pounds of big binoculars.

We were barely over the rocks when we heard the explosion and saw grayblack smoke swirling upwards. Seeing that only quickened Leggys strides. We kept up with him for stretch, and I kept tugging at him to stay with us a while.

"You aint got any listening device implanted in your brain or body, do you? Maybe we can help each other out. You know where young girls are kept? Maybe a couple lost boys?"

He ignored my questions. The area we were in was open and rolly with scattered rocks and a few dry washes, and Leggy was headed towards one of the wooded slopes to the southeast. He seemed to want out of the happy valley.

"I am just wondering since you are so set on shaking yourself loose from NewHarmony. You think youre going to be blasted apart by another baby bomber?"

He glanced once without breaking stride. Joe was off to the side, angling towards some rocks. He wanted to set up with his fancy rifle in case some more blacksuits came after us.

"Theyre coming after you, not me."

"Whos they?"

Leggy didnt bother to glance.

"You have no idea."

"Give me an idea."

He wasnt being too talkative, and I was huffing and getting tired of matching his leggy strides and his surly responses. I reached over and grabbed at his pack and then stuck out my leg, tripping him. He went down hard on his side but scrabbled back to a crouch, giving me a wild look like he wanted my blood. He had no guns, but we had missed the long black knife he pulled from a sheath strapped to his ankle. I took a step out of his reach.

"What is it with you blacksuits? You carry anything that aint

127

black? You eat black bread and drink black water too?"

He gathered himself up like he was ready to take a lunge at me, which encouraged me to take another step or two back, but before he could spring there was a loud crack and the ground next to him exploded. I waved at Joe, and he waved back. He was lying on top of a boulder a couple hundreds yards off, playing with his new rifle.

"You had better relax and drop that blade. Joe can punch out a fly buzzing in the wind from this distance. He likes your fancy rifle. Thats what its for, isnt it? Knocking people down from a distance? You ever kill someone close by?"

Leggy slowly got up out his crouch and replaced the knife. Then he turned to me.

"We are trained to kill. Thats awhat we do. Thats what they trained us to do."

"Whos they?"

Chapter 30

Leggy never told me who they were. But he repeated that they were coming after me and Joe. I didnt feel like tripping him again, and he made it to the pines quick enough. Without bothering to rest he slanted back towards the ridges southeast of us. I figured he was of a mind to head out of the valley and down to the old road. Once he got on that crumbly old highway he would meet up with something that would either kill him or take him in.

Which left me and Joe back where we started, stumbling around without Nell, without the lost boys, and without direction. It was Joes idea to let them come after us.

We set up in Joes rocks, which was a small mound of granite boulders and some stubby thorny scrub out in the open. We had a good sight of anyone coming after us. Joe was content to spend the night and all the next day waiting, which wasnt a bad plan, but I wasnt sure how long I could hold out. I was worried about Nell, and the longer we waited the more those worries tugged at me.

I wished Sid and the Deadman hadnt got shot up, and I wished that crazy Marena had stuck around. With them we might have had enough to take on the whole happy valley without having to hunker down in a bunch of rocks and thorns. I wished we could recruit some starving kids in the fields or out herding and all have a go at the big house. Putting together an army of children all wanting a piece of the big housepie wasnt a bad idea. Then we would find Nell and maybe the lost boys and then set fire to the whole happy valley. I hate setting around with nothing but worries to grind me down. But after a while I slipped into a little split between two large boulders and slept a little.

I dreamt about something that made no sense and about a place I had never been. There was a big slappy river and a bunch of young people trying to get across, and something bad was coming up the road to get them, and I couldnt get anyone to listen to me that something terrible was coming, and Joe was off someplace, and all I could do was run around doing nothing to stop what was happening, and I had lost my horse and pack.

Then Joe pulled me out of it and hushed me.

"You were starting to bawl out in your sleep."

"So? Aint nothing wrong with a couple good nightscreams. Ive heard you yowl a time or two." I wasnt quite fully awake, which made me contentious.

Joe hushed me again and started to moved back to his perch on top.

"Quit being ornery and come look at whats coming after us."

"I was hoping for a couple more little trucks. I bet I could drive one of those. I aint sure about that thing. I aint even sure what kind of thing it is. Its old military, aint it?"

I asked Joe, but couldnt tell if he nodded or shrugged. We were laying flat on top of a big rock watching something we hadnt ever watched before. It was late in the night, maybe a couple hours before light, and up ahead of us, back the way we had come through with Leggy, was a large squat vehicle with a rack of bright headlights pointing toward the east, cutting a wide arc of bright light for a couple hundred yards. It had three bigfat tires on each side, and a froggymouthed front, and sides that slanted out from the top and bottom.

"You think they sent that big froggy thing after us? Kinda like bringing a bucket to a spitting contest. Or like . . ."

Joe hushed me. The vehicle had stopped, and behind it, with a little light from the crescent moon, and we could make out manshapes spilling out and then spreading out in a small half circle, but two of the shapes went up toward the front in the bright light and huddled over a map. They had little brightbeamed headlamps, but they still dipped their map into the arc of froglight.

"I wish you had brought them big binoculars. Then we could read that map with them. Maybe theyre lost and need some help. Im feeling helpful, how about you? You want to go over and give them some direction? Maybe theyre looking to get out of this happy valley like Leggy. Maybe the whole place is pulling apart."

Joe hushed me again. A couple more of the shapes lit cigarettes, and we followed the red dots as they plodded around behind the vehicle. We couldnt hear anything but the deep unnatural sound of a heavy engine thumping a quarter mile. I strained to make out more of the vehicle. It was large, squarish, and bigbellied, and it had something sticking out its front above the headlights.

"They must have a lot of fuel around here. You think you could shoot out all those headlights in under six seconds. You want to bet a bottle of our best whiskey? Whats that odd shape up on top in front?"

"Some kind of big spitter gun, probably in a little turret that spins around. You keep talking like its open market on a meetup day and that spitter gun will spin our way," Joe whispered. Cradling the fancy rifle, he started to slide down. "Come on, you old blind fool, we are going to surround them and take them by surprise. You charge them from the front, and Ill come at them from behind. Catch them tobacco smokers before they finish puffing."

Once me and Joe did spring a surprise attack, or mostly Joe sprung it, and it wasnt a happy time. We had been up in the north hills with a string of four mules hauling gallons of white whiskey, swiggy stuff not a whole lot better than the worst rotgut dripping out of rusty stills, but it was drinkable, and so it was tradable. We had passed through a splintery crossroads inhabited by a few trolls living underground and a dozen or so whiskeysoakers, men of various ages and shapes and a couple of women who werent much different than the men. They seemed to live by hunting and scrounging, and maybe a few days work in between. We traded some, taking a handful of greasy silver for a couple gallons of our whiskey. But the soakers got so tanked and crackbrained that they thought it would be great fun to take the rest of our load.

But it wasnt much fun, not for them and not for us. A blustery day in the early freezings, a cold northwind had kicked at us most of the day, and on and off there had been snow swirling in the air. After stashing the mules I had taken refuge in a little concrete pump house by a lake a couple miles past the crossroads, but the soakers had searched me out and had come after me. They were laid about in a half circle above the shoreline, firing down on me, and taunting me. At first it was for laughs, and not so serious. I fired off enough rounds to keep them where they were, but I wasnt feeling much fight. They were just drunken fools too soakedup with bad whiskey to realize how stupid they were. They werent murderous, and at first they fired off as many taunts and threats as bullets, probably as part of what they thought was a good time. But then things got ugly.

After about an hour the gunfire and taunts attracted a few more, and then another handful joined the fun. But this last group wasnt there for the fun. They were a rough bunch, wackers who lived by butchering. I could tell there wasnt much connection between them and the soakers, as I saw a couple of the drunken fools slink off when they showed up. The wackers knew their business, and the threats and taunts stopped, and a ring of fire started up, and rounds started chipping away at the concrete and smashing through the front and side windows. A couple minutes of that and I would have

131

been dead, but then Joe went at them from the back.

Later when telling the story I might have magnified the numbers Joe took on, maybe mentioning fifty when it was more like fifteen. But whatever the number he came flying at them spraying cutter fire every which way, and then he was in among them jumping around faster than lightning, a violent uncontrollable storm of wild rage. As soon as I popped up and saw Joe I rushed out, and I came at wackers from the lakeside, and did my best to imitate Joe Cruz, though I suspect it was an infirm imitation.

But between the two of us we quashed the party. The soakers mostly dropped or scattered, and the wackers split apart and fell back towards the woods. Joe was all for going after them, but I held him back. Soon we all stopped firing and, for a moment, me and Joe stood there above that concrete shed a little surprised that we were still standing. There were five knocked down who would never get up and several more cut up and bleeding out. I helped those I could, but it was an awful bloody scene and not nearly as glorious as the story that later on got passed around the whiskeyshacks in Aurora and the dead city.

I knew Joe wasnt serious about launching a surprise attack on an armored vehicle with an undetermined number of men and guns inside and a big spitter gun on top. I didnt think our surprise would have much effect on a military vehicle created to crush little surprises like us. But I trailed after Joe.

We got about halfway to the vehicle when all the shadowy shapes piled back in, and it set off with grinding gears and a puff of smoke blacker than the night. It bumped over some rocks and then swung in our direction.

"You run at them from the front, and Ill take the rear," Joe said, and took off slanting west.

I stood there for a few moments listening to the huff and crank as that giant mechanical frog made its way toward me. It sounded unnatural. I wasnt accustomed to giant mechanical frogs, and I wasnt sure what to do, or what Joe wanted me to do.

But I live by trading, and I thought maybe I could exchange one thing for another, maybe do some haggling over what they wanted and what I needed. When the froggy thing huffed and cranked its way close enough, I stepped into the arc of light, raised my hands, and offered a universal appeal, dont shoot me.

Chapter 31

Two grabies were guarding me, and neither one would talk to me, but I knew they could hear me behind the steel door. I refused to accept their silence and kept up my end of our conversation. Sometimes you dont have to speak to be part of a conversation.

I offered a stream of Joe stories, entertaining my silent graby guards with some old tales, while polishing a few of the fine points, and then I started in whittling away on some new stories. I told them how me and Joe busted into the Magic Mountain with the wild boy and the brokenfooted woman, and I gave them a more or less careful account what went on inside those tunnels. Despite the bright lights and isolation, I kept myself occupied.

I had to occupy myself, as there was little else to do but fester. I wasnt sure how long I had been locked up. Somewhere between a couple hours and a couple of days. During this blurry stretch a little window at the bottom of my door had opened twice and little sandwiches had dropped in. I am fond of the sandwich when its constructed with good bread and identifiable meat with something tangy lathered on, but what rolled in was put together with stale pasty bread, something cheesy mushy, and a slice of dark meat that came off an animal I had never before encountered, and never hoped to. After the first one dropped I talked with my guards about it some, and I tried to imagine what sort of animal could be so sour, parchy, and leathery.

My cell was small, maybe nine by twelve, or maybe smaller, and aside from a metal bed that was bolted to the wall and floor, a too thin, stained pad on top of it, a little metal sink, and a little metal toilet, both also bolted into the wall and floor, there wasnt much else in there with me. Except for the bright lights. Set behind a thick metal cage recessed into the ceiling, and higher than I could jump, was a series of three large lights that never blinked, and never went off. There was no mistaking what my room had been created for. I wondered how many more there were, and why an orphanage needed a jail.

The journey from getting frog swallowed to getting spit out was also blurry, but I guessed it had been fairly brief, an hour or less. At first the frog had stopped a hundred yards ahead of me, I waved hello at it, and then I started heading towards it. We met in the middle.

I aint too sure of the next part, since I was rendered unmindful by handful of heros dressed in camo fatigues. They spilled out and knocked me down before I could say hello, and then to protect the happy valley they kicked, punched, and clobbered. When I came out of the fog I was bloodied and bruised and lying in the frogs fat belly bound with thin plastic cords, and every time I tried to roll around or sit up one of the frog soldiers battered me back down. I hazily recall being dragged out of the damn frogthing and into one of the side buildings near the big house, and then being hauled down a hallway and heaved into my little room. I had made better journeys.

After running the rusty sinkwater and flushing the toilet a few hundred times, I had started waiting for whatsnext, and then when that didnt happen I started storytelling. I knew the grabies were out there, because I could hear them scratch, shuffle, and sigh, and a few times the graby guards had been rotated in and out.

They were good listeners, but they lacked conversational capacity. I had asked once if, just maybe, it was the rustwater that had caused their throats to closeup, or maybe the drybread and cheeseypaste, but I didnt get any response. I had encountered better companions, but I didnt hold it against them. I thought they were probably trying their hardest to be good grabies, since their happy valley grabyworld was all they knew. I was hoping they might get a notion of something out of my storyworld.

My two interrogators, Captain Stein and Lieutenant Garnett, could talk well enough, but they still lacked conversational capacity. Talking is trading. You give one thing to get something back, but they were unwilling to exchange anything. I would have happily offered whatever they wanted to know in trade for what I wanted to know, but nothing got swapped.

"How large is your Princes military force?"

"What will you take for your writing pen? I will give you a boneyhandled foldup pocketknife with two blades for it. You like to carve ducks or dogs out of chunks of wood?"

The Captain dropped the pen on his scribblepad and looked away. The Lieutenant, about Leggys age, continued to stare at me. That seemed to be his only function, and he was handy at it. He had been wall leaning in back the whole time the Captain sat across from me with the plasticmetal table between us. Both the table and chairs were bolted to the floor. And I was bolted to the table.

"Say, yall have any furniture and housestuff that aint bolted down? After a time I start feeling scrunchy and need to shift around, lean back, and stretch. Maybe if you let me move around I will remember some of the stuff youve been pounding me with. That would be a start to a fair trade."

The older one returned his gaze. With his gray head nearly skincropped and a stern look, he resembled the late departed Captain Leo Sadler, though he had big ears and a pointy chin and seemed a bit softer around the middle. But the age seemed about the same. No doubt that, one way or another, he and the rest of the Captains and Majors had come through the Fires, and the more I thought about one way or another, the more I thought it possible that they had come through the hot times squirreled away in their happy valley, policing orphans and melons. But that didnt make much sense, the whole world getting scorched while all the Captains and Majors watched over a melon patch. I smiled back at the older one.

He had gruffly introduced himself as Captain NoFirstName Stein and his younger associate as Lieutenant NoFirstName Garnett.

After a squad of teenaged graby guards had shuffled me into the interview room and secured me to the table, and after a considerable wait, the Captain and Lieutenant had marched in and began flinging questions at me. But I wasnt about to say much until we began a serious exchange.

Indirectly, I had already provided them with a fair amount of information, since they had listened to my onesided conversation with the graby guards, and since they surely had heard what happened out on the road. Captain Stein had doggedly spent the better part of two hours hurling bits and pieces back at me, trying to sort out the true and notsotrue parts, and trying to root out a little more information about the Prince and Aurora, and about what had brought us into the happy valley. But my head was stuffed with more serious questions.

"Ive been wondering, are you all Captains and Majors around here? Can I be a Captain too? I would sure like to preside over marrying and burying services. Once during a cold snowy stretch I stepped in as a preacher and served up a range of platitudes till the thaw came. Maybe we can trade for one of your uniforms too. What kind of military are you anyway? Once up in Nineveh I had a uniform and some new shiny boots to march around in, and a new greasy cutter that hadnt ever been fired. I was pleased to be part of Gods army, but I soon had to retire from the righteous. You aint exactly old USA Army, are you? I see you aint sporting any of those old bars, stars, stripes, and eagles. I guess the Fires burned all that stuff off."

Captain Stein continued his blank gaze, offering no indication of his connection, or the slightest inclination to trade.

"What weaponry did your Prince take away from the US military installation he overran?"

I shook off the question and sighed.

"I told you an hour ago that he aint my Prince. I never took on ownership, even when his mother had a use for me. And I aint sure what he carried back to Aurora. I dont think he came away with any giant mechanical frogs. How many of those things do you have around here? Where do you get all the fuel for your vehicles? You know up beyond the pass people are still slogging around with horses and mules, except for maybe a rat or two on motorbikes. Did a motorbiking rat show up here a couple days ago?"

Captain Stein and Lieutenant Garnett stared silently at me. After a minute or so the Captain gathered up his pen and scribblepad and stood.

"Tomorrow morning youll be taken before a military court, where you will be tried for murder, a capital crime according to the laws of the National Recovery Alliance. I suggest you take your trial a lot more seriously than you have this interrogation."

Captain Stein pulled for the door, but I called after him.

"Hold on a minute, what murder? Who am I supposed to have murdered? I aint dispatched a soul in your happy valley."

He paused, and then turned. His wall leaning Lieutenant quickstepped out of his way to give him a clear shot back at me.

"Actually," he said, and let the word hang in the air before continuing, "you have been charged with three murders, the deaths of two civilian agents, Morrison and Stayton, and an NRA soldier, Sergeant Adam Lochlan."

"Wait, is Morrison the slaver and Stayton his tall stringy scout? It was that crazy woman Marena that took them down, and it was them that made her crazy. Didnt your graby squad tell you that? And last time I saw Lochlan he was alive and scampering off to the east. He didnt take kindly to getting babybombed, so hes probably a hundred miles past the pass by now."

Captain Stein was so enjoying his moment that he nearly smiled.

"Sergeant Lochlans body was recovered a couple hours ago. He had been badly beaten and then shot in the back of the head." The Captain stretched out his final moment in the doorway, before adding, "Tomorrow morning, after the court is done with you, you will be allowed to face your executioners."

I do not take kindly to death threats, particularly when they are directed at me. After the grabies hauled me back to my lockup, I brooded on my death. I was not resigned to whatever nastiness they planned for me, but without weapons or a way out there was not much I could do, except get jumpy and bothered. But brooding tires me out, and after a time I quit worrying. I didnt even complain too much when another moldy drybread sandwich rolled into my cell. There were better things to think about.

I thought about a lively man named Owen Sullivan, a man I watched die. The Princes father was set on hanging him as a thief and scavenger, but back then, back when the Fires were still smoldering, all of us were thieves and scavengers. Everyone was scuffling and grasping to stay alive. After the old couple who kept me a while had died, and after their neighbors had looted their apartment and turned me out, I attached myself to a crowd of throwaways, and we swarmed through the scorched areas like locusts, scooping up whatever we could that was eatable or tradable, and hiding from all the militias, crazies, and wackers. Anyone who survived the Fires had to scavenge and steal their way through those hard times.

But Sullivan worked on a grander scale than most. He assembled an unusually large gang of scavs and pickers around Aurora and the dead city, and even when the Princes father sent his troops after him, he and his crew kept at it. Lurkers and soakers around the whiskeyshacks told stories about Sullivan emptying the citys warehouses and stockpiles and filling up abandoned buildings scattered around the dead city with tons of leftovers, including hundreds of outofthebox brightly colored shoes, the kind people wore before the Fires when they wanted to look athletic. When half the people in Aurora began turning up wearing bright sparkly rainbow shoes on their feet, the Princes father got set on making an example of Sullivan.

As it often happens, someone told someone who told someone about where to find Sullivan, and all those someones got rewarded with a handful of silver, and Sullivan got caught. He had been hiding ratlike in a cellar hidden underneath the floor of an old burnedout building, but they found him and dragged him out, a little mucky and sooty but sporting a nice pair of bluebright shoes. Even the trolls and cave dwellers creeeped out in the daylight to glimpse Sullivan as he was dragged through the dead city.

Sullivan didnt go out quietly, and thats the part I liked best about his stories. He escaped at least three times, once bribing a couple of nightguards, once gouging and squeezing his way through the ceiling, and once setting fire to the building the Princes father had been using for a jailhouse. But each time he got caught and loaded up with more iron, though the jailfire took out most of the building and allowed half a dozen others to escape. The night before he was supposed to hang a group of his friends burned down the gallows that had been especially erected for him, and the event had to be delayed until another fancy trapdoor affair got hammered together.

I was there when they launched Sullivan, me and a couple thousand other people packed into the old Aurora park, and I swear most everyone was sporting the bright rainbow shoes on their feet. At first the city militia started arresting anyone with those shoes, but the crowd was so huge and so stirred up that they gave up the notion quick enough.

The afternoon was dark, rainy, and sulky with thick grayblack clouds hanging down low enough to make the world seem close and smothery. But Sullivan wasnt beaten down. I had wedged my way near enough to see and hear, and I heard Sullivan scold the hangman for not knowing his trade and then calling out to all of us that he was being murdered, not executed, and that it was hard for a man to die on a tree for anothers greed and deceit. Instead of calling for mercy in the next world or people to repent in this world, or any of the usual blather, he called on his accomplices not to get caught. The Princes father had set himself on his own little gazing platform, and he got so mad and flustered that I thought he was going to charge over and drop Sullivan himself. I never got any of those rainbow shoes, but I liked Sullivan. I thought if I had any last words I would call on Joe to shoot all the scumsuckers.

Chapter 32

After about a minute into my trial I concluded that my three judges deserved to be the first of the scumsuckers to get shot. They had decked themselves out with considerable brass, silver, and ribbons that declared their allegiance to the NRA, and they sat squatty and toadlike at the long table at the end of the room. There were several others in the windowless room, three older NRAers guarding me with cutters pointed in my direction and a younger grayboy poking at a computer off to the side. I hadnt made up my mind about shooting the guards or the boy, but the three toady judges were definitely down for eradication.

They had introduced themselves as Brigadier Fisher, Major Werth, and Major Murdinger, and as soon as they started reading off my charges I concluded their eradication was the only solution. In addition to murdering four people I barely knew and certainly did not slaughter, I was charged with criminal trespass, carrying illegal firearms, evading arrest, assault, theft of property, destruction of property, and something else that got spewed out so quickly I was not sure if it was subversion, sedition, or perversion. Then they finished up their catalogue with terrorist activity. I was not charged with public intoxication or public urination, though as I sat hitched to a table and chair and forced to listen to their babble I felt inclined to both.

I had tried to clarify the process, but evidently I was not supposed to speak.

"Excuse me, but could you go back over that first part about National Recovery Alliances jurisdiction? I am a little unclear as to why I have been invited to perform a part in this melodrama. I used to read stories and poems in whiskeyshacks for drinks and food. Yall going to trade for my acting a part in this theater?"

They ignored me, though Murdinger gave me a quick look. He was taller than the other two and had to hunch over to create the appropriate toadlook.

"Excuse me, I think we should exchange some basic information. Like, what gives yall the right to haul me in here, accuse me of a bucket of glop, and threaten my life? Yall know I havent harmed or threatened a soul in your happy valley. Me and my partner came down here in this crazy place to find something that was taken from us. Yall are accusing me of things youre guilty of. Thats a strange use of language. Shouldnt we be trading places? I would be a merciful judge."

It was the Brigadier that pinned with a stern look.

"If you continue to interrupt this process, we will have you gagged. You will be given a chance to speak during your sentencing. This place you refer to was bought and deeded decades ago, and in the absence of any previous federal or state authority the National Recovery Alliance has instituted its own laws and order."

He paused to self inflate and pinned me with another stern look.

"It is our right as free men to live by the laws we choose. This is our land, and you have violated our laws."

He paused again for another inflating. He was smaller and squatter than the other two, and when he spoke his upper lip tended to wedge up in a snarl.

"And for violating our laws you are subject to whatever penalties we choose."

"Yall aint free. People who keeps themselves hidden away from everyone else aint free. Youre just a bunch of loopy lunatics crouched under a bush hoping no one will notice you. Any deeds, contracts, or agreements you might have had for this happy valley got burned up in the Fires long ago. The Prince is going to come down here and purge you of this nonsense in no time."

We eyed each other for a moment, and I probably should have kept my mouth shut, but when some fool goes all blustery in front me, I cant help myself.

"And another thing, who are the we who are going to gag me. If you three warty toads lay a hand on me, Ill make each of you eat a table leg."

It was the guards that gagged me. They sealed me up with a long sticky piece of duct tape that got attached to both face and shaggy head. I could barely mutter and mumble my defense, but since my defense was a nonessential part of the circus, I didnt have much to murmur or mumble about.

Except when the little beaverfaced baldheaded idiot appeared. When the Brigadier announced District Manager Joseph Unger as witness, and the little fool strutted in with a couple more of his golden grayboys, I choked on my own laughter. He sat himself down at a table across from me, facing the three brassy toads, with two angel assassins behind him. Even stickyfaced and mute I would have preferred to face him, but he only glanced once and then directed himself toward the toads.

The beaverfaced fool had rehearsed his part, and after getting his cue from the Brigadier he launched into a colorful recitation of my crimes, though he curiously failed to mention either the lost boys or Nell. Mostly, I was a cheat, fraud, swindler, impostor, thief, killer, monster, and miscreant who had defiled everything I ever touched.

"He came at me with a knife, and it was only the courageous actions of my adjutants that subdued him."

"You and they and a handful more like you wouldnt dare to disarm me, you cowardly lying hornswoggling maggotbrained fool," I muttered as loudly and distinctly as stickytape would allow.

"He is a violent, murderous horse thief without loyalty except to those equally savage and bloodthirsty. He is an outlaw who has been convicted and condemned in settlements all along the front ranges, and it is only due to the lawless protection of the mountebank who claims to be the Prince of Aurora that he has escaped execution."

"When I get my hands on you, you perjuring dungeating blundering halfwit twit, Ill give you some savage and bloodthirsty," I mumbled.

Regretfully, I was not given the chance to get my hands on Unger, or ask him any questions. He and his blond grayboys marched themselves out just as soon as he finished his dramatic catalogue of my atrocities and iniquities. Though I rocked, strained, thumped, and muttered, the only blood I spilled was my own from tugging against the plastic binders that attached my hands to the table. But I had to give the little beaverman credit for using the word mountebank, which I vaguely recognized, and which I thought was be a better fit for fraudulent district managers than the Prince.

When you have someone helpless, whether chained, tied, or taped, and when youre holding a gun to his head, you get to say whatever you want, and whatever you say gets to be true, at least as long as your captive is helpless. I have never believed truth was absolute, and I have generally accepted that it was a raggy, knotty thing with a lot of loose threads that people tug at a lot of different ways, and each way they tug they think is the only way. Most times, at least without chains and guns, truth gets negotiated, bartered, haggled, and dickered by people balancing what they have with what they want.

But in that stale airless room there was nothing to be bartered or balanced, and I felt nothing but sputtering helpless rage, knowing that those three toads and that perjurous officious little mountebank beaverman could say whatever they wanted, even if the most crackbrained blundering nightscreamer could perceive that what they were saying was the opposite of what was true.

I vowed eradication and revenge, and thinking about what me and Joe would do to get things balanced made me feel better.

Chapter 33

My vengeful thoughts got churned up when I next endured the perjury of Colonel Alfred Eliot Lyingscum BabyBomber Stevens, who tearjerked his testimony so much that I almost wanted to convict myself. A twitchy sallow sickly fellow about the same age as the toady judges, he sat down without once looking my way, started drumming his skeletal fingers on the table, and, with a splatter of melodrama, proceeded to describe how he had listened over open line of the phone while me and Joe tortured both Captain Sadler and

Lieutenant Lochlan. He was particularly drippy when describing the screaming, shrieking, and death groans he heard as me and Joe heartlessly abused our helpless captives. If I hadnt been intimately familiar with myself, and if I hadnt known what a pack of brazen boldfaced lies it was, I would have condemned myself. It was a good show.

At that point, with my wrists hurting, and still bruised, blackened, and lumpy, I didnt bother to mumble or shake my objections. I was an object, a prop, forced to take part in someone elses ritual to justify my murder. I had little role in the spectacle.

Nor did I take part when one of the giant mechanical frog mapreaders, a little squirrely man identified as Lieutenant Pollins, testified that I had attacked them, and it was only by some mysterious courageous action on his part that I was captured and subdued. Just me, without Joe, attacking a giant mechanical frog fitted with a spitter gun and a gaggle of soldiers armed with automatic weapons. I was touched by my own bravery, but mortified by my greater stupidity. The thought was farcical, but not enjoyable. It would have been more enjoyable if Lieutenant Pollins had described how I had attacked his giant mechanical frog, or how he subdued me. But he left out the good parts.

That I had walked up and had given up didnt matter. I tried to stop listening and let it go, and even tried some of the little blanket mans deep breathing. Their version of me was too distorted to recognize as me, and theres only so much craziness that I want to fill my head with. I began to think about the next time I would visit a woman I favored back in Nineveh. We would sit in the sun out on the old Bishops porch overlooking the lake, and we would sip and eat and I would tell her about all the places me and Joe had been since we last visited. Those were sweet thoughts, much sweeter than my final sentencing, which I half listened to with my eyes shut and while humming an old song about a hardheaded woman. Joe would have poked me for acting so childish, but I thought my acting was appropriate.

Then the Brigadier asked me if I wanted to make a statement.

Sure I wanted to make a statement. I wanted to make a statement with Joe boiling over, a couple thousand of the Princes best Rangers, and a few dozen pieces of groundpounding artillery. It gets personal when some jacklegged fool threatens my life, and I wanted to declare my dissatisfaction with considerable display. I knew nothing I could say would matter, and I almost shook my head no. But then I nodded yes and waited patiently while one of the idiot guards untaped me without much concern for preserving hair or flesh. I made the toady fools wait while I rubbed off the sting.

"First, I would like to thank you for allowing me a small part in this pageant. It was packed full with interesting testimony of my crimes and outrages. But . . ."

I paused, trying to pin the toads with my killer stare,

". . . it was all a pack of shameful lies. And thats the most interesting part. You know, I know, that little keytapper over there knows, the guards know, and especially your most unreliable witnesses know, what a pack of outrageous falsehoods have been slopped out about me. The fact is you cockleburbrains have taken the truth and reversed it in every possible way, and you sit there like smug toads knowing what youve done, and its only the use of force and some damn ducttape that lets you get away with it. Youre the murderers. We ought to trade places. Let me put you on trial for crimes against humanity. You know youre guilty. Youve been guilty for a couple decades and probably a lot longer than that. Theres not one thing being recovered by your stinking National Recovery Alliance. Your only gutless authority comes from holding a gun to my head. Yall should be shot for language abuse."

My statement got me a headknock from one of the guards, the Brigadiers promise that I would be shot the next day, and a rough drag back to my cell. Had it not been for the headknock, I might have felt better after making my statement. But words dont mean much when no ones listening. Words are just noise unless someone wants to listen, and no one at NewHarmony wanted to hear what I had to say. All the hoopla and show was just to prop up a misshapen me to sanction their own bloated selfrighteous distortions.

Truth can be a blinding light, and I suspected that most of the NewHarmony caretakers preferred to hide in the dark. When beliefs get so tangled and snarly, they aint easy to straighten out.

So I spent some time trying to straighten out my own thoughts, but all I could keep in my head was the hope that come morning Joe would find a way to make his own statement. I chewed down another drybread sandwich, slurped some rusty water, and thought about Joe with that fancy sniper rifle until I fell asleep.

Chapter 34

I thought I was dreaming when the large happyfaced woman appeared before me, and so I waited for the dream to speak.

"My name is Mother Mary."

She settled herself down on a stool, but where either she or stool came from I had no idea. I figured it was best to let the dream go at its own pace without interruptions or questions. Except for her head, she seemed barrelwide from top to bottom, and she was decked out in a long black dress and a couple layers of blueygreen shawls and scarves and a fat clinky silver chain. She was heavier than me, but I thought if I had to wrestle a dream I could take her.

"I heard youre quite a talker. Aint you gonna talk to me? You should talk to me if you want to get out of this damn place."

From somewhere on her she produced a pack of leftover cigarettes, the kind in those little red and white packs that scroungers will kill for. She fiddled with a cigarette and lit up. Thinking I hadnt ever seen a dream smoke before made me sit up, especially after the smoke drifted my way.

"Who the hell are you?"

"Just as I said. I am Mother Mary."

I stared back at her without responding. Sometimes silence asks the loudest questions. She paused a moment, waiting for my silence to finish, and then plunged ahead.

"I am the Director of NewHarmony Farm. I came here a long time ago to provide a haven for lost children."

My silence spoke a little more.

"I have helped a lot of children here at the farm. My sister too, but she . . ."

I waited while she chose her words.

" . . . she is not longer with us."

I waited some more while she puffed, jiggled, and tugged at her silver chain.

"How come all you crazy people around here say one thing when you mean the opposite? How come you use good words for bad things?"

She tried to use my silence as her response, but she couldnt hold out long.

"Dont it always depend on who youre talking to. I aint lying to you. I have helped lots of lost children, and I have come here to help you.

I sat up some and wished I had some chocolate from Joes secret stash, or maybe some more of those hard peppermint candies he was carrying. I had a bad taste in my mouth.

"This aint no orphanage. I dont know what it is, maybesome kind of work farm. Or plantation maybe, but it aint no haven for lost children. Yall snatch children and carry them off here to water your plants and herd your sheep."

She accomplished a bit more of her puffing, jiggling, and tugging before responding.

"Like I said, it depends on who youre talking to. Theres plenty of young troopers around here who will tell you how much I helped them. Theyre grateful for my care. Many of the children love me."

I waited for my silence to gnaw at her.

"Listen, you want me to leave you here to get shot in the morning, or you want to hear what I got to say? There aint no one else around here gonna help you."

"When you say help, does that mean youre going to shoot me in the back of the head when I turn around? Yall use language in funny ways."

She fussed with herself some more and produced a small black femalesized pistol, which she pointed at me and smiled.

"My three toads aint going to like it if you shoot me now. Theyre fixing to have me play a final scene in their morning theater. Theyre probably listening to us right now."

She returned her little pistol from wherever it had come from and crushed her cigarette out on the floor. She was wearing a pair of old pointy western boots.

"Youre a little crazy, aint you? I dont know what toads youre talking about, but there aint no one listening. I got friends around here, grateful friends like I told you, and I had everything turned off so we could talk in private. But if you dont want to talk I will be leaving. Those old NRAers are gonna have you shot in the morning."

"The three toads all had names and military titles, but all they did was squat in a row and snap at little bugs with their long slimy tongues while they sentenced me."

She looked closely at me, wondering if maybe I was a lot more crazy than she first thought.

"I am just a poor trader. I move around the ranges dragging leftovers from one place to another, trying to barter a living from the ash heaps left after the Fires. Sometimes I tell a fortune or two, help find lost things, maybe do some doctoring or lettering, and sometimes I might borrow a horse, but mostly I barter and trade. What is it youre wanting to trade?"

She had me confused with someone else, but I let her go on thinking I was someone else, since that person was an advance scout for a thousandfold horde of savage bloodthirsty raiders about to overrun her happy valley.

"You get me someplace safe out beyond the pass, and Ill help your Prince. I know all the secrets about this place. This farm is just the tip of what really goes on around here."

"I keep telling people, he aint my Prince. Hes been his own man ever since he was old enough to ride horses and drink whiskey, which was about the time he decided me and Joe were a bad influence, at least in public."

She looked me and shrugged.

"Thats my offer. Ill get you out of here and away from the farm, and youll give me safe passage and work something out with your Prince so I can settle up north someplace, teach school maybe, maybe start an orphanage where the kids dont have to work in the fields and then beat on each other. You do that and Ill tell you and your Prince all about this place. Ill tell him where stuffs been hid since the beginning."

I didnt bother to correct her again about me and the Prince. Her thinking he was my Prince was a tradable commodity. I didnt have much else to barter but lies and misperceptions. As long as she coupled me to a prince and bloody horde of murderous savages I would keep working it to my advantage. The truth was my putting a good word in for her with the Prince wouldnt get her more than a shove toward the door, but I encouraged her to think otherwise.

"Maybe we can work out something. But first you tell me what secrets and what stuff. To make a trade, I have to know the value of whats being offered. And for starters, as a show of good faith, you let me have that little pocket pistol."

She lit another cigarette, and then jiggled and tugged some more before settling back to respond. She pulled out her little automatic and tossed it to me. She seemed working up to a dramatic effect.

"You get me safely away from this place, and Ill start telling you and your Prince all about what this place really is and whats been hidden away. But you have to get me out of here and set up some place safe."

I pocketed her gun and wondered what else I could get her to give up.

"Tell me more about this place and whats hidden away. Whats all the whats youre talking about?"

She took a moment to suck down some smoke and then slowly huffed it out. She looked at me and smiled.

"Gold, tons of gold. Those old men started hoarding gold out here years before the breakdown."

"Tons?"

She jiggled, smiled, and nodded.

"Tons."

Chapter 35

Me and Mother Mary struck a bargain, which in truth was diddle and deception on both our parts. Me and Joe were going to escort her out of the happy valley and get her set up with the Prince back in Aurora, and in return she would help us to harvest tons of gold from NewHarmony Farm. But it wasnt so much the empty promise of gold that was of value to me, but the bits and pieces I learned about both the farm and the NRA.

Me and Joe love to barter gold, since a little gold ring is worth more than a weeks soaking in the best whiskeyshacks around Aurora and the dead city. But other than rings and little pieces of old leftover jewelry, most people dont have any real weight. Those still scratching at life up in the mountains will generally have something small and shiny tucked away, an old bracelet or chain that got handed down and hidden away, but never the kind of gold she was talking about. That kind of gold gets buried and stays buried, and if it gets dug up it just gets buried again.

Back when the Fires broke out a lot of people were hoarding gold, thinking it would make their lives fireproof, and a lot of that got wacked away and fought over by endless storms of raiders and looters. Sometimes the old soakers in the whiskeyshacks spin stories about treasure troves of gold and silver buried someplace, and sometimes some pack of fools run off some place and start digging, thinking their secret map or secret information will turn them into princes overnight. But they never come back with anything except oozy blisters, sore backs, and foul dispositions.

If some poor fool actually stumbled over more than a couple ounces of gold, hed hide it as quickly as he could before the snatchers and creepers got wind of it and decided they were entitled to it. Hunkering down over any sort of mound aint ever worth the trouble. Thats what sends people underground and turns them into trolls. Better to trade away. Hoardings a fools game.

The bits and pieces I learned about the happy valley had more weight than tons of hypothetical gold. I had suspected there was more going on in the happy valley than a farm of snatched children, but I never expected what she finally leaked out.

"The farm and the NRA only exist to conceal whats really here. You take that dirt road out beyond the river, follow it three miles, and it will suddenly turn into a nice paved road and lead right up to a big fancy electric gate. Behind that gate are some of the biggest nicest houses you can imagine set on big green lawns. Some of the richest and most powerful people in the world built themselves a sanctuary out here, and when everything from before was breaking apart, they came out here and took refuge. They brought out everything they needed, including their own private army and tons of gold. The farms just their own private garden, and the grays who get sorted get recruited in their army."

I was feeling cramped and constricted, and I wanted to get outside. And not just outside but far outside. What she was telling me was that there was another set of toads hidden away somewheres, bloated scammers and schemers who had tucked themselves away in the happy valley to enjoy their own selfish little playworld while the real world got bloodied and scorched.

For years during and after the hottest Fires there had been a lot of armed communities, places where people had walled themselves in to wait out the blazings. But theres nothing that attracts packs of bloody wackers and wandering crazies more than walls and fences and the thought of whats safe on the other side. Me and Joe always thought that those supposedly safe communities werent ever so safe. Some of the most vicious battles we had ever observed were waged over walls. And once the walls came down, and they always did, there was never any mercy.

I was surprised. Theres still a constant stream of whiskey-shacked stories of sanctuaries hidden away, whispery tales of hidden governments hiding warehouses full of stuff, but most places got rooted out long ago. I was surprised that a place like the happy valley had held out so long. But in thinking about the scale of all the planning and scheming, I was less surprised. Whoever had hidden themselves away down here had erected a lot more than fences, walls, and a big fancy electric gate.

"You want to get out of this place or what? We got a deal?"

She fiddled some more with herself waiting for my reply. In the harsh light of the cell she seemed less happyfaced and more worn and haggy. There were still bits and pieces I wanted from her.

"Youve been here a couple or more decades. Why are you so hot to get out now?"

She shrugged off my question.

"I told you. I dont want to be around here when it gets overrun. Ive been here long enough, too long. Everyones saying your Prince is on his way, and hes got a big army, and now hes got a lot of old military stuff and is gonna blow this place apart. If thats what hes got a mind to do, Ill help him."

"You want to be on the winning side?"

"There aint nothing wrong with looking out for yourself. All these years Ive been down here working for those old men out there in those big houses, and I never got invited in, not like those old swindlers who sentenced you today. When they came down here they were nothing more than guards hired to protect the rich people. Now theres not much difference between them and them that hired them. And ever since my sister went off a couple years ago they havent trusted me. Somebodys watching every time I open a cabinet."

"Why now? Dont you think all your NRA troopers can hold out against the Prince?"

She threw a halfsmoked cigarette down and crushed it under a boot heel.

"This whole place is going to hell. Its falling apart. Things dont work the way they used to. I should have gone off with my sister. Theyre running out of fuel, and now those old fools are trying to run their cars and trucks with steam and manure. Bunches of the old guards took off long ago, and even some of the children and grandchildren of those that started this place have run off, preferring to live in the dark on the outside than stay inside. And now those old fools think theyre gonna organize territories on the outside, as if thatll stop whats coming. The Grays do most of the guarding and roaming, and they aint gonna stop a horde of . . ."

She let her sentence trail off, so I offered to finish it.

"Crazy bloodguzzling cannibals? Savage primitives? Ive heard stories about starving people coming through the Fires with nothing to eat but their neighbors. Ive heard once you taste it you get a desperate craving for it. Its a hunger that cant never be satisfied."

She quit rearranging herself and looked back at me.

"I dont believe that."

I shrugged. She was probably wondering if she had made a big mistake. I thought she probably had.

"I aint saying its true. Just a story I heard. You probably got music and movies that you can play by pushing a button. Most of us wild savages dont have anything better to do than sit around the fire and tell stories, that is when we aint slaughtering innocents."

She quit picking at herself and gave me another long look.

"I dont believe that either. I dont know what all goes on out there, but we get reports. We got contacts, we got dealings with outsiders." She paused and leaned in. "We need to quit talking and get out of here."

Other than taking me through a couple empty hallways and out into a cement courtyard fenced in with double walls rusty fence topped with razor wire, she didnt have much of a plan.

And much of a response when we got tackled. We got into the middle of the courtyard, and she stopped to look around.

"Theres supposed to be a gate leading out of here."

I took her bewilderment as a bad sign. There was no way out other than the way we came in and another door down a ways, and it was shut tight. I was just turning to head back when racks of overhead lights sparked on, blinding us, and before I could blink the door we had come out banged open and half a dozen or so notyoung grayboys spilled out, followed by the old toady Brigadier, who stomped out all swaggery and full of himself. It was quite a gathering.

The woman got over her shock quick enough. She heaved herself up and looked fiercely at the Brigadier. He smiled back at her.

"Mary, did you think we were going to let you simply walk out of here, and take this murderer with you?"

She looked at him a moment, let go a loud scream, and launched herself on the Brigadier. With her weight, size, and surprise, she took him to the ground, snarling and scratching. She had one hand on his face, and I thought she was trying to pop an eyeball. In an instant he was screaming for help.

"Get her off of me, get her off of me, kill her, shoot her."

Three of the grayboys grabbed at her and hauled away with handfuls of hair and clothing, but she kept scratching and snarling, while the Brigadier kept shrieking his getheroffmes. Then a fourth leaned in and smacked her on the forehead with the buttend of his cutter. That stunned her long enough for the toad to roll away. He popped up tattery, torn, and screamy with a long scratch on his face. Mother Mary was on her knees, her face bloody, but she started laughing. The Brigadier did not hesitate.

"Kill her, kill them both."

I had been edging my way back towards the open door, but when the toad spoke two of the grays turned to circle me. I smiled and pointed back towards the Brigadier, hoping to redirect their attention.

"Kill them, shoot them. Thats an order."

The grays hesitated moment, then one, still a boy but hot for blood, stepped toward Mary and let go, zippering her chest with four quick shots. She was knocked down and then lay still. For a moment there was nothing but silence and the recognition of death. Then the

Brigadier picked up his shrieking.

"Kill him, shoot him."

All six grays turned toward me, their cutters pointed. I stepped toward them, pulling out Mother Marys little black gun, wanting them to look me in the face, but also wanting to get close enough to express my complete willingness to die fighting.

Suddenly a shot exploded and with it the Brigadiers head. The two grays standing closest were splattered with blood and gore and fell back stunned, not fully deciphering. Before the others could react two more shots exploded, and one of the grayboys dropped, screaming and clutching at a bloody foot, and while the deluded mothershooter flipped around, dancing with a shattered hand. I was left with a semicircle of grayboys, as old as Sid or maybe a little older. Though dazed and unsure, they began to raise their cutters in my direction.

"Are you crazy? My partners hit everything he aimed at. Do you think hes going to miss you?"

A couple of the grayboys was reasonable and backed off, leaving one still pointing cutters at me.

Chapter 36

We stared at each other a moment, me and my maybe executioner, waiting for something to happen, but not knowing what would happen.

Then suddenly something did happen.

"Over here," a voice croaked.

We looked. The second door twenty yards down cracked open, and someone was leaning an arm out, motioning us over. There were no lights on beyond the door, and I couldnt see who was beckoning, but it didnt matter too much to me. It was a tight spot, and when a door opens, and there aint other opportunities to worry over, you go through it.

I grabbed and jerked my executioners arm, and we headed towards the open door. I cant really say why I grabbed him, only that we were a pair, and I thought it best to keep him close rather than leaving him behind. If you have to drag an assassin around with you, he was a likely choice.

We got to the door, and it opened wide enough to gather us in. We were in a small holding room, and on the other side was a double set of steel bars blocking entry into the hallway beyond. For a few seconds we all gave each other curious glances, and our beckoner got most of my glances.

He might have been a hundred years old, or a thousand years old. He was slight, silverhaired, and withery, but not so wrinkly like some old people, more tightskinned, shiny, and mummylike. He was brighteyed and amiable, and he seemed amused with us, offering a quick nod and a thin smile. Next to him was a man much larger and younger, but much older than the grayboys. He was headshaved, thickbodied, and suited up in black like the riflemen, and he was armed with a handgun on his belt and a cutter strapped over his front. He didnt seem half so amused with us as the little mummy man.

"Lets all move on before we cause further confusion," the old man said, and motioning to Shavedhead, who turned to the nearest wall and punched something into a keypad. Both sets of steel bars pulled back, and we tumbled through, the old man going first, my executioner and I following, and then the black hulk after us. We hurried down another hallway, through two more sets of steel gates, and then to a door. Each time we stopped for gates and door, the old man stepped aside to let Shavedhead punch a keypad. No one spoke until we were outside. Then the old man turned to my executioner.

"Whats your name, son?"

My executioner went rigid.

"Hopkins, Sir. Glenn Hopkins. Ive been a Gray for three years."

The old man smiled. Near us was another small vehicle, only this one was more carlike, having seats enough for four people and lacked any lettering or numbers. He walked over and slowly climbed into the front. Shavedhead followed and sat himself behind the wheel before I could offer to drive.

"Trooper Hopkins, would you do me a favor."

My executioner again went rigid.

"Yes Sir."

"Would you kindly stay behind and inform the Command that I have assumed responsibility for the captive?"

"Yes Sir."

The little mummyman wanted to know if Joe was going to shoot him.

"Your friend is quite a marksman. He isnt going to put a bullet in my head, is he? "

I thought it unlikely but shrugged.

"I cant predict his inclinations, but I dont think so. Youre a moving target, anyway."

We had set off at a fast clip, past the side of my jailhouse and another long building, before turning toward the back. There were several small clumps of grayboys and NRAers scrambling about, jumpy and agitated, and they clogged our path as soon as they saw us coming, but as soon as they got a closer look they stepped away. I felt like waving.

"Thats good, because Mister Gunther would be most dis-pleased if anything happened to me. Isnt that so, Mister Gunther?"

Shavedhead didnt respond. He turned us down another small roadway toward a field of something clumpy and bushy. It was still dark, but I could see well enough to trace the roadway up a ways to a small bridge over the creek. I thought it distinctly probable that Shavedhead wouldve been displeased if anything happened to the little old mummyman.

"My name is Morris Howard Gault. You may call me Mister Gault. What is your name?"

He twisted himself around toward me and offered another slim smile, but little else. He held his upper body stiff, and despite smiling he seemed grim. Since there were more important issues, I jumped over name game.

"A few minutes ago the Brigadier was intent on having me shot, so I am certainly pleased to meet you, Mister Morris Howard Gault. Your friend Mister Gunther isnt going to shoot me, is he? Im a little touchy with all the shoothims and killhims getting shouted out around here. I aint particularly dangerous."

The old man gave a small headshake.

"No, not unless I tell him to, and not while he is driving. Furthermore, I never shout."

He lingered a look a moment longer and then turned back towards the front as Mister Gunther clattered over the bridge. There were a few bumps and the old man gripped both the rollbar and a handhold as we went over the bridge and pulled onto the dirt road. I figured we were headed to the land of big lawns and big houses.

"I thought it might be to our mutual advantage to negotiate. I understand you came down here to negotiate. Is that not correct?"

"Mostly I like negotiating more than shooting."

I got to a place I had never been before, a world that hadnt ever been broken or burned, or charred, cracked, or stripped, a world filled with picture pretty houses that had big wide porches, high balconies, and lush green lawns with flowery gardens, sprinklers, and walkways leading to secluded spots where you could while away long summer evenings, resting or reading a book. I didnt think such places existed.

It all looked pretty, but it also looked eerie, empty, and life-less. The only people I saw were a few sleepyheaded graby guards strung out along the roadsides. And except for the twittering of a few birds and the slap of wheels on the roadway it was silent.

It was a world created to shut itself off from the rest of the real world, a little playground fenced off and gated from everything that surrounded it. Even the houses had their own fences and gates. I wondered if inside the houses there were more fences and gates.

We drove along a treelined road, passing a few houses before Mister Gunther pulled up to a big iron gate, punched a button on a little black box he pulled out of a pocket, and the big iron gate silently split apart. The gate was painted shinyblack and had swirly flowery designs along the top that ended in sharp points, and it looked heavy enough that I doubted a handful of men could lift one half section. I wondered what would happen if Mister Gaults electricity ever got cut off, but then figured he would have a dozen backup plans. I doubted he had ever got caught short in any kind of storm.

We rolled up a curvy driveway that led to a house constructed of several square blocks, some big and some small, all constructed of concrete, timber, and black iron. Curving around the side and back was a large green open space that crooked at an angle.

"Who lives here?"

"This is my residence," Mister Gault offered.

"But who lives here?"

He sideways around to look at me. He heard what I said, but not what I asked.

"Did you not hear me say that this is my residence?"

"Sometimes I dont quite hear what I am hearing."

"You dont understand my language? This is my residence, my domicile. I had one of the worlds most gifted architects of modernist design build it for me."

"Does he live here?"

Mister Gunther pulled up to a big box that leaned over the edge of the drive and punched another button. A huge door began to pull upwards. Inside was a cavernous garage that contained a couple more minicars like ours and in back a row of big cars, old cars from before the Fires. There were a couple big shiny sedans, one silver and one black, and several smaller zippier cars of various shades of red and blue, and all of them quite worthless.

"No, he does not. He could have come out here with us, but he was killed during the early days of the Breakdown."

Mister Gunther pulled into the garage, stepped around to Mister Gaults side, and waited. I wondered more about Mister Gaults language than I did about his cars and gasoline. I had never before heard the Fires referred to as a Breakdown. Sometimes, things that breakdown can be patched and repaired. But that wasnt the world I blundered around in. You cant patch or repair buildings that burned down, or lives that got chewed up. We sat for a moment longer.

"Who else lives here? Awfully big house. Does Mister Gunther live with you? Anyone else? The Prince could stick his entire Guard in a house this size, and they number more than a hundred."

"We need to talk about this Prince you refer to. As for my residence, there are three attached apartments. Mister Gunther and my administrative assistant live in one above this garage. My wards and their steward live in another, and my housekeepers and cook live in the third."

Mister Gault slowly started to climb out. Mister Gunther reached over to help him. Any blind fool could see that the little mummyman was dealing with some serious pain. I sat for a moment longer.

"My language aint quite up to yours. What are wards and whats a steward?"

Chapter 37

"You want a girl? What kind of girl? There are many girls at the Farm, and there are a number back here in the Residences."

We were sitting out back in an enclosed patio area complete with garden strips of strange bright flowers and a tenfoot waterfall. The water tumbled down over some rocks into a little splashy puddle pool at the bottom, and it was all surrounded by big leafy plants that wouldnt have lasted a day baking in the dry hills. It was a strange useless jungle to have built in the back of a house. But then the whole house was useless, nothing more than a museum of the dead.

"Would you like me to have the water turned off?"

I looked back at Mister Gault. He had caught me staring.

"What else can you turn on and off?"

He offered a thinlipped smile and sipped from a water glass.

"Most everything, I suppose. Now what about this girl."

I looked away from the waterfall and waited while he sipped again. He had offered food and drink, whatever I wanted, but I had declined, though at some point I hoped to return to what he had called his barroom. We had passed through it earlier, and I had noticed rows of shiny bottles, all in various shapes, sizes, and colors. It didnt seem fair to call them leftovers, since nothing in the little mummys world had ever been left over. Everything had been lugged down and set out for grave robbers.

I was still soaking in my surroundings and not ready to respond to direct questions. Most times when bartering you need to learn about where youre at and who youre with. I nodded toward the green belt beyond the patio.

"Whats that green strip out there? You got little planes you land around here?"

Mister Gault sipped some more water. I noted he was a particularly sippy man and thought maybe he was trying to wash away whatever canker was gnawing at his insides.

"That is the first leg of the ninth hole."

We shared a language, but he spoke in a strange tongue. I considered going back to the barroom and fetching a bottle, wondering if that might help our communication.

"I didnt know holes had legs. How many legs does your ninth hole have? Holes are usually identified by the amount of nothing they contain. In the dead city theres a big hole more than a mile around. Thats a whole lot of nothing."

I was playing the fool. I had seen pictures in old books and magazines of people knocking little white balls around, so I knew what he was talking about, but it seemed a good moment to appear ignorant. But I had never seen a golfy playland before that wasnt ruined.

"You dont golf then? This Prince you referred to, does he play golf? Are there any golf courses left where you come from?"

He dropped the words out slowly, like they were a bad thing, like I was a bad thing that came from a bad place. Shavedhead had disappeared, and we were alone, and I wondered what it would be like to toss him off his own waterfall. But I was feeling amiable, and I knew Shavedhead would not appreciate Mister Gault tumbling off into his own puddle pool.

"There were lots of golfy places before the Fires, but they got dug up and planted, or squatted on by shackers looking for a place to live, or just left to go wild and weedy. Most everyone was too busy trying not to get scorched to worry about golfing. Seemed like a big waste of space back then, especially when the water lines got torn up. Where yall get your water from?"

We both looked out on the empty first leg of the ninth hole.

"Our community is entirely selfsustaining. We have our own wells."

"Selfsustaining except for the labor of little people. You got to go outside for that."

Mister Gault thinlipped a smile and sipped his water.

"New Harmony Farm is an orphanage for young people in need of a home."

"Most of them had homes, and they got snatched by slavers like Morrison. Thats what brought me and Joe Cruz down here. Following that scaly miscreant."

Mister Gault stiffened up and closed his eyes. I thought maybe something inside him had gone twitchy, and I wondered if he needed a dose of meds to dull the pain. I thought about calling for Shavehead, but then the mummyman looked up and smiled.

"I understand you knew Mister Morrison. Brigadier Fisher had you convicted of his murder. Did you murder Mister Morrison?"

"That fat oily toad of a Brigadier convicted me of a ton of things, and most of them murderous, but I wasnt guilty of a one of them. It was all a pack of lies and flapdoodle. I havent killed anyone lately, and rarely ever. It was that crazy woman Marena that snuck up behind Morrison and dispatched him, both him and that creeper Stickman of his."

"Marena?"

Mister Gaults eyes were watery and red, but he kept smiling at me.

"A woman he kept and abused up at his place above NewPueblo. She tracked him down all the way here just to pull a shotgun up to his head. You want me to call Shavedhead, I mean Mister Gunther, or someone? You need something for your pain?"

He shook his head and looked off toward his lush green dogleg.

"This woman, Marena, what happened to her?"

"I have no idea. Once she had done her dispatching, she took off. I wasnt expecting her to appear out on that road just when your Mister Morrison was screaming for my blood. Yall had any fires around here. I think shes an igniter."

I paused for a moment while he reached for his water.

"Youre dying, aint you? How much time you got left?"

He drank, carefully replaced his water glass, and then smiled at me.

"Plenty of time. Shall we talk about this girl youre hunting after? Are you planning to snatch her away from us?"

"Her name is Nell. I aint sure of all the extended connections, but I believe she is the great niece of a rancher up above NewPueblo, a rich man by dead city standards, though he aint got a golf course or a waterfall. She came out with me to search after his favorite grandsons got snatched. Morrison took her, and either he or some of his gang took those little boys. I think theyre all down here someplace. Theres a steady flow of little people that gets relocated here, and me and Joe came to collect those that belong to the old mans ranch and take them back with us. The old man up there offered a monsterish reward, least by dead city standards."

He nodded and slowly stood up. Mister Gunther wasnt close by, so I reached over to offer a hand to steady him, which he gripped to pull himself up. He didnt seem like there was much weight to him.

"How many people use your golf course?"

He started off toward a series of wall switches.

"Not too many anymore, Im afraid. Many of my neighbors are gone now. Years ago we used to have wonderful tournaments among all of us living in the Residences."

He got to the wall and steadied himself. I didnt want to correct him about his word choice, but living wasnt a word I would have chosen.

"I was champion several years in a row. But that was back when I was a vigorous man. Now I am," he paused and looked back at me, offering another weak smile, "less vigorous."

He turned to a little silver square by the switches, pressed a button, and spoke.

"Mister Gunther, I think we are ready."

He turned back toward me and began his slow return.

"If I help you in your recovery project, may I assume that you will be obliged to help me?"

"I like to be obliging, but I also like to know what I am obliged to do. What kind of obliging you have in mind?"

He came back and I offered my hand to help him lower himself back into his chair. But he waved off my hand and lowered himself. I waited to see if he would answer my question. Off behind I heard a door open and shut, and then softly some steps approaching. There was a sudden cry in back of us and then suddenly Nell launched herself across the room and wrapped herself around me before I could pull my arms up. She didnt want to let go.

"You came for me."

I nodded, though I wasnt sure if she was asking or telling.

"You been kicking any rocks around here?"

She shook her head and gripped my arm tighter.

"You ok? Did anyone hurt you in any way."

She shook her head again.

"No, not really. I got grabbed up by that river and then tied up. They stuck a nasty rag down my throat until I choked and dragged me off. Those men you went to see, they did it, and that tall man was the one that grabbed me. They brought me down here and then left me at the farm. And then this man brought me out here from the farm."

She pointed to Mister Gault.

"Ive been locked up ever since with these two little girls and this sour old woman who keeps saying shes my teacher. Can we go now? I saw Jemmy off a distance back at the farm, but not Ben.

She started pulling me toward the outside patio door.

"Wards and steward, Im guessing."

I looked at the shrunken mummyman. Shavedhead had followed behind Nell and now stood next to his master.

"What are we exchanging, Mister Gault?"

Chapter 38

"We tried to save the best of everything."

"You tried to save yourselves."

Mister Gault looked out the big side window. We had moved to what he called his library, a massive room with high ceilings lined with chunky old books and fat leather chairs. There was a long waxy table by one wall with a bowl of apples and a bottle of whiskey set on top. On a side table there was a large elaborate statue of a horse and rider in full gallop. Out the side window there was more lush green lawn and a little stage surrounded by trees and flowers. The stage had its sides built up with thin wooden slats ornately woven together and two arched entryways. He called it his arbor. I called it useless, though not aloud. Curling in front and winding around to the back was a narrow manmade stepover stream. It was pretty, but more uselessness.

"We were the best of everything. We gathered forty of the worlds wealthiest, most talented, and most gifted people, all leaders of industries and the arts, all highly accomplished experts in their fields. There was nothing more we could do to stop the madness. Rioting had erupted everywhere. The idiot politicians had choked the life out of business and were at war with each other. The military had split into factions, and there were criminal militias putting up barricades and claiming sovereignty over areas no larger than a few blocks. People had gone crazy and were demanding what was no longer possible. It was madness. We stayed as long as we could, doing everything we could, and when there was nothing more left to be done, we came out here. We came out here to preserve what was best and create a model for the eventual restoration."

"Model, what do you mean? Like an example, something for people to imitate? But yall hid yourselves away in this happy valley. Dont models have to be seen?"

"There was nothing to be done until the madness had stopped. The government should never have attempted to regulate the rights of private citizens, especially in business."

I wasnt comfortable, and knew I should shut up, but I also knew I wouldnt. People who never doubt themselves scrape my patience away.

"Around the dead city most people generally blame both the old government and the corporations for all the greed and grasping that ruined things. Bad policies all around."

Mister Gault looked at me again like I was a bad thing. Nell sensed some tension and stopped eating an apple she had plucked from the table. She had moved a chair next to mine and sat as closely as possible, though she had relaxed her arm lock. Shavedhead stood next to his master, staring but not looking. I wondered if he believed the same foolishness.

"Thats a rather simplistic view, dont you think? Blame the corporations? The business world wasnt the problem. It was the damn politicians and government regulations. It was the greed and blind stupidity of those entrusted to guard our freedoms who obstructed the rights as free individuals to pursue our selfinterest."

The little mummyman stared sternly, and I coundnt stifle a laugh. I sipped some of his whiskey to hold back any more laughter. He had ordered the bottle to be brought out, and it came in its own wooden box. The whiskey might have been decades older than most of the little people pulling weeds or raking muck. It had a deep goldenred color, and it was smooth and mellow, almost sweet. I had never tasted anything like it before. I wondered how many bottles he brought out with him and what I could trade for a couple. There were probably dozens of miscreants lurking around the dead city who would slaughter dozens of innocents for a bottle.

I was trying to be polite and ignore the constant grinding between real and unreal. But Mister Gault wasnt through with me.

"Mans moral purpose is selfinterest, selfishness is a virtue."

He pointed a finger at me, and I gulped his whiskey. I thought maybe it was a language thing again with the meaning of words getting wrenched around. I waited a moment to enjoy the sweet whiskey burn.

"Me and Joe once came across a man who was known to have killed over a hundred men. Once he shredded a man with a dozen shots for sneezing. He didnt have much moral purpose. He was a prickly selfish sort and would have gone on killing if he had not miscalculated his capacity to take on both me and Joe and a handful of the Princes Rangers.

"You fail to understand. This man you refer to was irrational and criminal. Youre being simplistic again."

I didnt move to pour any more of the mummymans whiskey but held the little glass fondly. I thought my pursuit of selfinterest was probably a lot more cruder than Mister Gaults and his forty heroes.

"All of us that made it through the Fires are simple people. We blunder around worrying about where to sleep and what to eat, picking up leftovers, and hoping we dont get cut apart by some pack of crazy wackers. Simple solutions work best for us."

He was irritated with me, and paused to gulp some more water. I should have moved on to our real business, but I couldnt stop picking at him.

"Mister Gault, you and your bestofeverything people shouldve stayed where you were. It was when things went all crazy, when the firestorms started blazing out of control, that all your superior talents and considerable assets were needed the most, but you were gone. You had been planning to leave the whole time the world was tearing itself apart. After everything got scorched and stripped you still mightve helped, but yall wanted to come out here to your playland and be a shining light for nobody. How long did it take to build your golf course and waterfall? How long did it take to build that cute stepover stream out there? Did the worlds greatest architect design that too?"

Mister Gault stared at me and then motioned for Shavehead to lean down. He whispered something to him. I thought maybe I had scratched too deeply.

"But then maybe I am being simplistic again. You know howsimpleminded us ignorant savages are."

Shavedhead moved off towards the front of the house. Neither he nor the mummyman were inclined to mention what or who he was fetching.

"We came out here to wait out the Breakdown and then return. We thought a year or two at the most, and people would start to use their reason again. None of us expected what happened. We misjudged . . ."

The mummyman let his words trail off. There was probably no way to calculate the magnitude of what he and his friends had misjudged.

I waited a moment and then jumped head first into our business.

"Tell me, Mister Gault, what is it you want? Why did you bring me out here?"

Mister Gault smiled and clasped both hands together.

"I want to live forever."

Up to this point, he hadnt seemed like a sputtering foamymouthed lunatic, not like the screamers and mudbrains that bump around at night, but I started to wonder.

"Good luck with that."

He stared back at me and seemed to be enjoying himself, contemplating his forever. Since the Fires got lit up, me and Joe had encountered scores of crazies, from slobbering fools to bloodcrazed brutes, and some were so absurdly delusional and crackbrained that they lived in farcical worlds of their own creation, playing sorcery and swords, or spaceships and star travel, but I wondered whether any of them ever thought they could cheat death.

"I am sure you are aware, Mister Gault, that you want the one thing that you cant have."

He broke into a laugh.

"Dont be so sure, dont be so sure. I am a man of defiant will and sufficient resources."

We stared at each other, him enjoying his defiant will and sufficient resources, and me thinking it likely Shavedhead and the rest of household had to keep him from howling at the moon.

"In terms of our potential, we are still mewling babies. There is an entire universe of possibilities before us. You asked who lives in my residence. You should also have asked who lives in the residence next door, merely a few hundred yards away."

He paused, waiting for me to ask, but I didnt.

"I have three of the worlds most brilliant, most accomplished medical scientists over there, with full laboratories and staffs. Their work is miraculous, simply miraculous. In a few weeks, a month or two, I will transition, but I will not disappear. Not hardly."

He laughed again, and I wondered why no one had knocked him on the head and put him out of his misery.

Nell stood up and moved between the mad mummyman and me. She had finished her apple and was carefully holding the core. She had a special talent for choosing her moments.

"Can we go find Jemmy and Ben now? Is Joe going to meet us back at the farm or come to this place?"

I wished I could have answered her about Joe, but I didnt know.

Then I looked out and did know, and the sudden knowing made me smile like a raving lunatic. Joe was sprawled out in the arbor, his Captain Sadler killer rifle leaning next to him, and a cutter in his lap. Nell turned to look, and seeing Joe she flew out of the room. I wasnt sure if she found a door or jumped a window, but in a few moments she was latched onto Joe and dragging him toward us.

Shavedhead burst into the room holding a machine pistol, followed by a second man similarly armed, but Mister Gault the mad mummyman waved them back.

JoeNell came in attached, and the Joe part looked around, smiling.

"Nice room. I bet you love this place, being such a bookman."

He spoke to me but smiled at the mad mummyman, Shavedhead, and the third man.

"We are all friends here, aint we, soldiers of the righteous?"

He asked, but didnt wait for a reply.

"You read any of these books yet?"

I shook out a no.

"Havent had time. Mister Gault here was telling me hes not going to die. Hes got a whole house next door full of geniuses that are going to help him transition into a state of forever. Evidently theres going to be a whole lot more of him once hes transitioned. I am fascinated. He hasnt told me if his associate, Mister Gunther, is going to accompany him or not. But they go every place together. I havent met the third man yet."

Shavehead looked at me, and it wasnt a mild look. The third man smiled. He was on the small side but had a bellybulge and was thickbrowed with dark eyes. He also had his hair slicked back with something greasy and shiny.

"I presume you are the shooter who disposed of Brigadier Fisher. Welcome to my residence. I was not displeased to see Brigadier Fisher withdrawn from active service."

Mister Gault swept one hand across the room, as if he was offering something. Joe held out the killer rifle and offered it to him.

"I helped him transition, is all. Ill trade you this rifle for a couple of those apples."

Shavedhead stepped between them. He held the machine pistol down at his side, while Joe had one hand on the cutter strapped across his chest.

"Thats alright, Mister Gunther. I think its a fair trade. He can have as many apples as he wants, and I presume he has run out of ammunition for the rifle."

I stepped up to them and tried to pull Nell away, but she was sticking with Joe. I turned toward the mad mummyman.

"Mister Gault, this is Joe Cruz. Hes a famous man, at least by dead city standards. Up around the north hills and out in the high country, people tell stories about him."

Joe leaned the rifle up against one of the fat chairs and with Nell matching his strides went over to the bowl of apples. Shavedhead watched but didnt move.

"Youre a powerful man, Mister Gault. I could see that the way all the grabies scattered as we drove out here. But out beyond the pass in the cinders and ash heaps you left behind Joe Cruz is known to be a powerful man.

Chapter 39

Joe bit into his third apple, nearly taking half in one bite. The mummyman watched him, as if fascinated.

"Was Mister Gault right about the ammunition?" I asked.

Joe nodded and finished his apple. Nell had pulled a footrest over to him.

"He was. I used up all I had back at the farm and then along the creek road trying to keep those crazy grabies away. Some of those boys aint learned the lesson of caution."

Joe paused, wiping his mouth on his sleeve.

"Theres an awful lot of mistering that goes on here, aint there?"

"We are careful to abide by courteous usage. Mister is a polite form of address. Do you not wish to be addressed as Mister Cruz?" Mister Gault asked and drank from his water glass.

"Joes fine. I aint no mister, and I know he aint no mister either."

Joe pointed at me. I had been trying to look misterly.

"We are savages, burned to beserk in the Fires. Aint that right?"

Joe waited for me to respond. I had been contemplating the

whiskey bottle. I had given up sipping since there was bargaining still to be done, or harder work. But I hoped to borrow the bottle on the way out.

"Thats us, simpleminded brute savages, primitive and unenlightened."

"Yet quite lethal," the mad mummyman offered with a thin smile.

I would have preferred that he had posed his statement as a question. Joe dropped his apple core back into the bowl and stretched. He went over to a side table and peered closely at a sculpture of a horse and rider. The horse was straining while the man was twisted around firing a pistol behind him.

"Whats chasing him?"

The mad mummyman continued to smile. Joe continued to stare at the statue. Then he turned.

"I guess somebodys always chasing somebody. Me and that fool thats been gulping your whiskey have been chased all over everywhere. But I aint never hurt anyone that wasnt trying to hurt us or hurt someone else. Aint never. A more lethal man than me couldve knocked down a bunch of those crazy grabies, but I only encouraged them to hunker down behind some rocks and reconsider their direction. I aint no murderous wacker. Aint that right, Mister Brute Savage?"

Joe didnt wait for me to answer. He stood up and moved toward the door back to the front of the house. Nell latched on to his arm again, and he swung her along. Both Shavedhead and Slickedhair moved to intercept them.

"Come on, us brute savages got work to do?"

"Are we going to get Jemmy and Ben now?" Nell stopped Joe midstep.

"Them and a couple others."

"A couple others?" I got up to go with them.

"While you were out here apple eating and whiskey drinking, them NRA boys and a packful of grabies brought in a couple more captives in need of delivering. I came out here to get you. It aint right for you to leave me to do all the delivering."

With a little help from Shavedhead, Mister Gault stood up to follow us out.

"And who is it you wish to deliver from captivity, Mister Cruz?"

"A couple old friends. We are only going to take those we came for and those we know. Sure is a pleasure to find Nell here. We wont have to go hunting after her."

I had a bad feeling.

"What old friends?"

Joe looked back at me and smiled.

"That damn Sid and the Deadman followed us down here and got taken by a couple grizzly NRA boys leading a pack of babygrabies. Must have followed us out on the Marena road. Now we got to go get them. Too bad I run out of ammunition for that fancy rifle. I could sit off a ways and keep them all squatting while you rushed in to grab our friends."

Joe stopped and turned back to Mister Gault.

"You got any fancy rifle ammunition around here. Ill trade you a couple apples for some."

Mister Gault introduced the third man as Stanley Stricter, who he had brought out to help us locate the lost boys. A smiley man, he bobbed around like he was happy to help to us.

"He worked with Mary at the farm. Hes Director of Resources. He oversees all of the placements and work assignments"

Stanley Slickedhair smiled and moved toward me as if he wanted to take my hand, but Nell had grabbed a hold of both me and Joe, and I wasnt inclined to break her grip.

"Thats all right, Mister Stanley Stricter. Just tell us where those boys are, and we will make our own way."

He stopped and pulled out a piece of paper, which he carefully unfolded. Still smiling, he looked back at us.

"This is a list of all of the new orphans who recently joined

New Harmony, their assignments, and their quarters. We can . . ."

"Jemmy and Ben werent no orphans." Nell cut him off with her challenge. She had a fair supply of her own defiant will. Slickedhair looked at her and chuckled.

"Well, arent you a bright pretty girl. Wouldnt you rather come with me to look for your friends while these two take care of their business? I can show you around the farm." Slickedhair held out his hand, but Nell wasnt having any of it.

"Theyre my cousins, and I dont want to see any more of your damn farm."

Chapter 40

I wasnt happy with the arrangements, and I had voiced my complaints every time Mister Stanley Slickedhair swerved or went over a bump. For some reason Joe had made him drive, though he knew that it was my turn. The whole time Slickedhair was swerving and bumping he had babbled about all the good work they were doing saving poor orphans and about the good life they had on the farm, which made me all the grumpier sitting in back with Nell while Joe got to frontride. By the time he hauled us in front of a long gray box of a building, I wanted to shoot him.

"This is where all of the new boys are quartered."

He turned back around to smile at me and Nell. Joe had popped out as soon as we had stopped and had disappeared around another long box across the way. He had taken Slickedhairs machine pistol, though I would have preferred he had taken Slickedhair and left me the pistol.

Two older grabies came out of the box and moved toward us, both pointing cutters in our direction, but Slickedhair shook himself out of our little car and moved to intercept them. He draped an arm over the shoulder of one and huddled with them. There were a few raggy little people milling about, and a couple more grabies had stepped out to eye us. The afternoon shadows were starting to lengthen, and I wondered how long before all of the little farmers could quit their hacking and herding.

"Its all set. This girl and I will go in and look for your boys, but youll have to stay here."

I looked at him like he had muttered something unintelligible, which actually he had. I started to raise a cutter in his direction.

"You want to do what? Are you crazy? No, wait, youre all crazy around here. I aint letting you take off with Nell."

"Shes the only one who can identify the boys. All of the orphans are given new names when they arrive, so she will have to look for her cousins. But the grays wont let you follow us into the quarters. Its against farm policy to let nonresidents into the residences. Our children need to feel safe in their new homes. She will be only be gone a few minutes." He paused and then reached in to pat Nell on one of her bony knees. "Come on little lady, lets go find your boys."

Nell screamed like she was snakebit. "Dont touch me, Ill scratch your eyes out if you lay one more finger on me."

I hopped around the little car in a flash and grabbed Slickedhair by an arm, jostling him away.

"Now I am doubly sure youre crazy." I swung my cutter up to poke him in the head a time or two, but the two grabies moved toward us, so I swung Slickedhair around as a shield and pointed at them.

"Come on then, you cacklebrained clownbabies."

It was a foolish challenge, especially with Nell behind me, but I was angry, and sometimes I do foolish things when I get angry. I was trying to undo my foolishness when Nell grabbed a hold of my belt and started tugging at me.

"Let em go. Lets go find Jemmy and Ben and then go get Sid."

I had stayed in worse places, but Laurel House, as the oblong box was called, was no palace, just a big wood and steel human container with long open rooms lined with cots and with little personal space. There were young boys of various sizes and ages, most in little clumps but some off by themselves, staring off someplace at something only they could see. Most were raggy and grubby, except for the little globs of grabies we encountered on each of three floors. As we moved through hunting after the lost boys, bits and pieces of the raggy clumps broke off and began to follow us at a distance. It was a sad place and smelled faintly of rot and chemicals. We went through, Slickedhair leading and trailed by the first two grabies. Nell and I were objects of suspicion, though I was the biggest object.

I didnt like being followed around by two grabies armed with automatic weapons, but that was only one part of what I didnt like. It had been too easy.

Mister Gault had made few demands for plucking me from my executioners, connecting me with Nell, and then letting us go, even providing us with Slickedhair and one of his little runaround cars. We were to negotiate with the Prince to guarantee that the mad mummyman would be left alone when the hordes of dead city savages descended on the happy valley. Evidently part of his transitioning required that parts of him remain frozen for a couple centuries. I didnt bother to tell him that chances were slim the Prince and his Rangers would descend on the happy valley anytime soon.

I dont think it would have mattered to Mister Gault anyway. He was playing both sides, both us savages and the NRAers, doubling his bet, making sure that he came out on the winning side, and it probably didnt matter much to him who came out ahead so long as he was left alone to transition. He claimed he wanted to curb the NRAers, complaining that those he had hired as gatekeepers were now keeping him, but he would have gladhanded and backslapped the whole lot of them as he complained about all of us savages. Playing both sides is an art developed over considerable time.

But as soon as I walked out and got clubbed down from behind, and then looked up to see that snarly beaverfaced Unger and Captain babybombed blowntobits Leo Sadler smiling down at me, I thought maybe Mister Gault had wasted his time double betting on us savages.

Nell pulled at me to help me up, but the behindtheback clubber, one of our graby escorts, grabbed at her, trying to drag her away. I felt shaky, but I rolled up and tackled the little thug, and had the second of our escorts not cracked me again I would have tackled and mashed every single one of them.

A handful of grabies grabbed at me, and I tried to slap them away, but as soon as I tossed one off a couple more heaved onto the pile. I wanted to get to Slickedhair, who had wrapped an arm around Nell and was trying to drag her away. In my rage and desperation I believed I could shake off the grabies and tear Slickedhairs arm off before anyone else could react. But I misjudged.

Sadler and two more of his blacksuited buddies knocked me flat on the ground, and their combined weight and malice made further struggle useless. I watched helplessly as Nell struggled with Slickedhair, trying to bite, scratch, and kick her way free. She finally chomped down on a good chunk of forearm, and Slickedhair squealed, letting go of his bear hug, but before Nell could dart away he smacked her in the face. She went down, and he stepped over her, shrieking at her.

"Ill teach you, Ill teach you how to behave."

I knew then I would kill him when I got free, and I had not the slightest doubt I would get free.

Chapter 41

The little beaverman got in my face as soon as Sadler and his henchmen hauled me up. He was still smiling, and I added him to my retribution list.

"Your troublemaking is over. Youre nothing but a terrorist."

I ignored his stupid talk and looked around. Nell was up, holding a hand over one side of her face. But Slickedhair had been moved out of the way by a couple more NRAers and Ungers blond grayboys, who were guarding Nell in a tight circle.

Sadler stepped in front, and he was smiling too.

"Youre dead, you got blown up with one of your own baby-bombers."

"Your partner cut me loose. Taking pity on an enemy is a weakness. I am not weak like that."

I looked at him and added him to my list

"Ill keep that in mind."

Unger pushed himself back in front of me.

"You should have respected my authority. It is terrorists like you that we need to remove from the world in order to restore order."

I looked at the little beaverfaced fool, knowing he wouldnt hear anything I uttered. But I uttered anyway.

"Respect is earned. You dont get it slapping on a uniform or greasing yourself a title. You aint earned a damn thing prancing around playacting at something youre not. You aint got any authority over me. You aint got any more authority than . . ."

I looked around searching for the smallest and weakest raggy person, intending to point, but then I noticed that there were a whole lot more than one around us. We were surrounded by a crowd of little NewHarmony farmers, maybe near a hundred or more. They had spilled out of their containers, or left their chores, and were pressing around us. Some laughed, whispered, and gestured, but most just crowded around staring.

". . . than any of these kids you use out here for slave labor."

"Youre incapable of understanding. Order requires discipline. We are building, we are recovering, and you are exactly the kind of agitation and disorder we need to eliminate. These children need order and discipline. We are giving them a future."

I hoped Joe was near by. And I was achy and bloody enough to hope that he would knock down the whole pack of fools poking at me.

"Yall are screamranting crazy, you, Sadler here, those toads back my trial, Mister Gault and Shavedhead, and every damn graby that got sorted by beating on someone smaller and weaker, the whole lot of them and you, yall are bleating, babbling lunatics. The only sane people me and Joe have met in this happy valley were a couple of raggy shepherd boys out in the hills. We share a vocabulary, but yall jabber and rave in a language that makes no sense. Yall aint building a damn thing. Look around at these children. This place is coming apart faster than you can blink. Cant you see that your damn distorted little world is crumbling around you. You aint got any future to give."

Sadler pulled his cutter within inches of my head, close enough so that I could admire a small ugly scratch near the muzzle.

"I can take away your future."

The question of my future was interrupted when suddenly a small boy squirmed through the crowd and ran toward us.

"Nell, Nelly, here I am."

The small boy pushed through a forest of graby legs and wrapped himself around Nell. His eyes were wide and chest heaving. Holding on to her, he turned sideways, as if ready to fight anyone who tried to drag him away. Laughing, Nell hugged him.

"Oh Jemmy, I am so glad to see you. Is Ben with you?"

"They keep us separated. They gave us new names, but I hate mine. Are you gonna take us home? They make Ben work in the stinky dairy barn."

"Enough of this, get that boy away."

Unger screamed at the graby circle, and both his blond boys broke toward Jemmy, who started screaming back at them.

"Leave me alone, leave me alone, this is my cousin. Shes going to take me home."

I tried to break the grip of blacksuits and go to Nell and the boy. At that moment I felt nothing but blindhot rage and believed I could break loose of a dozen blacksuits, but before Sadler and his NRAers could correct my miscalculation a loud mechanical bell started clanging, and moments later a siren started blaring. The racket was loud enough to crack the ground open.

Our crowd of little people broke apart, some running in different directions, some yelling, "Fire, Fire." Unger pulled out a little pocket phone and started jabbing numbers. Sadler ungripped me and turned away in the direction of the big house. My rage suddenly drained away and I felt happy. I had a good guess as to the firestarter. Joe was partial to conflagrations, but then there was the rathouse fire. Either was fine with me. But I didnt have to wait long to find out.

Unger shrieked into his little phone when the reappearing Marena suddenly reappeared, shoving her way through a crowd of little people and raising her shotgun. Sadler turned toward her and received a full blast in his chest. My NRAers let go of me and moved toward her, but before any one of them could raise a cutter she fired twice more, dropping one of them while the second cringing fool jumped behind me to hide and fired a wild burst. I dropped and rolled on top of the one she dropped and came away bloodsmeary but holding a cutter he no longer had a use for.

Without pausing Marena dropped the cringer behind me and moved toward Unger, who had taken refuge behind his blond boys. She took one step when one of the blond assassins fired. Marena stumbled but fired again. Knowing there were still lots of little people around, I pulled the cutter bolt and fired low, knocking Unger and his escorts down, shattering knees and femurs.

Marena stepped next to me and leaned into me. Her breathing was gaspy and uneven. She was raising her shotgun toward the remaining grabies when that sleazy scumsucker Slickedhair came up behind her and fired a little pocket pistol into her back. She was slumping down as I turned and looked into Slickedhairs eyes. He was smiling as I fired, but the smile faded as he crumbled with a bloody line stitched across his belly and a look of disbelief on his face.

I whirled around and the remaining grabies scattered, searching for a better future. I turned back to Unger and his blond boys, but they were done with hostilities. Holding the collapsed and bloody Marena with one arm and my new cutter in the other, I kicked away all weapons near the three.

One of the boys was spurting blood, and I knew I that he would bleed out in minutes. Unger had a shattered knee on one leg and a calf wound on the other, while the second blond boy had a shattered pelvis and a nonlethal thigh wound. Marena and the first boy needed immediate help.

"I need some help here. I need help."

Nell and Jemmy came over, and then a third, an older cutterless graby.

I looked at him. He had been one of my knockdown escorts. I pointed to the first blond boy, telling him to keep pressure on the wound.

"Help that boy live."

While the older graby and I were trying to load the blond bleeder and Marena into our little car all the screeching of bells and sirens suddenly stopped, and for a moment I thought the silence odd and distrusted my senses. Off a ways I heard a couple short bursts of cutter fire and wondered if Joe was delivering or being delivered. There was no way to tell, and as long as someone wasnt shooting at me I had more pressing matters.

"What about me?" Unger asked. He was bloodsmeary and whiny, and he had rolled up to a sitting position and was holding his shattered knee. "You cant just leave me here. Help me."

My new graby friend climbed into the back with the bleeder to keep pressure on the wound. I had Marena strapped into the front. She had pitched over and I had one arm around her. She had started coughing up blood, and I wasnt sure I could get her help before she was beyond help. I wasnt even sure I could drive the little car. I ignored Unger and turned to Nell. She had picked up a cutter and had it poking out in front of her while holding on to Jemmy. She had already announced that she was setting off to search for Ben in the stinky dairy barn.

"You dont need that."

I put out a free hand and tried to grab the cutter barrel, but Nell stepped back. With the bleeder and Marena I didnt have time to climb out and chase her down.

"Listen, Nell, when you carry a gun, you can be sure that

somebody with another gun is going to come after you. Theres enough commotion around here for you to slip over and get Jemmys brother without carrying that cutter. Maybe you wont ever have to carry one. What do think?"

Nell looked at me fiercely, but Jemmy was tugging at her and she and her cutter turned away. I was about to shift the go lever and press the go pedal when Unger hitched himself up enough to grab a hold of the back.

"Damn you Unger, you mudbrained wormeating sleaze-bucket. You are the least hurt of anyone. You aint going to walk a straight line ever again, but you aint going to die. Now get off my car."

I considered poking a cutter at him, or backing over him, but thought the other blond assassin might get crunched. I hesitated a few seconds that seemed like forever and then leaned Marena over, got out, and helped both Unger and the shattered pelvis boy onto the back of the little car. I wasnt sure where I was going, and I wasnt sure I could get there, but I pointed the little car in what I hoped was the right direction and set off overloaded with bleeders.

Chapter 42

Mister MadMummyman Gault was screaming at me. I had driven past his useless playhouse and had hauled up in front of the closest house next to him. Except for the front steps I would have driven into the house. Gault had showed up within a minute.

"You cant bring them here. Take them back to the farms infirmary. This isnt a hospital."

"Get out of my way, crazy man. These people need help, and you got three geniuses inside. I am sure they can figure out how to keep these people alive. Marena here aint going to make it another hour without some serious medical help."

I had gotten out and was halfcarrying halfdragging Marena towards the front door. Our ruckus had attracted a knot of people around the front, and I was grateful that a couple labcoats had started down the steps towards us. There was a largeheaded older man standing in back smiling, seeming to enjoy the spectacle of a little car filled with bleeders appearing at his front door.

"This is the woman with the shotgun, the one out on the road? Let her die. She killed my son. Let her die."

A thought suddenly clicked into place in the back of my brain. When the labcoats got to me and shouldered up Marena, I pointed a cutter at Mister Morris Howard Gault.

"Step away or you die. She was protecting me, and now I am protecting her. Your son lived a bad life. He was a slaver and childsnatcher and a lot worse. You believe in karma?"

Shavedhead hurried up and began pointing his machine pistol at me.

"You want to live forever? You aint going to live another minute unless you tell Gunther to step down and back away."

The crazy mummyman looked at me in silent rage, but the issue was decided for us. A handful more of labcoated immortality workers broke off from the front steps and moved between us, taking up Unger and his two bleeding blond boys. I couldnt tell, but I thought the first boy was already gone. His skin looked fishbelly ashy, and he had lost consciousness soon after we began our expedition. The older graby boy was still clutching at him, pressing on him to keep life from seeping out. I was grateful for the boys help, and forgave him for headknocking me from behind.

Mister Crazy Mummyman Morris did not invite me back to his residence for apples and whiskey, but that was okay with me. I sat in the fancy front hall of the immortality house waiting on the outcomes of my bleeders when the largeheaded older man came out of a side door. He was still smiling.

"Are you one of the three geniuses who are going to keep that crazy man alive forever? Have you considered that crazy people maybe aint the best candidates for immortality?"

He shook his head and handed me a little pocket phone.

"Science makes use of whatever resources are available. Crazy men or rhesus monkeys are all the same. But here, you have a phone call."

After dropping the phone into my hand, he nodded for no apparent reason, and went back to his science.

Not being reconciled to talking to someone I cannot see, I held the phone a moment, but before I could decide what kind of phonetalker I would become, a voice began jabbering in a brusque ordermearound voice.

"We have your friends surrounded, and they cannot escape. We will kill them unless you tell them to surrender."

I wasnt sure of the most efficient phoneholding customs, so I took a moment to bring it up. It was a fancy little thing, and lit up like a tiny bonfire.

"Whos talking to me?"

"This is Major Werth."

"Judge number two, Hey there, Major Werth. How you? Hows your recovery business? Which friends are you talking about? You got any more Majors there with you. I am so sorry about the Brigadier, but it was an awful ugly moment of either him or me, and Joe did the best he could. Mister Morris Howard Gault said he was okay with the outcome. You okay with it? Youre not sore, are you? You still there, Major Werth? Maybe you can be the new Brigadier."

"Your impertinence will result in the deaths of your friends. Is that what you want?"

I doubted he really cared what I wanted, but I tried to be polite.

"Dont mean to be impertinent. Is that like being disrespectful? Me and your friend Unger were just talking about that. Hes here at the immortality house getting patched. He stumbled and fell. What is it you want me to do?"

"Your friends have taken hostages. I want them to release their hostages and surrender."

I thought it a reasonable request, except for the first and last parts.

"Are they doing any harm? Maybe you can just ignore them

and theyll get tired and move on. Its about time me and Joe headed back with Nell and the lost boys. We should probably take Sid too, but you can keep the Deadman if you want him."

Liking neither my suggestion or my impertinence, Major Werth screamed into the phone.

"Your friend has shot four soldiers."

"Were they shooting at him?"

The toad did not respond, which I took for a yes.

"Were they shot and killed or shot and wounded? I will bet you a bottle of Morris Howard Gaults woodenboxed whiskey that Joe winged them. He can shave the wings off a fly at three hundred yards."

Major Werthless continued to scream.

"I will have them all killed. I will destroy the entire building. We have ordnance here. I can have them fired upon and destroyed. I will sacrifice all the hostages if I have to."

I double added Major Werthless to my list.

"Aint much of a sacrifice on your part, is it?"

"Hey Joe, how you doing?"

Joe was less reconciled to phonetalking than me, but he responded quickly.

"Hey you old fool, how you? We are having a grand time here in the big house, the part that didnt get torched. Where you at? Get yourself over here and we can have some fun. These grabies are ok once you get to know them."

"Theres a toad outside named Major Werth that says he has you surrounded. He says that you need to give up the hostages and surrender."

"We got them NRAers right where we want them."

"He says he has artillery aimed at you and that he will destroy everyone there, if he has to."

"We got them at our mercy. I suppose you being so softhearted you want us to be lenient. Some of those NRAers are a fractious lot. They are as cranky as they are dumb. But the grabies are generally fine once you get them detached from their keepers. Why dont you tell this Major to surrender. Its time all these brassy fools got flushed out of here."

"Maybe so, but how are you going to deal with those fractious boys outside? They got spitter guns, canons, explosives. They dont need to be deadeyed killshots with that stuff."

It was a good question, and Joe took a moment to answer.

"I dont think all of them are that crazy. They aint going to destroy their NewHarmony just to save it from us savages. Besides, I collected a respectable number of guests, including a Major of my own. You know him? Maybe my Major can talk to your Major and talk some sense into him."

"All of these Captains and Majors are a destructive crew. Yours and mine teamed up with the Brigadier to have me shot. For a happy valley, this place is dangerous. And youre the fool who cut loose Captain Leo Sadler."

I told Joe about the Laurel House shootings. He cursed under his breath.

"Marena going to live?"

"Dont know. Theres some fatheaded genius around here experimenting on crazy men and monkeys. I will corner him and find out. If they can keep a mad mummyman alive, they ought to be able to handle Marena."

I waited a moment. The front area was silent except for a big standup clock ticking off the seconds. I have always admired intricacy of old clocks, but this one I wanted to kick apart.

"Joe, I dont want to leave her here if she makes it. We need to collect Nell and the boys and get out of this happy valley. You get to Sid and the Deadman?"

"It was messy, but I got them both here. The Deadmans crabby and complaining, but I got Sid propped up in a chair keeping an eye on my fractious few. He has got a couple cutters and clips and is ready to shoot someone. You got Nell and the boys?"

"Nell got a hold of Jemmy, and they went to find Ben in some smelly dairy barn. I bet theyre hiding out someplace. We need an escape plan. You got one?"

"Of course I do. You rush them from the front, and Ill charge them from behind."

Chapter 43

"Mister Gault instructed me to kill you to avenge his son, you, your partner, and that woman with a shotgun, all of you for his son."

Since Shavedhead was driving a big shiny likenew red pickup, and not holding any type of weapon, I tried to be polite.

"Is that so?"

Being polite required some attention. Shavedhead had appeared at the immortality house just as I had decided to give up listening to the old clock and head back to NewHarmony. I was agreeable when he offered a ride but clutched a cutter in case things suddenly became less agreeable. I had twice politely offered to drive, and had explained that I was a proficient driver, having recently piloted a carload of bleeders, but Shavedhead ignored my offers and mostly ignored me. Revealing his vengeful instructions had been about the only thing he said since leaving the residences.

Taking up both ends of the conversation, I prattled on about my proficiencies and his vehicle, while trying to pry him open about his intentions and as well his gas supply. He had a huge gas drum sloshing around in back, and I thought it likely he was preparing for a long journey.

"I had no love for his son, but Mister Gault loved him, though they didnt get along. Morrison ran off years ago. He wanted to be in the dark world. A couple times Mister Gault sent me out looking for him."

"But you didnt find him?"

Shavedhead pulled behind a long barnlike structure and shut off his engine. He looked over at me without much expression.

"I found him. He wasnt hard to find. I even dragged him back here once. But he wouldnt stay. He hated New Harmony, hated everything his father and the others had done down here. He set himself up like he some kind of warlord up in the Pueblos, and then eventually the Command decided he was useful. But he hated his father and he hated his name too. You know what Morrisons real name was?"

Shavedhead was climbing out of his truck, and I supposed I was to follow.

"I aint real good with names."

"Same as his father only with a different number. His father was the fourth, and he was the fifth. His father expected a lot from him."

I followed Shavedhead around to the front. He was suited up in black, holding a cutter, and packed with spare clips.

"Morrison was a robber, a slaver, a child stealer, and a killer, but that aint what the fourth wanted of the fifth, was it?"

Shavedhead poked his head around the barn entrance. He waved at me to quiet down. But I didnt.

"I didnt shoot him. I confess I am guilty . . ." I paused, word-searching, ". . . of impertinence, but not Morrisons death."

Shavedhead waved at me again to hush up, but I aint prone to hushing up. He zipped around the big doors and disappeared, leaving me to disappear or follow. I went in after him, and suddenly found myself in an open cavernous garage filled with military vehicles, including a couple big greenblack trucks, a one big ugly greenblack thing on eight chunky tires with a cannon on top, and three giant mechanical frogs like the one that had collected me. I pointed to one of the frogs.

"I want to drive one of those things."

"You think you can drive this?"

Shavedhead was pointing to an open fourwheeled vehicle topped with a spitter gun. It was a chunky looking heavy thing squared in the front and the back.

"You said you wanted to get your friends out. This weapon will punch a hole in a reinforced concrete wall in seconds."

I wasnt sure of his intentions, either short term or long term, or if he was seriously inquiring about my driving proficiency. The garage was mostly cleared out. There had been a couple older grabies and a few greasebabies, but they mostly skated except for the greasebabies, who sat on a box watching us. It took me a moment to realize that one of the greaseboys was a girl. I pointed to one of the giant mechanical frogs.

"How about that one? Its got a spitter gun on top too. I bet I could steer it along and make it go."

Shavedhead turned to consider and shrugged.

"Too big, too slow, and its probably out of gas. The fools used up a lot chasing you down."

But he went over to the frog and climbed in the back. Me and the greasekids waited. Suddenly the frog exploded, emitting a sizable black cloud of exhaust. Its engine clattered and clunked, and the whole floor seemed to shake. Still with little expression, Shavedhead emerged from the rear.

"Ill drive. You get up in the turret and see if you can manage that fifty caliber."

I didnt fall in behind him as he turned to climb back into the frog. While I paused, our two watchers came over. They looked me over and then the girl spoke?"

"Whatcha fixin to do?"

"I aint got the slightest idea. Ask him."

I pointed to Shavedhead. He turned back around to look at us.

"Whatcha fixin to do?"

Shavedhead waved the question away, but then paused.

"I am going to help him and his friends escape."

All three of us stared. I finally could not resist asking.

"Why?"

Chapter 44

The frog clattered and clunked along, and I actually could have gotten out and walked faster. When I poked my head out for a look I saw the two greasebabies walking along with us like they were part of the show. A couple other raggy farmers who had joined the procession, and the whole lot of them probably could have run circles around the frog as it clanked along.

I sat in the cramped turret considering my options while Shavedhead drove the frog underneath me. His whys had been generally acceptable, but not believable. I wasnt sure what he wanted or intended. The mad mummyman had started his transition, and according to Shavedhead his duties were discharged as soon as the three geniuses took over. Evidently all of the sputtering, fretting, and conspiring had hurried him along to his long desired conversion.

I was sorry I hadnt borrowed his woodenboxed whiskey and hoped me and Joe could take a run out to his place before we finally departed. Back around Aurora a couple bottles would have gained us considerable favor with the Prince and all his prancing, mewling attendants.

I suspected that Shavedhead had provisioned himself with a number of things his former employer wouldnt be needing in the near future. His pretty red truck was loaded with a duffles and crates, and I assumed he had his own supply of whiskey and gold stashed away. He wasnt leaving empyhanded, but I suspected that, despite his bluff and guns, hed get emptied soon enough. His pretty red truck was a sirens call for every wacker within a hundred miles. But maybe he knew that.

Like Mother Mary, Shavedhead had it in his head that the happy valley was about to be overrun by savages like me and Joe, and he had decided to head out before things got hot. He had been over the pass enough times to know a little about what was out there and thought he would make his way to NewPueblo. I wondered if he planned to take up where Morrison had left off. He wasnt an expressive gossipy man, but he was capable. Since there wasnt a ready supply of crazy old mummymen in need of personal bodyguards, I assumed hed find work that suited him. Either that or he would get knocked down by the first pack of wackers that crossed his path.

We rumbled up beside a large square building near the side of the big house. There was smoke and cinder sparking in the air, and I saw where one lower corner of the house was still smoldering. It had been a decent fire. Part of one wall was blackened and crumbly, and the ground was littered with bricks and debris. Shavedhead shut down the frog and poked his head around toward me.

"Your friends are on the second floor of the main building. Youre going to have to cut your way through a line of NRA soldiers and grays to get to your friends."

I didnt want to hear what I was hearing. I looked around and noticed that our procession had grown to more than a dozen little people, including a few grabies who had joined up to watch the spectacle. They didnt appear attached to any NRAers and werent carrying too many weapons, so I wondered if they had unsorted themselves. I thought more about them than Shavedheads suggestion.

"You hear me?"

I looked down at Shavedhead. He couldnt be serious.

"Heard but not understood. What do you mean, cut my way through? You arent really suggesting that I use this spitter gun to fire on a bunch of children who aint firing on me? I aint feeling inclined to slaughter today."

"Theyll fire on you, alright. Theyve been exchanging fire with your friends already. I am going to swing around from the side and give you a clear line."

Shavedhead ducked back to his controls before I could object, and in seconds the frog belched another black cloud, lurched forward, and began to pick up speed.

I thought he was too hasty for battle and considered my options. I had brought along a cutter, and I could shoot him. I could try to squeeze out of the turret and jump off. Or I could go along for the ride and hope for a better option. But when Shavedhead came out to the front of the building he pushed the frog forward as fast as it could go, and in a few moments it clattered along at a surprising clip. The rattle and racket were thunderous, and just as I decided I had enough Shavedhead pulled up to the side of the big house and began his run.

Packs of little people scattered before us, and I was surprised by the number. There was a large crowd out in front either crouched behind cover or standing off to the side areas. There were handfuls of the older NRAers and grabies, who had taken up positions in a moonsliver along the front, all carrying cutters, but there was a larger number of weaponless grabies and raggy little people milling around the sides and back. I felt like standing up and waving.

"Open fire, use that gun, scatter that line."

Shavedhead was screaming at me, but I wasnt listening. The NRAers and grabies seemed hostile, and though several pointed their weapons at us, none fired at us. From what I could see, most seemed more surprised at the spectacle of a giant mechanical frog hurtling at them than they were scared of me shooting them.

I enjoyed the ride until someone let go a burst of cutter fire that clunked and zinged against the side of the frog, and I ducked just as the end of the burst rose high enough to hit the side of the turret. I peeked back and saw a grayheaded NRA fool aiming at us, with that idiot Major Werth pointing, directing the fools fire.

"Shoot back. Fire on them."

Shavedhead had disrupted the whole battle line in front of the house and was turning to make another run, but I still wasnt heeding his directions.

"No, I dont think I will. That old fool fired by mistake. He didnt mean to. It was that Major Werthless hollering in his ear that made him jump. That Werthless fools already on my list. Ill catch up with him."

With all the clatter and clank the frog was making I couldnt quite make out what Shavedhead cursed at me, something that questioned my ancestry, which didnt bother me much, since I dont take much stock in ancestry, especially my own. Best to let the dead worry about the dead.

But then he slowed the frog and abruptly turned away from the fools crowding around Major Damn Werthless and went toward the big house. He circled back around in front facing the NRAers and grabies and then backed up until the frogbutt scrunched against the long porch.

"Youre on your own."

Shavedhead gave me a final unreadable look, and he then climbed out of his little driving perch and passed below me heading for the rear frogdoor.

I didnt mind him exiting, but there were a couple things I wanted to know.

"Wait a moment, Mister Gunther. Did you really want me to start slaughtering those people?"

He paused and looked back at me.

"You dont know anything about this place. Morrison and the NRA command were destroying everything his father and the old group had tried to create."

"Theres probably a lot about this place I dont want to know, but I was just wondering if you had something personal going on with those fools out in front of us, or you are just partial to bloody spectacles."

Shavedhead thought a moment,

"Yeah, it got real personal. The sons been trying to kill his father, he and those NRA bastards. And twice now theyve come after me."

He turned, but I called again.

"Good luck out on that old highway. Whats going to happen to Gault now that hes transitioning and youre departing?"

He smiled, and it was the first and only time I ever saw him smile.

"As soon as they can, the cockroaches will swarm."

The Deadman wasnt happy with me. I had taken up Gunthers spot at the frogcontrols, and I had even managed to jerk the vehicle forward, but there were too many levers, pulls, switches, and pedals for me to figure out. Yet I persisted.

"I can drive this this thing."

"No, you cant. Quit your lying."

The Deadman shifted himself behind me in the frogbelly. He was limpy and sore. The days between now and Morrisons place had not been easy on him.

"I aint lying. I am preparing to drive. These frogs need careful preparing."

"You aint preparing, and itll take another ten years before you figure out them controls. And while your preparing theres a bunch of people out front with guns wanting to kill us, and theres a hundred more of them than there is of us. That crazyman Joe Cruz of yours sent me down here to get you, but I aint gonna wait around any longer."

He started hobbling toward the back. I thought his assessment and decision were reasonable.

"Up at Morrisons I gave you some silver to take Sid back to the old mans ranch. What are you doing around here?"

He looked back angrily.

"I didnt agree to any of this mess, and I aint givin you your money back. Next time you want Sid to go some place, you take him. He held a gun to my head. I aint had any damn luck since I met up with you."

"Since you tried to wack me."

He looked at me, not so angrily, but not so remorseful either.

"That was different. That was business."

I gave up fiddling with the controls and looked out at the front. That fool Werthless had taken refuge behind a wall of grabies, minicars, and his NRAers. They were quiet enough, but they were trying to strangle us, circling around to cut off any retreat. It looked like some of them wanted a battle. They had brought up that flat car with the spitter gun and a couple small artillery pieces, and now we all were pointing at each other.

"Morrisons dead. Marena shotgunned both him and his Stickman. You never abused that woman, did you? Shes vengeful."

There was a burst of cutter fire splintering the front of the house and breaking glass, and suddenly Joe threw open the back frogdoor and squeezed in. He was smiling.

"Good thing none of them out there are accurate. I dont think theyve had much experience firing on people, especially those firing back."

I was glad to see Joe, even though he swelled up the frogbelly.

"Wheres Sid. He upstairs ready to gun down the hostages?"

"No, hes hopping his way down the steps. He didnt want me to carry him."

"You let the hostages go? If Major Werth knew that he would be sending in a crack team of NRA fighters to finish us off, or explode us with cannon and babybombers."

"Hostages? We aint got hostages, more like friendly spectators. A couple slid out when we got chased in, but most were happy enough to stick around and watch. Even some of the older grabies. Theyre still peeping out the front windows except for a handful trailing Sid down the stairs. They want to go where we go."

"Theyre going to get cut apart if those big guns out front open up."

"I warned them to keep way back, but I aint a commanding presence as yourself. You go tell them, and Ill drive this thing."

Joe looked around and eased back on one of the side benches.

"You lose your driver? Youre always losing things. Did you lose Nell too? Am I going to have to drive this clunker around delivering everyone around here?"

I nodded.

"Pretty much. Youre the commanding presence around here. This whole happy valley needs to be delivered. You got a plan."

Joe laughed, and I knew what he was going to say, but he said it anyway.

"Course I do. You rush them in the front, and Ill go at them from behind."

Chapter 45

By the time Sid had shuffled his way down the steps I had caught Joe up on the shootings and transitionings. Even though the spitter gun was a useful deterrent, we had backed our way out of the frog and made our way towards the back of the main hall. For what it was, the plan was to go down the unscorched wing, slip out the back, and hope there werent hostiles around. After that, the plan got sketchy. With Sid hobbling around, there was not much chance of scrambling out before anyone noticed.

"You might end up gimpy and onearmed for the rest of your life, if you dont rot up and die of infection."

I went over to Sid and looked at his shoulder and leg. The bandages were dirty and hadnt been changed in a while.

"You said I was young and strong and would heal."

"I said you would heal if you gave yourself a chance to heal, but you aint done that. I need to get you back to Gaults geniuses. Maybe they can grow you a new arm and leg. The Deadman needs a new leg too. Yall shouldve gone back to the old mans ranch instead of following us down here."

Sid looked away, defiant.

"Shes my cousin, them boys are family. I was sent out to help fetch them."

"You can barely walk or fire a cutter. If you dont get your bandages changed and get your wounds cleaned up, you aint going to be good for anything except wormfood."

Sid was still defiant.

"Yall go on then. Ill keep them from following you."

He had a cutter strapped across his good shoulder, which he carefully pressed into his side while be pulled back the bolt with his unslung arm.

"Help me over to the door, and then you can all leave."

I admired his spirit, but regretted his stupidity.

"No ones going anywhere until we find Nell and the boys, and then we are all going to leave together. That crazy Marena too if she lives."

Finding Nell and the boys was easy, since we didnt have to do any finding. Before we had a chance to slip out the back Nell and the boys marched up to the front, they and a couple dozen other little people who trailed after them. It was quite a sight to see them come storming through the crowd in front. Nell was leading her little troop, gripping Jemmy and Ben with both her hands, not once glancing at the idiot NRAers and grabies pointing their weapons at her. Someone screamed at them a couple times to get back, but Nell and her troop ignored the screamer and kept right on coming.

I tried to caution her that ignoring men with weapons was not a good policy. But she ignored me too.

"This is Ben, my other cousin."

Little Ben broke away from Nell and came right up to me and stuck out his hand.

"Pleased to meet you. Nell says you come to take us home. Can we go now? I dont want to work in the cowbarn anymore."

We shook hands while Nell and Jemmy launched themselves on Sid, and seeing them Ben broke off from me and joined the huggers.

"Yeah, can we go now?" Joe laughed from behind.

I wasnt sure what was so laughable. I was surrounded by host of little farmers and grabies. Just as soon as Nells troop followed her in a couple dozen more pressed in after them to see what was going on, and soon the front hall was crowded with little bodies of various sizes and conditions, some cleaner than the others, but most a bit raggy and worn. I was wondering how to break up the assembly and head out the back when a small girl came up to me.

She wore an old dirtblue work shirt several sizes too large that covered most of her. She looked a bit hesitant but then plunged in with her question.

"Are you going to take us home too?"

As soon as she asked, two more squeezed in behind her. They didnt have to utter a word to ask the same question.

"Yeah, are you going to take us home?"

Joe laughed again, teasing rather than asking, so I ignored him. Still wrapped around each other, Nell and her family clump shuffled over to me. I leaned forward to the workshirted girl in front of me and asked a polite question.

"Do you know where your home is?"

She nodded immediately.

"Where?"

She thought for a moment, and then she pointed out toward the side of the hall. I was turned around and had no idea what direction she was pointing, or if it was a direction rather than a hopeful intention.

"Lets get going. Lets go," Nell urged.

"Dont forget there men outside with guns who aint inclined to let us get going."

But I was wrong about the men outside. A handful of them had followed the little people inside and were pointing cutters at me.

Chapter 46

"Youre ruining everything."

Major Werth screamed at me, but before I had a chance to consider the extent of either ruin or everything, he screamed again.

"Why do you have to drag everything down to your miserable level?"

I took offense at his question. Although he was hiding behind a wall of NRAers, I felt a strong urge to clarify his use of miserable and level. But I eased up, realizing the last thing I needed to comprehend was a crazymans meaning. I looked around and realized that everywhere I looked there were young faces staring back me. In order to step anywhere I would have had to part a sea of little people. There were even faces peering in from the shattered front windows.

I was pretty sure Major Werth wasnt crazy enough to start screaming more shoot thems and kill thems with so many little people around, but then I wasnt completely sure. I tried to step around in front of Nell and the boys, but the little dirtblue workshirt girl grabbed ahold of my leg. I looked over at Werthless. His face was red and puffy, and he looked like he wanted someone to shoot me.

"Nothing ever stays the same. Nature hates the thought of conclusion. You cant hold on too long before something moves you away. Yall are transitioning as much as that mad mummyman Gault. New Harmonys tumbling down."

"We are building a new world."

Werthless was a screamer, and there was probably no way that I could get him to stop screaming, or get him to understand. The reasonable thing to have done wouldve been to smile, wish him luck, and move away. But I aint always reasonable.

"You wretched muckbrained blind old fool, you keep screeching, but your words dont have meaning. Youre not building anything. Youre trying to hold on to something youve already lost, and youre too foolish and deranged to know its gone. There aint no recovering going on here. Youre grabbing at something that got loose years ago."

I thought Major Werthless might explode. He got trembly and tightlipped, and then started flapping at his side for an old army fortyfive. He tugged on the slide to fire, but he was so agitated that I thought it likely he would shoot half a dozen little people before settling his aim on me.

It was a tense moment. A large front hall packed with little people and a crazy shaky lunatic wanting to fire a handgun that he couldnt hold steady and aim. Both Joe and Sid had cutters raised, and I expected one or both to fire.

I shouted to no one and everyone to get down. But then suddenly, unexpectedly, a raggy hand with a sooty brick appeared behind Werthless and cracked him on the back of his head. He dropped like a bag of rocks.

There were three of them standing over that crackbrained fool Werthless, and I had no idea which one dropped the fool. Two raggy farm boys and an older graby stood there, each one a possible headcracker, but behind them a dozen others surged forward, most clutching bricks, broken boards, and metal pipes. It was an odd assortment of weapons and young people. The NewHarmony Farm Rebellion had begun.

But before I could react the fourman NRA wall that Werthless had been hiding behind broke apart, and two of the fools began to point cutters at me and the three brickboys.

And then a second quite unexpected thing occurred. A sea of raggy arms washed over the NRAers, both little and big, girls with the boys, the whole crowd heaving at once, all pressing in, pushing and grabbing. In a moment the soldiers were nearly covered in raggy little people when suddenly one of the fools fired a cutter burst, and the raggy sea pulled back.

I raised my cutter to fire, but Joe was already on top of them, holding his weapon headlevel and steady.

"You want to live?"

Joe asked, but not one of the four responded. They were too busy examining the black hole at the end of Joes cutter barrel.

"You want to live? Then you better drop those guns and raise your hands."

Sid was hobbling over and trying to keep his cutter pointed at the fools, and even the Deadman had a cutter in his hands and was pressing in behind Sid.

There was a pause, and then the first old fool laid his weapon down and raised his hands. Soon he was followed by a second and then a third, leaving only one lone fool holding a cutter. The three closest brickboys moved towards him, but I stepped between them and the fool, hoping he had not shot anyone. But there was no bloody mess of rags and torn flesh on the floor. Just a splintery gash in the floor.

"You can let go of that gun now."

Though I wasnt feeling calm, I spoke in a calm voice. The man looked back at me, and I thought he was going to raise and fire. A lean scraggy older man with dark eyes and a hard look, he stared at me, and then turned to look at Joe, Sid, and the Deadman. He shook his head, and I wasnt sure what he was shaking at.

Some moments can last forever, but this one only lasted a few seconds until he dropped his cutter, and everyone let out a breath and relaxed.

I turned to the nearest brickboy.

"Didnt anyone ever tell you it aint a good idea to bring a rock to a gun fight?"

I was trying to get him to smile, but he was feeling too serious for that.

"Weve never known anything different."

He wasnt explicit, but I understood.

Chapter 47

Theres never a clear line between whats happened and whats happening. Werthless getting headknocked was both beginning and ending, but it took a good while to sort the two out, and we never were sure which was which, but it was clear NewHarmony was unraveling. After Werthless got headknocked there was a continuous line of beginnings and endings, and me and Joe had to make a number of stops and starts to get back to where we started. Our going was slow because a lot of NewHarmony started sticking to us.

Sometimes when things become so snarled and tangled its hard to get out of a place, and maybe near impossible. Getting out of a knotty place can be like slogging your way through a boggy low area. The more you start moving around, the more you get sucked down in the muck and mire, and the more you get clumped up with everything around you. Getting out of the happy valley was like that. We mucked around and everywhere we went stuff started sticking to us.

Part of the load was our own foolish fault. We weighed ourselves down with a sizeable NewHarmony gift collection that included a two cases of woodenboxed whiskey, a few more cases of other exotic drinkables, a bag or two of gold coins we found lying around, a few mementos we found lying around unclaimed, an extra load of automatic weapons and ammunition, and a heap more of NewHarmony than we bargained for.

For reasons I did not know and did not want to guess, Joe hauled away the mummymans statue of the old cowboy racing his horse and firing a pistol over his back at something terrible chasing him. I aint much of a statue man, but this one was nice enough with a lot of intricate detail, even in the fierce eyes of the rider, though everyone knows you aint going to hit squat firing one of those old clunky revolvers while bumping along on the back of a horse racing over uneven ground. Joe said I shouldnt worry about the little statue man hitting anything.

We took a few other things too. We took about every horse and mule we could to help haul away packs of leftovers from those fancy useless residences, but also to pull five flatbed farmwagons, one loaded with food and garden stuff, including a couple crates of melons and apples, two loaded with the breakables and drinkables, and the last two loaded with hurt people.

I dont like setting off so loaded down. The first band of screaming wackers come charging down a slope, and youll lose most of what you got, if not your life. But we didnt have much choice in the loading. A lot of stuff just stuck to us, and the more we started gathering to leave the more stuck we got until it seemed like most of NewHarmony was set on coming with us. Which is practically what happened.

Our first stop was the immortality house, where that big-headed whitecoated smiler met us at the door.

"You know, we are not that kind of medical doctor."

I thought his reference and numbering were slightly dopey, and his tone peculiar. I pushed past him into the front hall and for a moment considered the possibility of borrowing that old standup ticktock clock. Bighead stepped in behind me, hovering, waiting on me to say something.

"What kind of doctor is that?"

He looked at me like I was stupid, which is a look I get often enough from people when I ask dumb questions, and I ask a lot of them.

"Why, practicing medical physicians with experience in emergency surgery."

"Are you a doctor?"

He again gave me another youresostupid look and launched into a discussion of his degrees and specialty, something about genetics and geneticists.

"I dont want to hear it. Theres hundreds of savage cannibals armed with automatic weapons coming out to loot all these fancy houses. Maybe you and all your labrats need to take off your white coats and find some new work. Out over the pass theres more need for doctors who can treat gunshots than those who play with rich deadmen." I tried to be polite, but the fool just gave me one more youresostupid look.

I found the bleeders in a back room with a pretty view of the mummymans useless golf course. Unger and his blond boys were awake and bandaged. They were out of danger, even the neardead boy, but it would take a good while to get over the pain and discomfort.

"You are ruining everything."

Unger was sitting up with one leg raised and immobilized. He had spit out his youword like I was personally responsible, but I didnt have time for idiocy and started to move past him.

"I will have you shot."

That stopped me long enough to laugh.

"You aint the first to blame me for something they done, or the first to threaten. You need to be more original. Maybe next time you could say something like, you damned misbegotten spawn of hell, you have violated all that was sacred. I aint heard that recently. You should work on your vocabulary while youre laid up. And your originality."

I started to move off toward a side room but then turned back. I couldnt shut up.

"Who are you going to order to shoot me. All your NRAers are out looting all these fancy useless residences, and the remnants of the mummymans superior people are all in hiding, except for one poor fool who thought too dearly of himself and that got himself shot dead on is front steps by one of those hed been paying to protect him."

Unger was moving his lips but at first no words were coming out, but then he coughed up a final threat.

"Ill get you."

Marena was in the side room, silent and still with tubes running in and out of her, and she was hooked up to some blippy machine. I wasnt sure if she was breathing or the blippy machine was doing it for her.

Big Gene the Geneticist followed me in and hovered, waiting for me to admire his work.

"We have done all we could for her."

I leaned close and called to her. For a moment she opened her eyes and looked at me. She looked for a moment and then closed her eyes. I took her looking as a good sign.

"Shes heavily sedated." Big Gene was being helpful.

I wanted to know if she was going to live and, if so, when she could travel, but Big Gene wanted to lecture me about anatomy and medical marvels before confessing that he didnt have a simple answer to my simple question.

"Ill come back tomorrow to check on her."

We left Marena in his care with a suggestion that their lives were connected. On the way out he offered to show me the mad mummyman transitioning, but I was tired of both his bighead and his medical marvels. And there was gathering to be done.

Chapter 48

The mad mummymans steward was named Oliver, and he wasnt happy with us.

"Colonel Stevens called and said I should capture you. He said he was sending out a squad of Troopers to have you shot."

"Ive been getting that a lot lately. You got any good plans on how to capture us?"

Neither me nor Joe were pointing a weapon at him, but he slowly shook his head and dropped a small caliber reolver on the couch next to him.

"I never liked Colonel Stevens much."

Oliver was efficient and reasonable, and after some encouragement he was almost obliging. Every time me and Joe started to bust open a locked cabinet or door he produced a key or tapped some magic numbers into a keypad. He hadnt been overly hostile when we showed up to take compensation for our work, though the gold coins required some persuasion. The mention of an imminent invasion of savage cannibals probably helped to move him towards cooperation, that and the realization his playland world was crashing around him.

After a while, after we had explored the barroom, he had taken himself off to the fancy library and sat staring at the little twisty stepover stream. Joe had already emptied the apple bowl and was tugging at the statue, and I was considering the fat leather volumes, wishing I could transport the whole room.

"Back in the capitol we hosted heads of state, even the President. Mr. Gault was a powerful man."

Oliver was an older man, thin but not skeletal. He had one of those happy faces that look pleased even when there was nothing to be pleased about.

"He aint so powerful now, is he?"

I plucked a tall thin leather book from a shelf and looked back at Oliver. He smiled at me.

"Thats a rare folio, one of the rarest in Mr. Gaults collection."

He didnt seem to care if I borrowed the volume, or about the statue or whiskey or much else. Having watched Shavedhead pack up and then having watched his master packed off in ice, hed been expecting us.

"You know he aint coming back. No one ever does."

Oliver looked out the window again.

I had already tried to encourage him to gather up a few things of his own and transition away, but he wasnt inclined to leave. I put the folio back where I had found it.

"All this stuff, everything that you and Gault and everyone else has around here is going to get picked over and torn apart. Theres going to be waves of looters and wackers and eventually all these big houses are going to get torched. Big Gene the Geneticist next door is already packing. Maybe you better help me pack a few books and come with us. The Prince could use a man of your refinements."

Oliver politely shook his head, but he helped me find the keys to one of the big shiny cars in the garage. Joe wanted to argue about who got to drive. He had hauled out his statue and a load of bottles, apples, coins, and kitchenstuff, and he was in a rush to load up and drive away. But I kept my car by directing him to a second big shiny car, which got his attention. We left Mister Oliver to wait for what was coming.

I am proud to say that, by the time we pulled up in front of the smokey big house, my big car had fewer scratches and dents than his, having only slightly scraped along a stone wall that suddenly jumped in front of me.

Out on the creek road there was a bit of going and coming, with little cars carrying NRAers, grabies, and raggy people passing both ways, in a hurry to go one place or the other. We passed that third toad, Major Murdinger, who poked his head up when we went by. I waved, which caused that disagreeable stone fence to get in my way, and which then abruptly concluded my waving.

By the time we got back to the big house, most of the NRAers, including the skulking Stevens, had taken themselves elsewhere, leaving a crowd of little people who seemed not displeased to see us. Several had raided a kitchen somewhere and were consuming leftovers out of a variety of large cans and containers. Two raggy boys each had an arm wrapped around a sizable can of peanut butter nearly as big as they were, and they offered us a gob or two. Since they were shoveling handfuls into their mouths, and since I could not identify what their hands had been shoveling before the peanut butter, I declined, but Joe found himself a clean stick and helped himself.

We were just starting off to ascertain our return transportation when Major Murdinger reappeared, having turned around to follow us.

"Weve been looking for you."

He had my erstwhile interrogaters with him, Stein and Garnett, who seemed less than happy with the sudden transitions. In the second little car that pulled up behind him there was another grayheaded fool of an NRAer and two older grabies.

I thought his use of we was inflated.

"I think your troops have been whittled down some. Whose your we?"

He and his small posse ignored me and were focused on Joe, who had unstrapped a cutter and was pointing it at them. I stepped in front of Joe to redirect their focus.

"Youre not going to threaten to shoot us for NewHarmonys ruination, are you? That aint going to happen. This place is coming apart all around us. It was probably coming apart for years while waiting for Howard Morris Gault the fourth to launch his transition. Yall had better gather up a few things and get out before you get knocked on the head. Theres a wild band of savage cannibals on the way, and theyre hungry."

Major Murdinger was a reasonable man. Once he sized up the general chaos and collapse, we came to a quick agreement not to get in each others way, which was convenient since we were headed in different directions. He and his hurried off to the residences while me and Joe looked around the farm.

I never directly lied about the imminent incursion of fleshcraving cannibals, or even about the impending storm of the Princes Rangers. We had in fact actually said close to the opposite, but belief is a funny thing, and once people get a notion stuck in their heads its hard to get it unstuck. No matter their size, shape, or measure, most NewHarmony people had it in their heads that me and Joe were advance scouts for something terrible coming after them, and we let them keep on thinking that, and maybe once or twice we nudged it forward. Getting people to believe something is a necessary part of any exchange.

Me and Joe believed that we pretty much had a clear path back to the old mans ranch and our reward. We just had to gather up and pull out. But just after Murdinger and his army of five departed, we realized that we had miscalculated the extent of gathering up and pulling out, and it was Nell that made us recalculate.

She came up holding the hand of the little blueshirted girl. Jemmy and Ben followed, and behind them a bedraggled group of a couple dozen more young people, a crowd of raggy NewHarmony farmers and grabies who had unsorted themselves, aged from little to not so little. In a few moments we were surrounded.

"We need to eat before we leave."

When I looked around and found all the faces looking back at me, I realized I had miscalculated. But I asked anyway.

"Whos your we?"

A long time ago, when the Fires were heating up, and when I was a little throwaway kid starving out, I ended up begging in front of a sandbagged warehouse where food was still being sold. I dont remember how I got there. I was still handholding age, and I think I had been taken up by a pack of older throwaways that were scrounging and scavenging in the wreckage. I imagine I was planted in front because I was so small and so pitiful. I do remember men with cutters guarding the building, and every so often someone would go in and come out. Then an old woman came up escorted by two guards, and maybe because I was the smallest and most pitiful someone shoved me in front of the woman.

It was cold and rainy, and I was wrapped in dirty canvas and soggy cardboard, as miserable and tearful as the most wretched of the throwaways, which in truth I probably was. I remember the old woman smelled like flowers and had red waxy lips. When she started to move around me, one of her guards pushed me down, which made me more miserable and tearful. I was probably a howler back then, and I probable let go wailing as loud as I could. The old woman stopped and turned, and I might have raised my arms for her to pick me up. But she didnt. She leaned down and looked at me.

"I dont care about you. I dont feel anything for you. I have my own family."

She turned and disappeared into the entrance, followed by her guards. Not one of them looked back, while the other guards in front looked away.

I could have given up and crawled off to some hole to die, like so many others that gave up and slumped over. But I got mad instead, a tiny miserable skinandbone throwaway furious at the unfairness and the indifference, furious at the old woman and all of the other fenced up, walled away people eating while I starved. I worked myself into a burning rage that lasted more than a decade. I wanted a gun, and I wanted to get that old woman and her guards. I wanted to get all of the men guarding that food, and I wanted to get inside and take whatever I wanted. I fed on that rage for a long time.

Maybe I did die that day. Maybe that little poorpitifulme child died right there in the mud and rain while begging from heartless people who thought they deserved to eat while others starved. Maybe I died and got reborn. Maybe I learned a harsh lesson. I think maybe that stupid unfeeling waxylipped old woman did me a favor.

I hoped all those young faces wouldnt have to learn that same same lesson, or feel that same burning rage. I looked at Nell and our two lost boys, at the little blueshirted girl wanting to point her way home, then I scanned the crowd all around me, thinking that they hadnt been singed in the Fires like me and Joe. None of them knew that survival was rough work and that sometimes, one way or another, someone would push you aside, letting you know they didnt care about you.

"Ok, lets all go find something to eat."

Chapter 49

We left New Harmony stringing horses and mules loaded up with a few things we thought were useful, five flatbed farmwagons, and an army of eightysome little people who stuck to us. It was quite a procession.

The going was slow, and got slower when we ran into the two shepherd boys out on the road to the pass.

"Where you going? You got any food?"

Staffboy looked about the same, though a bit soggy from a recent rain. He stood in the middle of the road in front of us, while Rifleboy was off a ways with the sheep. Joe had gone off early in the morning, and I thought it likely he had run into the boys, letting them know that the childrens crusade was coming through.

"Theyll give you something back on one of the wagons. You like melons or apples?"

Staffboy hurried past without responding, waving Rifleboy to follow him. I tried to call him over but he ignored me. The sheep generally ignored me as well.

A couple hours later, as we started up the pass, Joe appeared. He was smiling.

"You have a taste for roast mutton?"

I ignored him.

The old woman with the big garden slowed us up for several days. She, the brokenfaced boy, and their little crew were waiting for us when we finally got up to the house, the we being me, Nell, and a small handful of happy valley refugees who had made the trek up from the old road with us. I had been wondering about the woman, and I didnt want to pass by below without making a stop. After telling Joe the what and where, I headed up the hills on foot. Nell followed, and then a small group of NewHarmony refugees followed after us. Maybe they had also been wondering about an old woman with a big garden.

After we got over the last hill and closed the distance to the house three of the little raggy children screamed and broke off from the pack, running ahead. By the time I got up to the house the three had wrapped themselves around the old woman, a homecoming away from home.

The old woman was ready for me, and not particularly happy with me.

"Where you taking these children?"

"I aint taking them anywhere. Theyre accompanying. Me and Joe are taking Nell here and her two cousins Jemmy and Ben back to the big ranch. All the others, these and those down with Joe and the wagons, set out with us when we left. NewHarmony is in transition."

"Whats that supposed to mean?"

I thought my words were adequate but tried to explain.

"It aint what it used to be, and it aint yet become what its going to be."

"That dont tell me nothing either."

She stared back at me, edgy and uncertain. The brokenfaced boy stood next to her with a cutter strapped over his front. I thought we maybe should ease back a notch or two.

"I suppose its a doubtful word. Aint we all in transition? Why dont we give these little people some water, and then Ill tell you about NewHarmony. Its changed since you left it."

She started to headshake a no but stopped.

"You have a sister down there, called herself Mother Mary?"

She looked away south. With the rock and hills you couldnt trace the road up and over the pass, but you could follow the high

211

ridges to the cleft where the road passed over.

"What happened to her?"

The old womans name was Meg, and she had three little ones, two girls and a boy, an older girl about Nells age, and Joshua, the brokenfaced boy. She and her little troop had pulled out of NewHarmony after a particularly brutal sorting that left Joshua with a torn face. His opponent had worn a couple brassy rings the size of large acorns.

"How come those doddery NRA fools wouldnt let you wrap your hands around something heavy and sharp?"

Joshua angled his unscarred side toward me, shook his head, and then left the room. He hadnt exchanged words with me, and didnt seem inclined to. Meg hadnt said much either, though she had offered a stringy outline of their departure. They had come upon the house in the hills by accident, having left the old road to escape the packs of NRAers and grabies sent out to fetch them back. They had only planned to stay a short while but had been there a couple years. They were all a bit bony and gaunt, and I wondered how they got through the snows.

"You should go back to NewHarmony and make use of whats left. Theres a fair number who stayed. Yall could put together some kind of real refuge for lost children. But youll have to boot out that fool Unger and a couple more zealots who think theyre in charge. Maybe send Big Gene and his crew packing. They aint doing much good worrying over whats left of Mister Morris Howard Gault. You could make a go of it down there."

The stubborn old woman wouldnt go, and no amount of prodding could budge her. The house in the hills was where she ended up, and that was where she was fixed. She went as far as the old road, where we loaded her up with food, leftovers, and a couple NewHarmony farm boys who decided to stay on. Some of the younger ones would have stayed too, but she wouldnt hear of it. Too many to take on, she said.

Yet she took Marena, which surprised me, and which didnt displease me. As we were preparing to lug her stuff back up the hills, she climbed up on the back of our ambulance wagon and spent a moment with those laid up and mending, even Sid and the Deadman. She spent more than a moment with Marena, who was still wobbling between here and beyond. They had exchanged a few words before Marena nodded off. It had rained some during the day, and Marenas blankets were still wet.

"Youre killing this woman."

"No, I am trying not to kill her. I am trying to save her. If we had left her back in New Harmony the best she could have hoped for was Big Gene keeping her spliced to some kind of blippy machine, and thats if Unger and his boys didnt find her. She did some damage down in the happy valley."

Meg looked at me and shook her head. She didnt seem to listen when I expanded on Marenas damage

"Shes staying with me."

Building a stretcher and lugging Marena up the hills was slow work, so it was the middle of the next day by the time we got her and everything else up to Megs place. Meg trudged along with us, cautioning us over rocks and thorns, and when we finally made it up the house with Marena none the worse and a fair supply of provisions and useables, she didnt seem especially beholden.

She came out after seeing Marena to a room in the back and handhipped herself into a posture of impatience. I had used a posse of twenty happy valley refugees to haul Marena and all else up the hills, and we were tired. And I might have been a bit cranky.

"Dont you tell anybody where were at. I go up to NewPueblo two or three times a year, and I make sure no one knows and no one follows."

She spoke sharply enough to get me up out from the patch of shade where I had been sprawled.

"Are you always so vexed and disagreeable? You could thank us for what we done."

She stood fixed and handhipped. Joshua came up next to her and sideways a glance in my direction.

"I seen too many like you. Men with guns and no steady life and no families."

"Where you seen these people? Im looking for them. I got misplaced during the Fires and have chased after a family and steady life ever since. I would be obliged if you can tell me where you seen these people."

She gave me a grim look and started to go back into the house.

"I aint no wacker or killer. You got me confused with someone else."

Meg stopped.

"You aint no farmer or carpenter either."

I followed her into the house, but Meg was done with me. Marena was only slightly more sociable. She was awake when I went in, and one of Megs girls was giving her some sippy water out of a giant orange plastic cup. She had been holding the cup with both hands. They both looked at me like I had violated their space, but the girl quickly set the cup down and went out.

"You want some more water?"

Marena shook her head. Her eyes were red and her face was pale. She had suffered from the lugging and bumping.

"You did a lot to help me and Joe."

She shook her head again.

"I wanted to get back at them that hurt me. It aint right what they done to me."

"Theyre dead, gone."

She closed her eyes and shook her head a third time.

"Theyres others up there that took turns."

Sometimes a few words can say a lot. I wished there was a way I could heal her.

"Let them go, let it all go. You got a chance at a new life. Let go of the old one."

She tried to raise herself and winced.

"It aint that easy, is it? We all got a lot of scars."

I started to tell her that everyone gets nicked along the way, but stopped, thinking my words would have little meaning for her.

"You sure you dont want any more water?"

I picked up the big orange plastic cup and offered it to her, but she just stared back at me without a nod or a shake. The cup was nicked and scratched, and I couldnt make out the faint traces of what had been some blue lettering.

"Its a big ugly world, but its getting better, and theres lots of good places and good people. Dont go judging all of creation just because you got cut up in real nasty patch of thorns. Every days a promise of something better. Youve got a chance at something better. You ought to give it a go."

She closed her eyes and whispered something I couldnt hear. I leaned closer and asked her to repeat what she had said.

"You go."

Chapter 50

I had better luck with the people in NewPueblo. Once the childrens crusade pulled into town, we got popular real quick after a handful of crusaders got recognized and claimed. The town council werent too riled to hear that Morrison had transitioned either, and they invited us to a dinner. Despite being gimpy and grumbly, the Deadman had himself a good enough time to get himself drunk and sappy. He lurched around the town center handshaking and thanking people for welcoming him home, having forgotten that hed been one of the buzzards up at Morrisons roost that had been pecking at them. Sometime during that first night The NewPueblo City Grocery got itself plundered and burned. It was a nice fire.

We stayed two more nights and spent the days trading a little, digging through what was left of the City Grocery, but also hunting around for more crusader connections. The people of NewPueblo were real helpful and kindly, offering to take on most of our happy valley refugees. Some of our unconnected accepted the offer to stay on. The Deadman decided he would stay on too.

He was leaning on a crutch someone had given him, surrounded by a couple former refugees, when me and Joe were gathering to head out. I asked him if he was fixed on remaining.

"I aint had no luck with you."

"You want me to knock you on the head with a rock?"

"No, and I dont want to get shot or stabbed neither, so dont go asking me any dumb questions. But for all the trouble you give me I will take some of that gold you got, and some those black sleepy pills, and maybe some of that crazy mans whiskey."

Joe was impatient to load up and head out. Nell and lost boys were leading a group of our unconnected out front, and they were all in a huff to get on. I had a small group with me, and there were others spread out with the wagons. It was time to go. I gave the Deadman one gold coin I found in my pocket, some silver I found in another pocket, and a bottle of woodenboxed whiskey I found in my pack.

"You sure you dont want me to put you out of your misery?"

Ignoring my question, he clutched his bottle, adjusted his crutch and box, nodded goodbye, and hobbled off. For a Deadman, he wasnt a bad sort.

Chapter 51

"I appreciate you bringing our boys back." He said it, but he didnt mean it. There was no warmth in his voice, no depth to his smile.

I was back where I started, up on the big porch overlooking the ranch, only the old man was gone, and the skinny curlyheaded soninlaw Henry had taken his place. Him and a handful of men who seemed to have nothing better to do than pet their cutters and stare us down.

The homecoming was not what we expected, and not what we all had talked up the whole time since heading out of NewPueblo.

Jemmy and Ben had chattered excitedly the whole time, grandaddying this and that, and Nell and Sid were just as excited, though Sid tried not to show too much of it. When we got to within a mile below the ranchhouse Jemmy and Ben had busted loose and took off running and screaming, racing to be the first to find the old man.

But now they were off a ways, stooped and motionless, quiet and subdued, their mother Jena hovering over them, whispering what I couldnt hear but supposed was about all the evilness festering the world. Nell had disappeared to find her own parents, but Sid was perched on a porchstep surrounded by a few of his former crew. He was quiet too. Jena had already dosed him with her whisperings. Except for the petters and their oily weapons, no one seemed particularly happy.

But what scratched me the most was that Henry wasnt the least bit appreciative.

"We had an extra Sid charge."

"A what?" He grinned back at me like he had heard something funny.

"A Sid charge. The old man offered a big reward, and then offered to double it if we took Sid along with us."

"I dont know anything about any agreements you had with Grandaddy. He was already getting heartsick when you were nosing around here last spring and in no position to make any agreements. I sent Sid out to hunt after his brothers, and he came back an invalid. You want me to reward you for that?"

There wasnt much use in continuing. You cant make sense of nonesense, and you cant make a fool stop being foolish. Henry was offering a handful of silver to compensate me and Joe for our time and troubles in returning the lost boys, who were hunched under their mothers whisperings and seemed as lost as ever.

"Grandaddy got so heartsick and weak he had to retire. Weve had to rearrange the ranch business. Grandaddy hadnt paid much attention to his accounts for a long while, so weve had to make some changes. Whatever agreements you had with Grandaddy got voided when he stepped down."

Henry smiled at me, and had I something handy and heavy I wouldve smashed his smile and broken his teeth. But I had nothing, having come up to the big porch thinking I would be appreciated, and not realizing that a cutter and few clips would have made me more appreciable. Joe was off down below somewhere with the rest of the refugees. They had quickly been herded off to a bunkhouse for food and rest, but that was before we realized that the old man had been deposed and Henry was rearranging.

"Whose your we?"

"What do you mean?"

"I mean exactly what I am asking. Whose your we? You keep saying we did this and we did that. Whose your we? These boys you got hanging around petting their guns, are they part of the we? Are they family? Wheres the rest of the family? Why are you sitting up here and not someone else?"

Henry favored me with another empty smile.

"With all the confusion and with Grandaddy suddenly getting sick, I had to step in as the temporary acting head of the family."

"Had to? No one else around? The last time I came through I heard there were three daughters and a son. What happened to the others? They get voided too?"

Though he wanted to cancel my account, Henry kept smiling.

"Some of the family have left the ranch to look for better opportunities elsewhere."

I looked off a ways. The horses and cattle that I had admired before were gone. I kept looking for Joe, hoping he could help strengthen our bargaining positioning by swatting away a few of Henrys gunpetters.

"Whered they go? They hustled off to NewHarmony? We didnt pass anyone on the road, and NewHarmony aint quite what it used to be. It got rearranged too."

I stood up and stretched, feeling tired and sorebacked. It was a hot day, and had been on the porch for half an hour, and had not been offered a glass of water. I thought about going down to the pump and soaking myself in the cold water. Maybe make some mud balls. I could either go without making a fuss, or I could fuss.

"Henry, you aint nothing more than a cutthroat and sneakthief. You spoiled the ranch that gave you a home, sold off your own children for slave labor, killed or run off most of the family that welcomed you as kin, and betrayed the old man that accepted you, and you done all that so you could set up here like you were something special. But you aint special, youre just damn ordinary. I am going to swat you off this porch."

I moved toward Henry, who recoiled suddenly, knocking over his chair as he moved out of my reach. Before I could step after him his gunpetters converged. Two of them from behind buckled my knees and pushed me down. Two others stuck cutters into the back of my head. Once I was down Henry moved back in front of me.

"You want to die here in front of children, or will you let these men take you out behind the barn." Henry was smiling again.

"Neither. What are my other choices?"

"You have no other choices. This is the end for you."

I tried to rise but got pushed down again.

"No, theres always choices, and endings get so slippery that you never can be sure whats stopping and whats starting. You think youre setting square on top, but the wheels about the turn and give you an unexpected drop. Dont look now, but somethings coming up behind you."

Henry turned and looked but saw nothing he suspected. He brightened into a big grin and pulled out a little sixshot pocket revolver. At a distance it wouldnt hit much or do much, but up a close headshot would mash my brains to bloody goo.

"Heres your ending."

He pointed the barrel into my face. Jena started pulling Jemmy and Ben over to watch.

Suddenly a burst of cutter splintered the porch and wall behind Henry, making him and everyone else around duck and cringe.

I looked over and smiled.

"Hey Sid, hows that shoulder feeling? Still sore?"

Grimly, Sid limped over the top step and moved toward us, keeping his cutter pointed at Henry. Behind him his barnyard crew followed, each holding an automatic handgun. For a moment both Sids crew and Henrys gunpetters sized each other up.

"Sid, put that down. I am your father."

Sid moved closer and bellypoked Henrywith his cutter.

"Fathers dont sell their children."

"Thats ridiculous I . . ."

Jena let go of Jemmy and Ben and came over to grab Sids cutter and jerk it away, but he held on to it.

"He is evil. He needs to die. He and men like him are corruption."

Sid twisted his cutter out of his mothers grasp and stuck it back into his fathers belly.

"I seen evil out on the old road and down in NewHarmony, and it didnt look anything like him. It looked more like that man Unger you were talking with every time he came around with his pretty boys. You let Trader go, and we will all go with him. You can have this stinking ranch. You aint a real father."

I tried to remember the boy I mudballed and bootbattered, but I couldnt quite recall what he looked like.

"Sid, think about what youre doing. We are family."

"They aint family." Sid didnt look away, but gave a slight headnod towards the gunpetters. For a moment we all just kept staring where we had been staring. But then a voice came through the big front door behind us.

"I aint family either, but Nell here is."

Henry dropped his smile, but I opened up mine. Joe came up behind the gunpetters holding a cutter on them, with Nell following.

"You boys best put your weapons down and keep looking off towards those pretty hills out yonder. Nell came out to invite me to join this discussion, but it looks like we better end it before anyone gets too excited."

"Evilness. This is pollution." Jena spoke, but no one paid her much mind. Nell came around and grabbed Jemmy and Ben to pull them out of the way.

"Trader, what are you doing squatting down there?"

I pushed myself up, taking a hold of Henrys little revolver as I stood.

"I was just looking at some porchcracks, but I am done with that. I think this whole porch needs a good sweeping. You boys mind helping?" I spoke to Sids crew, who obliged by moving forward to disarm the gunpetters.

"Joe, Ive been expecting you. I came at them from the front but was waiting on you to sneak up from behind. Took you long enough."

Chapter 52

When we finally found the old man, he wasnt in a good way, but he got better quick enough.

The little cabin where theyd stuck him had a small back porch, and we found him there creaking in an old rockingchair, staring at nothing, waiting for whatever. Me and Joe came around the back first. The old man looked at us with surprise.

"They said you had been killed down south on the old highway."

Joe thumped his chest.

"I aint been killed. What about you?"

Joe moved to thump me on the chest, but I eased out of his reach.

"I aint been killed either. What are you doing way out here? Up at the ranchhouse they said you had gotten sick and retired out here to rest. You done resting? Theres a ranch that needs looking after and some accounts that need to get evened out."

"They pushed me out here. They said I had some kind of heartsickness and needed to rest. They said I was getting too agitated worrying over them boys."

"Whos they?"

He never got a chance to answer my question. At that moment Nell and the lost boys came tearing around the back and flung themselves on the old man. Sid came stumbling after them as best he could and joined the heap. For a heartsick old man, he withstood the storm and clenched them all back.

I had never seen such a homecoming. Soon Nell and the boys were teary, and then the old man tearedup along with them, all hugging and crying and slaphappy. Sid was trying to stay stonyfaced, but he mightve gotten weteyed too. They got so giddy and jumpy they knocked over a little table by the rocker, and nearly knocked themselves over. Joe had to lean in and right them up.

But then a curious thing happened, and maybe the best thing. All the rest of our unclaimed refugees came crowding around the back, nearly two dozen of them, all silently watching all the hugging, jittering, lipsmacking, and laughcrying. For a few moments no one in the jumble noticed, but then the old man looked over and straightened himself. He looked all around and realized he was surrounded by lost children.

Nell broke loose from her family clump and went over to the still unclaimed blueshirted girl. She took the girls hand and led her over to the old man. A half dozen other refugees pressed in after them, and then all the others closed the distance. The old man was soon hemmed in on all sides.

The old man looked over at me and Joe for some sort of explanation, and I wasnt sure there was one.

"We thought if you were offering so much for two we would bring along a few more. Give you a special discount rate on lost children."

The old man looked around at the children, pondering the possibilities. I thought he might try to push his way through the crowd to some place less crowded. But Nell tugged at him and he bent down to her and his lost boys. The little blueshirted girl started crying. He reached for her and then, straightening, reached out to all of them.

www.ingramcontent.com/pod-product-compliance
Lightning Source LLC
Chambersburg PA
CBHW020401030726
47496CB00007B/2254